Extium

Katie Rha and Emery Gewirtz

ISBN: 0615921841
ISBN 13: 9780615921846
Library of Congress Control Number: 2013955500
CreateSpace Independent Publishing Platform
North Charleston, South Carolina

For our families

PART 1: Beginnings

One

Wren

I steadied myself and listened to the rapid thumping of my heart. It was whacking against my chest in an erratic frenzy. I took a few slow breaths to try to get it to return to a natural *thump-thump.* They'll be able to tell, I reminded myself.

I tucked away the last few items I thought necessary to bring into my rucksack: some blankets, a knife, a stun gun, several canteens, compact tents, and files from the restricted section of the Prime Minister's office. I hadn't dared to look at them yet.

A bead of sweat dripped down my forehead and I wiped it away. I needed to calm myself. I was never going to make it to the forest if I kept acting this nervous. Though, I knew my plan was nearly foolproof. Why would such a high-ranking government employee like myself ever be questioned?

With one more deep inhale I left the confines of my government quarters for the last time.

The government building was bigger than one might have thought. It was confusing and exhausting to navigate. Nearly all the walls were a bright white and the doors seemed endless. Luckily, I had my place here for several years and knew without the slightest of hesitation, which doors led where.

I took the last door at the end of the hallway. This one held a staircase that would take me all the way to the garage if I continued down long enough. And that was precisely where I needed to go. The government was always teeming with countless officials and other workers of our society of Laiden. But it was late into the night, so many less were roaming.

I crept down the staircase, with silent footsteps and a silent breath, pushing away any remaining thoughts convincing me not to go through with my rash decision. There was no time for them. Focus, Wren. I was almost to the bottom.

I pushed open the last door with a certain authority. It led to a massive room, perhaps even the biggest single room in Laiden. It had bright lights that were almost blinding if you stared at them for too long. Wall to wall, the garage was lined with hovercrafts as black as the night.

Over in the corner, tapping on his tablet's glowing screen, was Jarem, the night patrol officer in charge of keeping track of each hovercraft. He was an old officer who was known for his meticulous behavior. As I strode over to him, he looked up from his work, hearing my footsteps.

"What brings you down to our parts so late, Wren?" Jarem's gruff voice asked.

"I need a hovercraft for a last minute delivery to the bunker located due west outside the North Gate."

My voice didn't even catch on the stark lie.

"Sure thing, Wren. But are you sure you're taking it to the bunker? No one is stationed out there this late at night."

"Prime Minister Iris's orders," I replied.

No one questioned Iris's authority.

"Alright then," he replied. Pulling out his tablet again, Jarem began to record the vehicle's release form, checking boxes and scribbling signatures. "When will it be returned?"

"After the distribution is complete."

The lies became easier as I told them.

"You aren't going to oversee the distribution of the pills?" he asked in a truly shocked manner.

My face grew cold, but I forced out a chuckle. "I've seen enough of the those white capsules to satisfy a whole lifetime."

"I reckon so. Congratulations again, Wren. You should be proud of such accomplished work at such a young age."

I nodded my thanks as he handed me a small silver disc that activated the controls on my assigned vehicle. I looked at the key with unease. The feeling of lifting off and suspending in air made me nauseous even thinking about it.

The old official caught my hint of worry.

"Haven't ridden in a while, son? It's tricky to maneuver the hovercraft when you're out of practice."

"It's been a couple months," I admitted. And with that, I sauntered across the garage toward Hovercraft 16, feeling Jarem's eyes on my back.

I hadn't realized that lying would come so easy. But after years of working in a government whose foundation was built on lies, I guess it made some sense.

It was a lie that I needed to go to the bunker.

It was a lie that I was on Prime Minister Iris's orders.

The only thing that wasn't a lie was the fact that I had seen enough of those wretched white pills that were crafted by my own hand.

I hoisted myself up into the hovercraft, punched in the coordinates for the bunker's location, and pounded my thumb on the silver disc to start the ignition. The hovercraft whirred to life under my sweaty palms. I nodded to Jarem, and he pulled down the lever that retracted the warehouse roof, revealing the evening sky. I swallowed my fear and ascended to the stars, ignoring the rubbery stench of the engine.

I still had trouble grasping the concept that it was only yesterday I made the life-altering decision to leave Laiden. The conversation that had catapulted my decision kept coming back to me in perfect clarity, but I could no longer push my thoughts away.

I stood in whiteness. Blinded for a brief moment, I shifted my gaze to the East Wing corridor of the white-walled laboratory. Day in and day out as far as the eyes could see were rows and rows of pearl-colored capsules. After a long testing period, everyone was now ready for the distribution process to begin.

The laboratory doors slid open and men in white coats filed in, in a synchronized rhythm. Prime Minister Iris followed them closely behind. Iris, with his black eyes blinking, darted across the room. His suspicious gaze hit everyone, as his lips curled into an unattractive sneer. I glanced at Iris as he veered toward the cases of pills, where I was standing. Alert and impassive, he inspected every inch of the room.

My relationship with Iris was based on false cordiality and a lack of respect. It was getting old, but I knew what Iris was capable of. His grip on the people of Laiden was overpowering, and I did my best to loosen his hold over me.

"You've done well for one so young, Wren," he said with a mocking tone as if it was by mere chance I, of all people, had succeeded over my superiors.

There was no avoiding his deep gaze. "Thank you," I muttered somewhat cautiously.

His tone was quiet, but powerful and almost too mesmerizing. "As I'm sure you are aware, a meeting will be held tomorrow for the public eye. And as the top advisor of the pill, Extium, it is imperative you are present. Understood?"

"Yes," I whispered back, only audible for Iris to hear. I had most definitely understood.

I gave a curt nod to a few of my co-workers and exited the lab in spite of the rare celebration. Guilt ate at the pit of my stomach. It was at that moment the right choice became evident. I wouldn't be keeping my promise to the Minister.

My thoughts lingered on this horrid truth. Tomorrow really was Distribution Day, and the day the whole society would change for the worse. The irony was the fact that they all believed they'd be changing for the better.

This extraordinary idea of "the Extium pill" had lived for a half of a century, toying with the minds of ingenious scientists until I finally managed to put a balance to the equation. Disguised as the "Cure" to every solution, every problem, and every disease in what was really masked in simple terms— a mind molder. When dispensed to the whole society of Laiden, all citizens would have to succumb to the ideas of Prime Minister Iris. Only Iris's most faithful and useful government workers would be excused from taking Extium, not that my track record with the Minister was so perfect.

I knew that if I were to be found, Iris would unhesitatingly leave me as a victim to my own cruel invention. I knew that I would be forced to take Extium.

The hovercraft neared the edge of the gated community of Laiden. Though I was at a high altitude, I could still see the structure of center-city Laiden quite clearly. Cut to a perfect circle, Laiden's streets were devoid of life and our small population of about five thousand slept within the lines of their identical government-issued houses. Besides the murmur of my hovercraft, the city rested peacefully in silence. The only movement that could be detected was the timed rotations of the guards around the perimeter of the steel gates, meant to protect Laiden from a rumored "dangerous" forest. A lie that I could bet had been started by Iris, it acted as a security for the government. It ensured that citizens would stay away from the barrier. The greenery stretched for miles upon miles from the main city of Laiden to the borders of the barrier.

The government building, which included Laiden's high-facility laboratories where I had come from, lay outside of the center-city and directly outside of the South Gate. Iris could keep an eye on his citizens from a distance. Where I was headed, was the direction of the North Gate.

From my bird's eye view, I could only see miles of trees in every direction. No barrier. But I knew it was there, invisible to naked eye. The barrier both left room for no escape in Iris's sickening circle of life and separated us from another "rumored" dying world.

If someone were bold enough to try and reach the barrier, they would have to go through the forest first. I hadn't known anyone that had come close to the barrier anyway. Until now. It was the barrier that I truly wanted to reach, not the bunker. This left a problem with the hovercraft in part of my plan, but a detail not left amiss. These hovercrafts were embedded with trackers; so I knew I would have to set it down close enough to the bunker without causing unnecessary suspicion. It also gave me enough time to get a head start before, inevitably, the government would be after me. With fortune of the night on my side, no one would be in pursuit of me until the next morning.

Luckily, I wasn't tiring yet. Adrenalin pumped furiously through my veins. The hovercraft was fast, not even half an hour had passed, and it was already time to set down the vehicle.

I didn't trust Iris. I didn't trust the government. I didn't even trust myself. As I lowered myself onto the ground, I realized there was no turning back on my decision. The whirring of the hovercraft lulled to a stop and I leapt out, tucking the silver disc into my pocket.

I turned away, leaving my getaway craft behind me. I started out slow, but sped up my pace quickly. It was time to abandon my other life. It was time to be a tool of the government no longer.

Two

Wren

Night wore on and I was tiring. Hours of running and hiking had passed since landing Hovercraft 16 at the bunker. Alone with my thoughts, I toyed with my true intentions for leaving Laiden. Was I crazy? Maybe. I had no idea what I was getting into or what my mind was even capable of when I became the head scientist. Did I know how many lives would never be the same? Did I even know that my own life would be turned into something I could never imagine? No. The Extium pills were beyond me. They were beyond everyone.

Nevertheless, Distribution Day was tomorrow, and there was no possible way I could stop Iris now.

Emotionally and physically drained, I began to settle down for the night. Hiking to the top of a small knoll nestled in the forest, I resolved myself to make a small camp despite my intense desire to sprawl across the downy earth.

I readjusted the foliage around my shivering, sore limbs, and laid down in an attempt to release the knots coiling at the pit of my stomach. I felt Iris's hands clutch around me and scrape at the nape of my neck. I felt the insults from my family and my co-workers thrown at my chest like weights, jabbing my pressure points. I felt cold sweat running down my face mixed with tears of anguish. Somewhere in the fight between myself and the world, I suppose I fell asleep.

Three

Lennon

My name is Lennon Kincaid. I'm seventeen years old. And until yesterday, I was perfectly normal.

Laiden was abuzz with chatter now that Distribution Day was tomorrow. I half-heartedly joined in the discussions, but didn't care all that much. My mother had impatiently reminded me that morning that Distribution Day was supposed to be an exciting time.

She sent me on my way with the morning's rations. My father had already left for his work. I was taken care of fine enough, but for being an only son, you would have thought I would've been given more attention.

As usual, my eyes were drooping from a lack of sleep the night before, and I sluggishly acknowledged exchanges of "hellos" and waves between several of my peers as we all gathered in a uniform line to head into our morning classes.

We stood in front of a sign that read, "The Learning Institute of Laiden." It was the building we swarmed to each day for our education, teaching Laiden's bright and young generation about the fragility of our world. It taught us how lucky we were that we had a society to take care of us as well as it did. And we all believed it.

Across the building's tall, mirrored, steel walls was a massive eye. It was the prominent insignia of Laiden and was therefore etched ornately into the front of the complex. You couldn't escape gazing at its cold hard pupil no matter what angle you stood at. A group of my school friends always joked that it was merely there to remind us all that Prime Minister Iris was always watching, but to me it seemed like something more, something sinister.

I swiped my student tracker at the entrance of the school. The center of the band had the same creepy eye, and its pupil flashed a bright red as it "beeped" in harmony with a small scanner. A set of sliding doors opened for me as I walked in.

The soles of our shoes clicked with the cold, white tiles of the Institute.

The History of Laiden, taught by Professor Alegorn, was one of the more tragically dull courses I took. Mandated for all students each year, it was with good reason that we all became uninterested. Besides, there wasn't much history behind Laiden. The world died and our dome of Laiden survived, keeping us safe from the last remnants of desiccating life. Yadda-yadda-yadda, I yawned. I never paid attention in his class much. In fact, the only thing that kept me from dozing off was knowing that I'd have to face the looming stench of Alegorn's breath if he leaned over me one more time.

The day went pretty fast anyhow. They sent us immediately home after the last class. All people of Laiden had to be accounted for that night to ensure everyone would receive the Cure the next morning.

I went home to what would probably just be another monotonous night sitting in my room. I enjoyed going to the Institute. Too bad I'd never go again.

Four

Masen

Yeah, that's me— the one who wrote the book about self-absorbed fathers. I awoke to nothing but a quickly scrawled note taped to my bathroom door. It didn't matter much what it said. We both knew neither of us cared.

I grumbled and stepped into the icy shower, hoping that the discomfort of the cold water would interrupt any further trivial thoughts.

At least Wins was supposed to meet me outside in a couple of minutes to go to the Institute. Culver and Evelyn, her two siblings, would be walking with us. My best mornings were when I was with them. It was the only time I felt like I kind of had a family, but enough about that. There was no need to be depressed so early in the day.

I combed my hand through a mess of jet-black hair. Good enough. I grabbed the tasteless gray biscuit off the table set aside for my morning meal, and was out the door, anticipating that Winslett had already arrived.

She had.

Evelyn bounded along beside her, but Culver was missing.

"He went into the Institute early for extra special work," Winslett told me, rolling her eyes in a good-natured kind of way. Winslett loved her brother and sister more than anyone, except perhaps me.

Evelyn carried a small book sack and she impatiently twirled her dark pigtails around and around. She looked more like my sister than she did Winslett's.

It was days that I could spend like this that made me think I didn't have it so bad. Even so, when Winslett went home she'd still have two other people there with her. I was always welcome at Winslett's house, but I didn't like to intrude where I didn't belong.

In a short time, we arrived at the Beginner's Institute, a learning facility that educated the youngest generation in Laiden, and where we would be dropping Evelyn off. It would be several years before she joined Wins and me at the Institute.

"You have your ID scanner, right?" Winslett asked Evelyn as she readjusted the gray bows keeping her hair in place.

"Mm-hmm." The little girl smiled as she rose up her wrist with the blank eye.

"Good. Have fun at school." Winslett kissed her on the cheek and Evelyn scampered off down the pathway with the other little boys and girls.

"Bye, Evelyn!" I called after her.

She stopped in place to turn around and wave to me.

"Come on!" Winslett grabbed me as we hastened our pace. "Professor Darys isn't going to like it if we are late."

I wondered if that morning would have been different if we knew what was to come.

Five

Wren

The pastel hues that colored the sky seemed rather peaceful in contrast to the corrupted society lying underneath its soft glow. As far away as I was from the government building, I could see dots of white lab coats scattered across the city, indicating that the officials were beginning their morning rounds. Not only could I make out their images, I could see them in perfect detail down to the freckles on their noses. Gray to green to black, I shifted the dials of my Farspects and leaned toward the edge of the peak I was now resting on.

Peering through the thin lenses, you would have thought I was standing next to those officials. My old colleague, Fahad, knocked on the door of House 1 and gave a forced smile to the young woman who peeked through a crack in the door before swinging it quickly open. It was eerie to see the hesitance in her body language as she called to her husband and children. Seconds later, a burly man with gentle features sauntered to the door to join his wife, resting one hand on her delicate shoulder and another hand out to the officials. I watched as Fahad let four pills slip from his loose grip and drop into the calloused hands of the man. Another official, with Fahad, handed the family their morning food rations on a silver tray.

I felt sick to my stomach, yet the ill feeling mixed with a strange sort of pride. I despised that I felt this way, but the scientist in me watched with anticipation, wondering if the government could pull this off.

The officials stopped at every house until they reached the end of the street. Around House 72, I strapped my Farspects back on and focused once more as the door swung open.

A young couple opened the door with expressions of pure elation and relief. An uneasy smile formed around the lips of the comely woman as she knelt down to whisper softly into her child's ear. As the boy quickly left the room, the woman stood next to her husband and he enclosed his hand in hers. Then they too, took pills of their own. The small boy came barreling back next to his mother, tugging the sleeve of his younger brother's shirt, bringing him where his parents stood in the front parlor. The younger child hid behind his mother's legs as the government officials crept closer, handing him a small white capsule. The small boy seemed ill and limped, growing more lifeless with each step. His father proudly watched, thanking the officials as his son gulped down the Cure.

Little did they know, the pill would set the mind back to a primitive state, one that would be able to absorb newly fed knowledge, even if it wasn't the truth. This wouldn't help the boy's physical condition. Instead it would leave him, and the rest of Laiden, stripped of most emotions to the point where they were devoid of what made them truly themselves. This was what led me to believe the government actually had much worse intentions behind the mass production of the pills, and the reason for my flee.

I witnessed the immediacy of the effects of Extium reel through the child's mind. I saw the blank expression he wore, and the dilation of his pupils, as the child's eyes turned from gray to green to black. Without looking back, the officials moved on.

HOUR ZERO

Six

Lennon

Let's play a game: two truths and a lie. It's simple. I'll give you three things that happened to me the morning my family and I took the Cure, and it's your job to figure out which are the truths… and which is the lie. Ready?

1. My family had no reaction when Prime Minister Iris ordered an "unscheduled holiday."

2. I don't recognize my mother or my father, because I believe their bodies have been abducted and their eyes replaced with blackness.

3. I fed my pet Piffer my "supposed-to-be" school lunch.

If you guessed the third was one of the two truths, you'd be dead wrong. I don't even own a Piffer, and even if I did, it probably would have died by now from all of the mushy, gray school lunches I would have been feeding it. If you guessed the first two, you would be correct.

The moment the small, white pill fell down my throat was the second Prime Minister Iris's voice came on our living room speaker. I listened from my seat at the kitchen table.

"Attention citizens of Laiden. Today is to be an unscheduled holiday. The only obligation that must be performed is a mid-day gathering in the Central Square."

I looked around for my family. My mother stood silent and my father stared at the speaker as if it was Iris. They showed no signs of relief. They did nothing. Nothing at all.

I bit my tongue from questioning their actions.

"Mom?" I called from the kitchen table.

"Yes, Lennon? Have you gotten ready for the meeting?" she replied in a monotone voice.

"Umm, yes. But do I really have to go?" I laughed tentatively.

Her eyes swelled and she sharply scolded, "Lennon!" She then reverted back to a false sweetness. "Of course, why would you even ask such a silly question?"

Taken aback, I turned to walk up the stairs to the haven of my bedroom. But it was not my mother's swift change in mood that struck me as so dissonant. It was her eyes. Her eyes had not been the same blue eyes full of depth and warmth. They were both curiously and frighteningly black now. I turned to glance at my father, facing me now. Those eyes. Those same black eyes had replaced his own.

This was more than weird. A muffled conversation that was being held beneath the stairs took my concern away from the black eyes briefly.

I stopped to listen. It was my mother on the phone with, by the sounds of it, a government official.

"Yes, I'd like to report immediately of a potential defect in inhabitant number #453456."

My Laiden identity code? What had made my mother not even use my real name, but refer to me as a number instead? It was an unspoken rule in Laiden to never address someone by his or her number. But more importantly, what did she mean by defect? I picked up the other end of the line and listened closer as an unrecognizable voice said, "We'll have our best officials come to collect the boy. Everything will be sorted out. There is nothing to worry about Mrs. Kincaid."

The conversation ended with a click. The house stood silent.

"Lennon," rung my mother's voice beneath the stairs.

I reeled toward the direction of my bedroom and quickly shut the door behind me. My vision grew hazy and my heart beat from my chest so loudly, my mother could probably hear it from downstairs.

I gripped the edge of my bed. It could have been nothing. They might not have been talking about me. I'm not in trouble. Beads of perspiration lined the back of my neck. I wiped them away and closed my eyes and took a deep breath, only to be further discomforted. The image of the blackness that had replaced my mother's once-beautiful eyes ingrained itself into my head. Those petrifying, onyx eyes stared at me and at the speaker. I pictured Prime Minister Iris's eyes and then my mother's. I switched my focus between the two, and soon was no longer able to tell whose eyes belonged to whom. I rubbed my head furiously, but it was my hearing that was failing me now. The official's words rung in my ears like a hammer to a metal plate.

Come and collect the boy? Forget about convincing myself of a false reality. I had a situation on my hands.

"Lennon," called my mother again.

This time, I could hear the stairs creaking beneath her feet.

"Uhhh, yes?" I asked.

"Come downstairs and sit with me at the table like a good little boy," she replied plainly.

My mother's attempt to comfort me only secured the waves of panic beating against my chest, but my urge to flee had diminished. The officials would take me away. There was no doubt about that. But a new question arose. What had I done to cause enough trouble for the officials to take me away? What made me different? I racked my brain for clues.

I made sure I acted as a model citizen. I never spoke out and never rebelled, in an outward fashion at least. I had friends, my professors loved me, and I was active in the society. I knew how to mold myself to what Laiden wanted. Who could ask for a more perfect son?

A knock at my bedroom door quieted my noisy thoughts.

I looked up and prepared myself to see those stoic black eyes. I was mistaken again. An official in uniform stood at my bedroom door.

This was not a lie.

Seven

Masen

Government officials arrived at my door with the Cure. I ate my rations, and listened to the announcement from my house's speaker, just like every other citizen in Laiden. I wasn't too psyched at the prospects of going to the meeting alone, because who knew where my dad was this morning. But just because I didn't have the luxury of a parent that seemed to stay in the picture, I couldn't say that the idea of a day off didn't lighten my mood.

I peered out of my kitchen window, and noticed people already filing out of their houses to the Central Square.

Great, I thought. I fumbled for my jacket and hastily left my house. I glanced toward the people leaving from houses thirty through forty; I hoped one of them wasn't Winslett. Praying that my friend was still home, I brushed through the crowd. The hairs on my neck stood on end, and I bumped shoulders with a man who quickly grabbed my arm.

"Watch it!" I said with a little more disdain than I meant.

Instead of an angry rebuttal, his black, dead eyes locked with my green.

“You need to get to the meeting,” he stated dryly.

“I just need to see my friend first.” I pulled my arm away.

His grip was firm and didn’t loosen. “You need to get to the meeting.”

Anger built up inside of me. With all the strength I could muster, I yanked my arm free.

“Alright, I get it!” I yelled, which earned me some tentative glances from nearby.

Something was off, that much I could sense. Yet, instead of following the promise I made to the man, I dashed off in the opposite direction, knowing I needed to reach Winslett. As I was running, I allowed myself one quick look back at the man. He had all but forgotten about our brief row. He simply walked in step with the others.

Eight

Lennon

The official strode forward, peering at me curiously.

I rose from the edge of my bed and stared back at the official.

"What is your name, boy?" he finally spoke.

Glancing at my mother, who stood at the door with a blank expression, I responded reluctantly, "Lennon Kincaid."

The official nodded. His features were sharp, high cheekbones, thinly cut eyebrows, and small eyes. He had a crew cut, like all other male officials. His forehead was unusually large, but matched his bulky figure.

He pursed his lips. "How old are you, boy?"

"Seventeen."

He narrowed his eyes, scanning me from head to toe. I almost felt violated. Finally, he clicked his tongue and beckoned for another official standing outside of my room.

The second official, much more round, and clearly much more green, stumbled in. "Fa-Fahad says to bring the boy to the bunker. I ha-have the coordinates on the GPS."

"We'll be done here shortly. Clear out the house, and make sure these people get to the Square for the meeting," the first official barked.

The second official nodded and made his way out of the room, leading my mother away.

I felt this was a good time to plead my case. "I swear I didn't do anything wrong!"

The official narrowed his eyes toward me again. "Tell me exactly what you did this morning. Don't leave out any details."

I let out a breath, trying to calm my racing heartbeat.

"The government officials knocked on my door, and handed each member of my family a small white pill."

"The Cure," he corrected.

"Right. They watched us swallow down the Cure, and then left. After that, the announcements came on and that's when things started to get weird."

"And you swear on your mother's life you swallowed the Cure?"

I nodded my head vigorously.

The official moved fast, grabbing the crook of my arm and pushing me toward the door. He growled behind my ear. "I'm taking you in for another round of questions. Your filthy lies won't get you anywhere, boy."

My heart picked up speed and the back of my neck began to line with sweat. "But I told you everything! I took the pill! I swear!"

My pleading resulted in another push from the burly official. "Down the stairs and out the door."

I took each step slowly, in spite of the official, which resulted in another push.

“Don’t toy with me,” he warned.

“Well, I’m going to die anyway,” I mumbled.

“What was that?”

“Nothing.”

He pushed the front door of our house open and strode outside, dragging me along.

A strong gust of wind whipped my hair backward, and I shielded my eyes from the flying dirt. Peeking through my fingers, I gasped. An enormous hovercraft had landed outside of my house, its wide steel wings spread across the pavement.

I turned to face the official who moved behind me.

“What’s happening?” I shouted over the intense whir of the hovercraft.

He smirked back at me and shoved a cloth against my eyes, blinding my vision.

“Hey!” I exclaimed.

With yet another push from the official, I found myself on my hands and knees on a hard surface. Was I inside of the hovercraft? I could feel my face turn hot as my breath quickened.

“Buckle him in,” a voice yelled over the loud motor.

A rough pair of hands grabbed my shoulders and pulled me onto a seat.

“Where are we going?” I screamed.

Without an answer, we ascended into the sky.

Nine

Byrde

Clutching Mommy's arm, I skipped along with the rest of the crowd into the Central Square. Mommy's white lab coat touched the floor as she quickly walked.

Before we left our house, Mommy said it was very important for me to stay quiet. If someone asked me a question I was to either nod my head yes or shake my head no. Stay very still was her final word.

We finally stopped when we reached the entrance to the new stage set up the night before in the Square. I recognized some of Mommy's friends, wearing the same matching white coats, as they came up to greet us. I could feel Mommy's hands getting sweaty as she tightened her hold.

"Reina, are you ready for today? It's a new beginning!" the lady with dark hair exclaimed.

"Of course," Mommy chuckled. "We have been waiting for this day for quite a while, have we not?"

Another added, "Yes indeed. Iris seemed most pleased."

Mommy paused a second, though I wasn't sure why.

"Yes, I most certainly agree." She spoke with less confidence this time.

I started to fidget. This conversation was taking too long. "Mommy, are we done yet?"

The crowd of white coats jumped back. Out of the corner of my eye I saw one of the women dart off.

"Reina! This is a direct disloyalty to the Minister!" the lady with the dark hair cried.

"What on earth provoked you to not give your daughter Extium!" a man with a gruff voice shouted.

Everyone was mad at Mommy. I, in the middle of the confusion, was forgotten. That is, until the woman came back. This time she came with company.

I felt a hard push from behind me, but Mommy caught my wrist and tugged me tight to her body. A burly man with a mean face began unscrewing a bottle of white capsules as he came closer. I didn't know what was happening. I couldn't keep track of my surroundings. I couldn't focus, mumbled voices echoed around me, and hands grabbed for me. Mommy's face grew pale as tears began to leap from my eyes.

Then my face burned. Mommy had whipped her hand across my face in a quick motion, leaving a red mark on my cheek.

"Listen, stop crying," she leaned toward me and whispered. "I gave up everything for you, even your father. Remember what he taught you."

Mommy screamed as she backed away from the government officials closing in on her.

"RUN, BYRDE! RUN!"

Ten

Lennon

A pair of hands ripped away the cloth covering my eyes and shoved me onto a soft, cushioned table. It pressed against my aching back, as I looked up to see a florescent ceiling and white tiled walls. The floors were white too. Everything was white— except for the cases of small, brightly colored tablets and neon liquids in pocket-sized bottles on a wall not too far from my feet. The containers lined the dozens of shelves in color order, each with a pasted label on the front. I looked around the rest of the fairly condensed room. A computer with a glowing screen sat in the corner, documents were strewn across a desk, and paper overflowed out of its drawers.

A voice spoke to my immediate left. "Lennon Kincaid. Age seventeen. House 532. Family of three. No pressing health issues."

I blinked and peered at the voice's owner. A man with mousy brown hair and glasses resting on the bridge of his nose sat on a spinning chair, scrolling through stacks of papers in a manila file. He wore a white lab coat that reached the back of his heels, confirming his short stature. I hadn't seen him come in, and I immediately tried sitting up.

"Uhhh," I groaned. "Where-where am I?"

The light was giving me a headache.

"The Health Wing," he answered, not looking up from his work.

"Are you going to kill me?"

The man let out a few humorless chuckles. "No, son. Death is not a fair punishment to the innocent."

"So you believe me?"

"Innocent until proven guilty." He clicked his tongue and held up my file for me to see. "I need to ask you a few more questions and then we're going to do a little check up. After that, you get to go home." He spoke with a false enthusiasm similar to that of my mother's.

"You mean, you're going to turn me into a robot and give me black eyes like the rest of my family."

My interrogator clicked his tongue again. "Let's start with the questions, son."

I sighed and turned away from the man and looked up toward the florescent lights.

"What do you know of the Outlanders?"

I was caught off guard. The Outlanders were only rumors, rumors of people who lived beyond the barriers of Laiden. They were only used as a reference to tease the few delinquents or outcasts in school.

"The Outlanders?" I repeated, "Seriously? They're not real. I don't know what you're expecting me to say here."

The interrogator scribbled on the margin of my file and muttered something inaudible.

He then held up a picture of a glowing sphere. "What about this?"

I was stunned again. "I have no idea. Why are you asking me these questions?"

"Sir," interrupted an official with a trimmed beard. He had walked into the room.

My interrogator waved him away. "Not now, Gill."

"Sir, I apologize, but we have an emergency," the official interrupted again.

Turning toward the door, the interrogator let out an irritated sigh. "What is it now?"

"The young scientist is nowhere to be found."

The interrogator leapt out of his chair. I could see how short he was now. Five feet, two inches… maybe. "Are you certain?"

The official nodded. "Yes, sir. The scientist had reported a delivery be made to the bunker at one thirty last morning. The hovercraft he flew is stationed inside the garage, but no signs of him are in the bunker or back at headquarters. We-we believe he fled, sir."

The interrogator scurried out of the room, cursing and barking criticisms, while the official ran closely behind.

The chair the interrogator had sat in still spun slowly in circles.

I wiped the sweat off the back of my neck and my forehead. Pushing myself off from the table, I planted my toes on the tiled floor, and slowly walked toward the door. No officials seemed to be on guard in this wing.

Was it safe to leave? I backed away. Where would I go? What was the point? No, I had to take a stand. If I couldn't find the courage to escape myself, at least I could muster the courage to escape for the will of my family. Carefully taking a few steps, I wandered out of the Health Wing and into a dimly lit hallway.

"Hey! What are you doing? Who are you?" an official down the hall yelled.

My heart began to race again.

"Ummm- uhh," I stuttered.

"You're the maintenance kid. Aren't you? You got fired last week! What are you doing back here?"

I couldn't believe my luck. This was my best bet to stay out of trouble. No doubt the interrogator would be back soon. I played along. "Just checking back up on a couple things."

The official rolled his eyes. Grabbing hold of my arm and dragging me down a short hallway and into a garage, the official strode to the end of the room and opened a steel door with a silver key.

"Get out and stay out kid. Walk home," he barked, pushing me onto the wet grass.

I landed on all fours and spun around quickly enough to see the smirk on the official's face. He slammed the door.

It was nighttime, but light enough for me to make out the outline of the tall trees to my right and the flickering lights of Laiden to my left. I looked at the two directions, swiveling my head right and left, left and right.

Brushing the dirt off my knees, I stood and ran.

I chose right.

Eleven

Winslett

The feeling of anxiety and misery on the day I had found out my parents had died was the same kind of edgy feeling that was suspended in me now, though I wasn't sure why. I uneasily gazed out the window at the trees dotting all the way to the barrier. Despite Laiden's effervescent skies, I still felt as if gray storm clouds were threatening to make an appearance.

"Winslett," the tone of Culver's voice shook me from my thoughts, "come on."

I jerked around and was face to face with him.

"Culver! Way to scare me!" I joked, pushing him playfully away from my face.

"It's really not that hard," he teased, tossing an orange to me. "Get dressed, we have to go to the meeting."

"Ugh, it's not such a big deal. Why can't we skip the meeting?" I asked.

"Sorry, kiddo. After what happened with Mom and Dad, you know they're always keeping a close watch on our family. Grab Evelyn, and let's go already!" Culver shouted behind, as he left and reached the door handle.

I grabbed my book. Prime Minister Iris's meetings were always boring and I needed something to preoccupy my mind, besides chewing on my hair.

I've always been told I was a spitting image of my mother. We had the same slender face, and long, dark, wispy, red hair. Culver and Evelyn looked more like our Dad though, dark hair and tan skin. The only similarity between the three of us was the same frosty gray eyes, shared along with our parents. Still, I was definitely the odd child out.

"Evelyn, let's go!" I shouted up the stairs.

Technically, we weren't supposed to know the truth behind our parents' execution when they had defied the Prime Minister. The government told us they had died in a tragic accident, something we wouldn't have been able to understand. Knowing my brother and his hatred for authority, I knew he wouldn't take such a vague answer. In turn, his skills as a computer-hacking genius scored us a few files about our parents' death. Before he was caught that is. The government fortunately didn't want to make a scene, so Culver was let go with a warning. Our family has always had hard feelings toward the government. We were our own kind of "Outlanders." And to be honest, I kind of liked it that way.

"Evelyn! What's taking so long?" I shouted, running up the stairs.

Her room was left ajar, so I burst in. "Eve…" I halted mid sentence.

She wasn't there. I searched in Culver's room, our parents' old room, and my room. I fled back down the stairs and frantically spun around the whole house in search of the little mess of dark hair.

"If this is one of your tricks, Evelyn, I'm warning you!" I exclaimed.

I grabbed the door handle and pushed it open. Outside, Evelyn stood next to Culver.

I reached over to grab her arm. "Evelyn, were you here this entire time? I've practically torn the house down looking for you!"

"It wasn't her fault," Culver glared sternly at me.

"Okay, I was just making..." I began.

"Stop making excuses, Winslett. Why do you always have to be like this?" Culver accused.

"Whoa, okay, I'm sorry!"

This was way out of line. Culver was never like this. It was really unusual to see him so upset. I had only remembered when he freaked out at me when...

I stopped, meeting my eyes with his. Something about those eyes didn't seem right. I was used to looking at Culver's gray, soft eyes. His were now solid black. What was going on?

"Evelyn, I'm sorry. I guess I've been pretty out of it," I apologized, dazed.

Culver relaxed his shoulders and put a forced smile back on his face. Evelyn turned to face me, with the same gleaming, black eyes.

She reached for my hand, and squeezed it tight. In her sweet, angelic voice she said, "Winslett, why have you always been such a pain? I mean when's the last time any of us have cared about what you think?"

"Ouch," I whimpered.

Tears began to brim around my eyes, and frustration bubbled inside of me. We were all each other had and without them, I was nobody. I backed into the front door, my emotions swimming around my head. I didn't want to cause any more trouble.

"Hey guys, you know what, I'm really not up for this meeting anymore. I think I'll just lie down and rest some."

"I really don't think that's a good idea," Culver warned.

"Oh yeah, when's the last time you two ever cared about me, according to Evelyn over here," I replied. "Whatever, I'm going inside."

I reached for the door handle.

Suddenly, Evelyn grabbed my arm and jerked me around, with a strength I never knew she was capable of. Culver reached for my wrist and pulled it hard. I felt a crack.

I screamed as the splintering pain shot up my arm. I kicked Culver away, swinging my leg at his side. He fell backwards onto his arm and glared at me. What was happening? I couldn't believe it, but before Culver began spiraling back toward me, a gentle, firm hand reached for mine and pulled me away.

Twelve

Lennon

The slightest sound from the undergrowth made me fidget. Hearing a rustle, I jumped backward and stepped on something sharp. It was a rock. Thinking it could become useful later, I picked it up and tucked it away into my left back pocket. I sighed with relief when I realized the noise had simply been a Mauge. Out from the bushes its brown, squashed-in face gazed up at me in disdain. Its fat prickly torso turned away from me as I dodged its equally prickly, disc-like tail. I continued on with my trek.

It felt as if I was being watched and the image of my mother's over-dilated eyes left an everlasting mark. The picture seemed to haunt me, as I doubted my decision to leave.

Brushing some branches aside, I finally found the type of spot I sought after. I meandered over to my newfound campsite when I realized smoke was billowing only a few feet away. The leaves of a willow tree cast a shadow down over my head shielding me from view. As I edged toward the glowing flame, I peered over a small shrub to scrutinize the place.

That was when I saw the rucksack. Someone else was out here? Aghast, I stumbled over a tree root. I quickly caught my balance, pushing the thought of company out of my head. However, the feeling of being watched lingered on.

That was when I heard the click of a trigger. I turned around too late.

Thirteen

Masen

The streets of Laiden were tiled with slabs of thick, dirt-colored stone. Our shoes patted against them as we ran past the aisles of houses. Ninety-seven, ninety-six, ninety-five… I kept pace with Winslett as we dodged the crowds of citizens marching toward the Square and their equally unforgiving glares.

"Winslett, running away any farther won't do us any good. What was that back there?" I pressed.

Winslett held her hurt wrist close to her chest, giving me no answer. I let out a breath of frustration. I got enough silence treatment from my father. Winslett wasn't about to start with me.

I looked at her face and immediately softened. Her eyes, watered with pain, leaked tears across her face.

"We can stop if you want."

She shook her head and let out a few mumbles.

"Sorry, didn't hear you there."

"I don't have any idea what's happening! Culver and Evelyn, their eyes were so black and Culver tried to hurt me after I found Evelyn downstairs and…" she trailed off, out of breath.

Winslett sounded saner than the average schizophrenic.

She halted, breaking the flow of our run. "We have to go back. Come on, they need us!"

"Whoa, ok. We're a couple of streets from the Square. Let's just think things through there," I said with as much certainty as I could muster.

"I just don't know what's going on," Winslett began again. "Something is definitely wrong. You saw Evelyn. If something really is happening, I don't think I could leave her, or Culver. I need to apologize. They need me." Her voice broke on the last word.

We hopped the next two streets, just as the sky began to dim and the pitter-patter of rain echoed across Laiden. The slabs of stone, now spotted with the tears of the sky, blurred beneath us. The Square began to come into view, and our pace slowed.

Not far from the doorsteps of the nearing homes, the border of the Central Square lined with government officials' offices that dealt with Laiden's centralized problems away from Iris's headquarters. The floor of the Square, big enough to fit Laiden's population of roughly five thousand, was made of the same slabs of stone and formed geometric outlines rather than the dull parallel lines in the streets. Not only did the government use the Square for our standard town meetings, but also it acted as the arena for public display of punishment for those who committed treason against the government. From torture to hanging to public whippings by the government officials, the citizens of Laiden were forced to gather in the Square and watch. Almost as a form of punishment itself, having us watch those people fueled Iris's growing source of power: fear.

"Come on, over here," I whispered over to Winslett.

She followed my gesture as we ducked behind the row of people farthest from Iris. We snaked through the rear of the crowd, crouched and silent.

"Our leader and our guardian," the crowd suddenly chimed in unison.

I made an abrupt stop. Winslett bumped into me with her wrist and I could hear her sharp intake of breath. Slowly straightening my legs, I peered over the shoulders of a lanky boy— somewhat around my age— and directed my eyes toward the front. A wide platform stood atop the height of the crowd, built with an enormous screen projecting the face of Iris. Dressed in a sharp, black suit and polished shoes, the actual Iris rose from his chair on stage and stalked toward the front of the platform.

I glanced over to Winslett, and her already pale face had turned a more ghostly shade of white.

"We, citizens of Laiden, are humbled to stand in the honor of your presence," the crowd continued.

I looked above the platform, toward the projection. The blown up, virtual image of Iris was still enough to make me shudder. His beady black eyes held a wicked sparkle as he addressed the crowd.

"Hello, faithful citizens of Laiden. You are the lucky ones." His voice boomed and demanded the attention of the crowd, even without the help of his microphone.

A "Thank you, Prime Minister" echoed around the Square.

I scanned the crowd. This was no ordinary meeting. Not one person fidgeted, not one child tugged on their mother's shirt, and not one person even checked their watch. Thousands of black pairs of eyes laid intently on Iris, clinging to his every word.

His grin grew so wide that each of his pointed canine teeth was fully visible. "We are the last of the living. The world around us has died. The barrier erected is the only thing separating us from the remnants of what once was and the horrible diseases that plagued the old world. But you are cured! Be grateful my citizens!"

"We are grateful," the crowd beamed.

"I, Prime Minister Iris, am your savior. I have not only brought you to salvation, but I have a bright future planned for you. Only if we act and think as one solitary unit can our new way of life function. I will bring you to your full potential. With me as your leader we can have a perfect society. In Laiden, there is no conflict. There is no strife. There is simply you and me. And in this friendship, we have the perfect society."

All this chanting and talk of friendship was ready to make me wish I hadn't eaten my morning rations only a couple hours ago. I searched over the heads of the crowd. I had no clue what would be up Iris's sleeve next. If we wanted to leave unnoticed, this would be the time to do it.

I turned to Winslett and tugged on her arm, motioning my head toward the back of the Square and out of the crowd. She nodded reluctantly, although it hadn't stopped her eyes from scanning across the crowd, most likely searching for her siblings.

"We can talk behind one of the government administration buildings," I whispered.

She nodded again.

I ducked again, silently thanking the lanky boy and scooted away. We backed further away from view and deep into a dark corner between the sides of a daily rations building and a government official check-in building. Taking a hold of my forearm, Winslett crouched down and motioned for me to do the same.

"We are loyal citizens of Laiden. We accept this as the truth. We obey Iris above all else," the crowd continued to chant.

"You do hear this, don't you?" I hissed with disgust.

Winslett nodded in equal annoyance.

"I don't think it's safe for us here. It's obvious we don't fit in with Iris's weird mold. Officials are always on street watch and… and I think we should just leave."

Winslett propped the base of her palm against her forehead and let out a sigh. "We've learned in the Institute all our lives that there's nowhere else to go and you know that. I'd like to see you try getting out of Laiden."

"Wins—" I started.

"And why would you? There's nothing outside but rotting bones and dead air. No water. No food. No homes. Right?"

"Come on, you're the one that always rambles on about Outlander stories," I replied.

"Those people don't exist. There's no proof."

Winslett stared off into the crowd. It wasn't like her to not have faith in a wild idea, especially concerning life outside.

"You always went on about myths beyond the barrier and exploring. What's the sudden change in heart?" I asked.

She shook her head in disbelief. "It would be different if we had Culver and Evelyn."

"We don't, though, Wins. For whatever reason, they're stuck in some kind of trance."

"Maybe you're right. But even if you were, how, when, and where are you planning to leave?"

"Today. Maybe we could stay near the edge of the woods? Around the barrier?" I thought aloud.

"The woods?" she chuckled humorlessly.

I snapped back, "It was only an idea."

"You can't be serious. Masen, the woods are forbidden. No one knows what's out there and worse— we wouldn't make it a couple of hours out there."

"Which is why no one would find us."

She seemed even more unconvinced.

"Do you suggest we hide in alleys and steal food from dumpsters the rest of our lives? There's more of a chance we'd get caught laying around here than fighting for our lives in the woods. Listen, Winslett, everyone knows there's a North Gate and a South Gate around the walls of Laiden."

I drew a map with my finger against the hard stone.

I continued, "The government building is positioned directly outside of the South Gate. Our best bet is to leave through the North Gate and take cover in the woods there."

"We can't just waltz out of the North Gate like we're going on a picnic."

"Why not? Can't we just take a look?"

Winslett faltered.

"It's worth a try. What left do we have in here?"

More silence. More thinking.

"That's a reckless idea, but I'm willing to go if it's our best bet," she conceded.

I was pleased Winslett was slowly showing signs of her spontaneous self.

"Listen, Winslett. You know this is goodbye then, right?"

"No. It's goodbye for now. But whatever's happened to them, whatever sucked the color and life from their eyes might be able to be fixed. I have a feeling." Winslett said it with such assurance I almost believed it myself. Almost.

"Don't look at me like that, Masen," she began again. "It's true. Before my mother died, she told me something. She told me how the government was made of people I could never trust, and that they were always looking for ways to have total control. This must be it."

"Well, why didn't it affect us?" I asked fervently.

"I don't have a clue. I really don't, and I'm not sure I want to."

I inspected us both from head to toe. Our shoes were tracked with mud and our hair was drenched from the rain. I had never suffered worse conditions, but couldn't have been more thankful I wasn't alone.

"Okay, Winslett, let's think later. Everyone's attention is on Iris, so we need to leave before the meeting is over," I said in sync with Iris's next booming words.

"This is a new age and you will all be an essential part to it!" he proclaimed.

Ugh. In disgust, I began to move away from the dark corner, back toward the direction of the houses, until something smooth brushed my arm.

I snatched my arm away from the disturbance as a cold nerve struck the back of my head and the beat of my heart raced to follow. I was greeted with big, milky brown eyes red from crying. It was a little girl who couldn't have been older than nine. She crept closer into the light and I could see her fair, blonde disheveled hair and her dirt-smudged face. I tried out a smile but it may have looked more like a grimace.

"Winslett..."

Winslett was still listening to Iris on my other side.

"Look at this," I hissed, hearing the tremble in my own voice.

She jerked her head around and stifled a gasp.

"Shhh," I spat.

Winslett looked over to me, eyes wide and frightened. But with a quick exchange of looks, Winslett and I were on the same page. This girl was the only one so far, besides Winslett and me, whom Iris wasn't controlling. This meant that the strange girl now needed us.

Calming the fear in her eyes, Winslett looked back at the girl, and rested her good hand on the girl's shoulder.

"I'm Winslett," Winslett said in singsong voice I've heard her use with Evelyn. Just when I thought the girl was mute, she murmured in an equally sweet tremor, "I'm Byrde."

"What are you doing here all by yourself, Byrde?" Winslett asked gently.

"Mommy told me to go," the girl said like it was the simplest thing ever.

"Why did Mommy say that?"

"The bad people were coming."

"Who are the bad people?" Winslett asked with more concern.

There was a long pause before the girl pointed to the stage where Iris stood speaking.

"Byrde, what do you say about coming with us? Masen and I are going to try and get away from these bad people too," Winslett suggested soothingly.

I began to protest, but Winslett nudged me roughly with her shoulder. I stayed silent.

Byrde stood up, no taller than the dumpster, and nodded eagerly. My mind raced. Escaping with Winslett would be like punching Iris in the face— impossible, psychotic, and deadly. Add a little girl who just lost her mother on top of that? There was no way the three of us would be able to pull this off. I had to talk some sense into Winslett.

But just as I pulled her away from Byrde, the crowd uniformly rose and started to file robotically out of the Square. The only sound to be heard was a thumping of thousands of pairs of feet. We had missed our chance to leave the Square undetected.

Without wasting any more precious time, I grabbed the arms of Winslett and Byrde and filed in quickly with the rest of the crowd toward the homes up ahead, and toward the North Gate.

I let my eyes quickly flit to the stage where Prime Minister Iris stood watching his new minions disperse. And for a moment, I could've sworn his black eyes flickered to lock with mine, or maybe it was just my imagination.

Fourteen

Masen

After twenty minutes of marching uniformly with an ever-so-stiff crowd, Winslett, Byrde, and I broke out of the formation to continue to the gate. We were nearing the last row of houses, but the thought of officials coming around their nightly watches still shook me up. I quickened my pace.

"Do you think they have officials guarding outside the North Gate?" Byrde asked, walking in between Winslett and me.

Winslett shrugged. "I don't know. I've never been close enough. Have you?"

She looked over at me.

I shook my head. Crossing another aisle of houses, we walked with an awkward silence. It wouldn't be long now.

"Well, maybe there aren't any guards," Winslett suggested. "Maybe he doesn't see why any of us would want to leave."

I scoffed, "You really think Iris is that naïve?"

She looked slightly abashed. "No, Masen. But people feel safe here. Besides, it's the only part of this world that isn't spiraling toward death."

I rolled my eyes. "Or so they say."

Byrde started to drag her feet, but now wasn't the time to slow down. Officials could start their nightly check up any minute now. We needed to reach the gate.

"Come on, Byrde. It's not that much farther," Winslett cooed. "Look, don't you see the trees over there?"

She was right. The Square was long gone, and the further we moved away from Laiden's center, the more green sprouted under our feet. I could even start to see the first row of trees only meters away. The colors of the trees were like nothing else in Laiden. The rich greens seemed so full of life compared to the dull, gray houses. On one of the closer trees, I even saw a pink flower. Pink. Would Byrde even know that color? Though Laiden was bursting with life, it wasn't a vibrant life. I wanted to reach up and pick it, but a color like that deserved to stay.

We walked around the side of the last house, and finally, the North Gate came into view. Although, it wasn't "technically" a gate; it was more of an entrance, because the rest of Laiden was surrounded by twenty feet high steel walls. The North and South "Gates" were the only ways to possibly escape the city of Laiden and into the woods. But like Winslett had said, the woods weren't exactly an enticing reason to leave.

"Look!" exclaimed Byrde, pointing toward the gate.

"Shhh!" I hushed, cupping my hand over Byrde's mouth.

I looked to where she had pointed and out of nowhere, a dark-skinned official came into view, planted his feet in the dirt, and stared off in the woods, his back facing us. My heartbeat quickened and Byrde reached to hold my hand, which I shook away. Neither of us said a word as a long three minutes passed. Suddenly, he began to move again. I exchanged a glance with Winslett, but remained stiff. Another minute passed, and a new official walked into the dark-skinned official's previous place.

Winslett shifted to tap my shoulder. I looked over at her.

"Do you think they are on a rotational system? That way they can cover all the spaces in between the stations of the officials?" she whispered.

"Maybe."

Byrde chimed in, "Can we just run in when the first guard leaves?"

"It can't be so simple. Iris would station more officials if it were only that easy to get out of this place. Plus, we'd probably be in the second official's line of sight."

"Another two minutes and he'll move again, if we're right about it," I added.

"Masen, I don't have any ideas. We can't exactly attack him or confront him."

I didn't respond, not right away. I had an idea myself, but I didn't want to run it past Winslett. She would shut it down immediately. And if it went wrong, it was going to go horribly wrong. But then again, we were pretty limited on our options.

I looked around and spotted what I needed. Picking up a medium-sized stone lying next to a patch of grass, I brushed my hands across it. I straightened my legs and ran toward the gate, beckoning for Winslett and Byrde to follow. From the devil look on Winslett's face, I knew that not telling her about my reckless idea was a good move. But they reluctantly followed, and silently, the three of us reached the gate, so close that it was within arms length.

I crouched down. My legs were tired and my throat was dry from the lack of fluid, but I remained silent, waiting, and counting down the seconds. Ten- nine- eight- seven… I could hear Winslett muttering curses under her breath. She was holding Byrde close to her side... four- three- two-one. Right on cue, the guard began to move and just as he did, I chucked the rock as far left as I could. A clattering sound echoed in the distance, and the official bolted in the direction of the sound. I was positive his replacement had as well.

"Now!" I stood up quickly, and ran toward the trees.

"Masen, that was reckless, and stupid, and crazy, and…" Winslett hissed as she sprinted beside me. I was impressed Byrde was keeping up too.

I said nothing. She was right of course, but I knew I had made the right decision. Here we were, three juveniles, running into a forbidden forest, defying Laiden's norms, and free of Iris's crazy mind-controlling games.

It was dark enough that Winslett couldn't see me smiling.

Fifteen

Wren

The boy just lay there. I wasn't really sure what to do with him. I wasn't really sure how he could even be here. I knew what today was, and if my calculations were correct, everyone would now be gathering in the Square. How was it possible this boy made it all the way to the outskirts of the woods? I rummaged through his pockets and found some leftover morning rations, a sharp rock, and a picture of his family…how sentimental of him.

I took his rock in case he would prove to be a threat, but honestly, it wouldn't be so bad to have some company. Still, he had to have taken Extium. He should have been forced to take Extium. He shouldn't be here.

I leaned against an entrance to one of the government's outdated shafts, once used to transport citizens of Laiden into the government building. Its use had long expired, but the shafts hadn't been completely destroyed.

Almost two hours later, I finally heard some sign of life in the boy.

"Finally come around, have you?" I asked.

Terror filled the boy's eyes when he saw me. Absentmindedly twirling his sharp rock around in my fingers, I almost chuckled. I placed it beside me reluctantly. I needed answers and I needed him to give them.

"How did you get here?" I asked.

The boy looked pretty stupid sitting there trying to grasp a sense of consciousness.

"You shot me!" he exclaimed in pure alarm.

"Yes, I did, but as you can see you're fine. Just answer my question."

"Fine, I walked," he said sardonically, as if I couldn't have figured that out.

"Yes, but why aren't you with the others, back in Laiden?" I continued patiently.

"Listen," he said bitterly, "my mother called an official to take me away after I told her I didn't want to go to the meeting. They brought me to some sort of safe house outside of the gates and then kicked me out. So then I ran, is that okay with you?"

I still didn't understand how the circumstances were feasible, but I could already tell this kid didn't want to have anything to do with me.

He glared at me, doing some scrutinizing of his own. "What are you even sitting on?"

I looked down at the shaft's entrance.

"It looks like a door," he continued.

"Because it is a door. If you open this cellar and go down the stairs, you'll see an underground express shuttle that'll take you to the government building. Several are scattered across the forest."

He looked skeptical. "Where exactly would it take me in the government?"

"Each leads to a separate room, but I guess Iris could've changed them to his liking. Anyway, the shuttles have been closed down since an anti-government coup tried to overthrow the government decades ago."

The boy didn't seem to be completely hearing me. "Are you lying?"

"Nope, people used to live out here in the woods in small communities, before Iris took control over Laiden."

He raised an eyebrow. "You mean Prime Minister Iris?"

I nodded, "Prime Minister Iris, whatever."

He sighed and I continued with our original conversation.

"Who are you?" I asked him.

"Well, who are you?" he asked with a smirk.

I rolled my eyes, but answered him. "I'm Wren Casterra. And did it occur to you that I could turn you in for being in this unregistered territory? If you don't start giving answers, this stun dart is going to make a reappearance."

This was a bluff of course. I could never turn him in without turning myself in as well. I had committed close to what would be an act of treason, meaning I would be executed. He, of course, didn't know this.

The boy muttered, "Don't call me a kid. You can't be that much older than I am. But fine, I'll answer your questions. Then, you'll have to answer some of mine too. I have no idea what is going on."

This time, I knew he was being sincere.

"Trust me I will, but answer mine first. Who are you and why are you here? I can spot a liar— so don't stray from the truth," I persisted.

He sighed. "My name is Lennon Kincaid. Some officials came to our door this morning and gave us the Cure. Like I said, things got weird. My family wasn't the same, and I ran after an official had taken me to a safe house outside of center-city Laiden."

This kid, sorry, "Lennon," was smarter then he looked. But, one problem remained. If he had taken Extium he shouldn't have been able to formulate opinions or trigger emotions. He should have been in Laiden with the others.

"Are you sure you took that pill?" I questioned tentatively, careful not to use the word "Extium" around him.

"Yes, of course. The officials practically shoved it down my throat if I didn't pick it up fast enough! There wasn't a choice," he said with a gulp. "This wasn't actually a cure was it?"

Lennon asked this with the innocence of a child. He had just shattered the veil of the most highly constructed lie Laiden ever fed the society. Lennon's darkest confession was what made me decide I could trust him.

"You're right. It's not, Lennon. It changes people and their ways of thinking." I paused, thinking of how to condense an explanation of Extium into the simplest terms. "Think of the pill you took this morning as a mind molder. Now, think of the brain of a newborn. The Cure reverts the brain of those who digest it similarly to the mind and simple thinkings of a newborn. With this new power, Iris has the ability to practically nurture the citizens of Laiden as if they were his own children. He will teach them manners of behavior he finds suitable and eliminate any further intentions of government resistance. The way you see the citizens now, obedient and emotionless, is the first stage of the Cure's effects."

"There's more than one stage?" His jaw opened slightly.

"Yes, the Cure is a gradual process. The people of Laiden will soon forget their families, friends, memories, everything. Now, Lennon, I've decided to trust you and take your word that somehow the pill doesn't work on you. Perhaps it is you alone, but if anyone were to find out that you weren't like the others, you'd probably be dead."

"But I don't understand," he interrupted. "Why would the government make us take the Cure? Weren't things okay the way they were?"

I shook my head. "Not for the Prime Minister. The Cure gave him a sense of security that ensured no anti-government or rebellious groups would ever form again."

"But that was ages ago!"

I shrugged. "He and his scientists have been working on the project for a long time."

"Well, I hate every one of them. They deserve a piece of their own medicine." His indirect amount of contempt toward my co-workers and me was not surprising.

"Not many people are either brave enough or stupid enough to wish ill upon Iris in public."

"I'm not *trying* to act brave."

"So, stupid then?" I smirked.

He shook his head. "Neither, okay? I mean, we've learned at the Institute to revere the ways of the government, but I mean… this is unforgivable. Who wouldn't hate them for what they've done?"

I turned away and changed the subject.

"Nevertheless, it's going to a be huge adjustment, for both you and me, to get used to living without the luxuries of Laiden." I paused. "So, are you with me?"

"Yeah, I guess so. I don't suppose I have any other options now," he said with a strong front but with a slight hint of regret.

"I hate to be so harsh, but there is no turning back now. Your family and friends are gone to you," I reminded him.

The sky had turned suddenly dark and I looked upward as raindrops began to hit my face. I brushed them away as I told Lennon I would pitch a tent so he would have a dry place to mull things over.

When I had come back to him, I could tell he was tired, like any day of running would make you. I was about to tell him to go in the tent and take a rest when he abruptly broke the silence.

"Wren, you seem like the kind of guy who knows what he's talking about. I'm with you," Lennon paused. "I can't go back, not to a place of people who aren't themselves."

"Good decision. Why don't you take a rest?"

"Wait, what's our plan?"

"Lennon, you just got here. We don't need to talk about plans just yet."

"Why not? We need to figure out where to go from here."

What would I answer to this? I couldn't divulge all I was thinking just yet. Firstly, I wasn't sure myself and secondly, I didn't know if I wanted to drag anyone else into my risky plans. I only knew I had to right the wrong I had done.

I followed up with a more honest answer. "Our plan is to survive."

Lennon gave a curt nod. He then turned quickly to head into the tent, but I still saw the misery that welled in his eyes.

I sat by the fire a little longer for I knew the rain would soon put it out. I pondered over my newfound alliance with Lennon. It still worried me that Extium didn't work on him and I told him that, but as smart as he seemed, he looked over the one obvious question. If I told him Extium only hadn't worked on him, didn't he wonder how I was here? Nevertheless, I was glad he didn't ask. Because that was one answer I didn't know I could ever give.

Sixteen

Winslett

The woods weren't nearly as ominous as the rumors had always said. The trees sprouted tall and thick from the fresh-soiled earth. Green was everywhere, and plants germinated all around us. We had to be careful not to entangle ourselves in the unknown life, but it was exhilarating to be among such naturalness. If only Culver and Evelyn could see this with me too. Evelyn, especially, would have been in so much of a trance, Culver would have had to lift her little weight onto his back. Evelyn would've held my hand and played with Culver's kept hair as we walked, calling out unusual plants and animals that passed us. And if she had seen a flower, god forbid, we would have had to stop until she was satisfied we had all sniffed and admired its beauty aloud. I could imagine Culver gently placing a flower with small, bright petals, behind Evelyn's dark, smooth hair.

I smiled at the fantasy. But as soon as the smile came, it disappeared, and I resumed the impassive expression over my face.

Masen, Byrde, and I were a little ways into the forest before I let us stop to catch our breath. We were all panting heavily and I knew hunger would soon take over. Mauges, creatures I had only ever seen in textbooks from the Institute, prowled the ground, looking for strange insects. I thought I had even caught a glimpse of a small bushy tail of what was possibly an orange-backed Riiber skittering up a tree for the impending night.

"Listen, I'm hungry, and I know Byrde probably is too. Let's actually try and find something to eat," Masen said in exasperation.

"Geez okay," I said, and once more ran ahead, "Come on!"

I turned behind me to grab Byrde's hand; only she wasn't behind me anymore. I swiveled my head, scanning the forest.

"Masen, wait!" I called.

He turned to look at me. Reading the panic washed over my face, he grabbed my shoulders with both his hands.

"What's wrong, Winslett?"

"Where's Byrde?" I exclaimed.

He pivoted too, searching for some sign of a small, blonde head.

"Wasn't she with you?" he asked.

"Yes, I turned around the next second, and she was gone!"

"Maybe she just went ahead?" he inquired calmly.

"Byrde!" I screamed out of exasperation.

"Let's just go straight," Masen said. "She had nowhere else to go. She'll find us."

But I wasn't so sure. I didn't know all the creatures that lived in the forest, and maybe Byrde had been caught by the worst.

Masen and I jogged at a brisk pace in search of the little one.

Suddenly, a rustle broke out from one of the bushes a short distance from where Masen and I were. The branches shuffled again, and I looked at Masen. He nodded, and we both made a mad dash for them.

Reaching the greenery, I picked a twig from the dirt and poked the bush timidly. Masen was more daring, and walked through the bush with little effort. He held the branches to the side for me to cross, and I looked down. Sure enough, Byrde was there chowing down on some purple berries with odd yellow dots. I exhaled a sigh of relief. I had certainly never seen this odd fruit before, and quickly joined her in the undergrowth, popping several in my mouth.

"Mmmm," I agreed.

Masen interrupted my bliss. "What do you two think you're doing? Those could be poisonous!"

Byrde chimed in first, "These are delicious! Don't worry, Masen!"

Hunger must have eventually gotten the best of him, or the fact that neither of us had dropped dead yet. Running his fingers through his hair, Masen tentatively sat down with us.

He picked up a berry and slipped it into his mouth.

"Yum," he declared.

And we all laughed. It felt good to laugh.

Seventeen

Lennon

Night was approaching and the once heavy rain had been reduced to a slow drizzle. I was on Wren's order to collect firewood for the night and I was slightly annoyed. It was hard for me to come up with an impression on the guy. I mean he seemed reliable, independent, and strong, mentally and physically. But how could I trust a guy who practically killed me with his stun dart?

Frankly, I was still on the fence whether to trust him or not, for the more than obvious reason. I shifted my glance back to camp and looked at Wren. I shook my head and continued collecting firewood.

Wren was also mysterious. After a grueling hour of spilling my life story out to him, it irked me that he was still hiding his. The more I thought about it, I actually knew nothing about Wren, except for the fact he used to be a government worker and was never taken seriously by his co-workers. He would not elaborate any further, even when I tried pressing him on the subject.

I eventually gave up, and we went back to our old habit, silence. I had this weird feeling that Wren knew more than he seemed to let on.

In mid-thought, I froze. My nerves quickly turned to ice as I glanced up to spot a wisp of fire that had raced a far distance away.

"Wait, that wasn't fire," I whispered to myself. "What was it?"

I sidestepped into the back of a nearby fir tree, with my knife at the ready. The "thing" came closer. I heard a crack from a tree branch I had dropped. It had split underneath its feet. The sound was followed by a loud thump onto the ground.

"Crap!" it mumbled angrily.

I swiveled around quickly to see what had spoken, and found a girl with fiery red hair, in a face plant, right in the dirt. About five feet away from the soles of my shoes, she cautiously looked upward into my eyes. I could tell, even though I had no idea who this strange girl was, she was about to scream for help. I sprinted toward her and clasped my hand over her mouth. It was just in time too. I muffled her cry. I quietly chuckled to myself, until I felt her teeth clamp down on my finger so hard, a trickle of blood swelled quickly. I gasped, and she pushed me to the ground.

"What was that for?" I exclaimed.

"Well, why the hell would you suffocate me?" the fire girl shot back in a mocking tone.

I took note of her equally fiery attitude.

"I was only saving both of our lives. These woods are filled with more than Bavines you know," I said.

She glared at me.

"Who are you anyway?" the girl pressed.

"I might just have to ask you the same question," I replied back. "What are you doing out here?"

"I was *trying* to get some dinner, until I tripped over this stupid branch," she explained, tossing it aside.

"Well, let me help you with that."

"No, I got it, thanks," she replied immediately.

After a brief silence, she asked somewhat rudely, "Well are you going to answer my question?"

"Hmmm?" I inquired.

"Who are you?" she persisted, aggravated.

"Lennon, you?"

She ignored my question.

"Are you from Laiden?"

"Of course I'm from Laiden, where else would I be from?" I replied, surprised she had even asked. "Are you?"

"Yeah," she answered, although her facial expression faltered suddenly.

"Are you going to tell me who *you* are, or what?" I asked.

"Maybe," she replied slyly.

A gust of wind picked up, and carried Wren's voice. "Lennon, where are you?"

Footsteps moved toward us.

I looked back into the mysterious girl's face, and her eyes rose with panic. She began to sprint off as Wren crept closer into view.

"Wait!" I yelled after her.

But she was gone, her fire chasing after her.

Eighteen

Byrde

I sat as far away from him as possible, the one with the rock. I wasn't sure how he got it and I wasn't sure the edge could've been any sharper. He sliced it against the smooth stone again and again while staring me down with those green eyes. I had made up my mind. I didn't like him. I missed Mommy and Daddy, and Winslett too. When would she be back?

She hadn't even been gone long, but being alone with Masen for even a second could seem like hours. I guess I was happy they had found me, but now how would I get back to Mommy? Was this even any better? The grass was soggy from the pouring rain. All we had were some logs around us. No blankets. We were all cold. Truthfully, I wasn't even sure these two knew what they were doing, no matter how much they tried and acted like they did.

I decided to hum my poem, the one Daddy always told me. Every night he whispered the story, until the day he never came back.

"Byrde," he said the last morning I saw him. I looked up at him. He was in his work uniform. Daddy was a special scientist. Prime Minister Iris was always with him.

"Byrde," he said again, "my child, be brave for me. One day the world will find use for you, and that is when you need to remember me. Don't forget what I taught you."

Looking back, it seemed like he knew he'd never see me again. I was only five then. All I did was nod and smile.

"See you later, Daddy!" I grinned.

Through my smile, he probably didn't know I noticed the tears in his eyes.

What would he think now as I sung about the stars? I snuck a side-glance at Masen. Yup, still staring at me. This time he had a different look. I guess he thought my song was weird. That was when I saw it, a prickly beast with black eyes crawling toward him.

My poem ended.

"Masen!" I screamed.

His reaction was fast as he swiveled around and flung the rock right at the animal. I held back a yelp. The creature wobbled toward Masen before falling over on its side. I knew the animal could be dangerous, but I didn't want him to kill it! And as if the kill meant nothing to him, he flung the rock at the poor animal again. Redness began to leak from under its ear, and tears began to drip down my face.

"Oh it was just a Mauge," he said with an odd crack in his voice. He quickly cleared his throat.

"You didn't need to do that!" I cried.

"Well I don't mean it was *just* a Mauge. Their bites can sometimes be poisonous. It's how they try and kill prey. We learned about them at the Institute in tenth year. It was in a restricted nature book. I owe you one."

"Oh. I guess you do owe me one, then."

"Hey, don't go getting too big-headed," he said, smirking back. "You looked pretty terrified yourself."

"Did not!"

"You so did." He shook his head.

Maybe this guy wasn't so bad after all.

Nineteen

Winslett

I must have looked like a fool. Who face plants in the dirt from a couple of twigs with someone standing right in front of you? The worst part was for a split second I thought the boy in the woods had been Culver.

Out of frustration, I shoved my shoe into the ground and a small cloud of dirt drifted into the air. It was stupid to think my brother was somewhere in the middle of the woods. No. He was somewhere in Laiden under Iris's control. I couldn't be having these hopes of seeing him out here. Neither Culver nor Evelyn would be coming to rescue me from the wilderness.

However, I couldn't push the thought from my head—people, besides Masen, Byrde, and me were out in these woods. Had they run for the same reason we had? Or had they been here all this time? And if this guy wasn't bound to the government, why couldn't it have been Evelyn or Culver instead?

I focused my frustration toward the boy, Lennon, with his stupid toffee colored hair that hung slightly above his eyes. His eyes. His soft light brown eyes with golden flakes made me swallow any kind of former resentment. Of course, I went ahead and bit him. Really, what was I thinking?

I patted my cheek, reminding myself to snap out of this trance quickly. I would never see this guy again, and he was not my priority. My only focus was to save my family, whatever the cost. No distractions. Which was why I wouldn't tell Masen what happened.

I broke back into a run. I had been away from our makeshift camp for too long, and I knew he would be worried. Jumping over piles of fallen leaves and aimless twigs, I dodged past old oak and fir trees. I was flying through the woods until, once again, I tripped over my clumsy feet. This time, at least I had the decency to catch myself before falling over a rough brown piece of something. Grabbing a fallen branch off the ground, I prodded the obstruction until it flipped onto its backside. It was alive! I knelt next to the brownish figure. Wait, no. It was very dead. Fresh red blood leaked from its side and onto my ankle. Stifling another cry, I swallowed down a hard lump in my throat and inspected the creature closely. From what I could tell from any of the nature books I had ever read, it resembled a Bavine. Its wound looked as if something or someone had killed it recently. I gently picked up the animal by its flat tail, wanting to avoid any contact with its mashed-in face and sharp teeth. I decided I would bring the Bavine back to Masen and Byrde. Who knew when we would eat again?

I rounded into the clearing and saw that the two had already started a semi-fire and seemed to be cooking. And by semi-fire, I meant a small ditch with twigs and grass settled between a couple glowing embers. I also noticed a patch of blood on the ground. What had happened here? I sighed and sat down shakily.

"Where were you?" Byrde asked, before taking a bite of the unknown meat.

I directed my response to Masen. "Trying to get us some dinner, but it seems like you already took care of that." I nodded toward the food.

"Hey, Winslett, the Mauge found us. And considering our situation, I thought it best not to waste anything." He shrugged, watching me as he took a juicy bite. My mouth was watering. It seemed like it had been so long since I last ate.

"So you caught a Mauge?" I asked, as I held out my Bavine.

"Actually, he hit it with a rock," Byrde piped up.

I couldn't help but laugh. Masen killing a Mauge?

"How'd you manage that?" I asked him.

"Hey, don't underestimate this," he joked.

Grinning, Masen snuck me a side-glance and whispered, "I was scared to death. I just flung a rock at the first thing that moved. This one over here did the screaming for the both of us."

"Hey!" Byrde giggled, handing me a piece of the hot meat.

I was eager to taste the creatures. Any variety was better than our standard issued food in Laiden.

"How'd you make that fire?" I asked Masen, suddenly realizing it wasn't as chilly.

"Asher Brigale."

"Huh?"

"That kid in fifth year? The one who got chastised for playing with the twigs and making sparks?"

"Oh yeah," I recalled, "and it worked?"

"It took about the whole time you were gone to actually make a single spark. I was pretty convinced it wouldn't work."

"Nice job." I stretched out my hands toward the low orange flames near some slabs of the meat.

Food was designed to give us all the nutrients we needed to survive as humans, not for taste or appearance. Mostly the food was too dry or too moist. Colors were dark with an occasional orange, green, or red hue. I just kept staring at them, not sure what to choose first.

"Dig in," Masen urged.

"Thanks," I replied. I looked over at Byrde who couldn't seem to stop eating, even to breathe.

I bit into the Mauge and then the Bavine. I was ready for the rush of flavors to consume me.

"This is great!" I said, lacking the feeling the others had had.

None of the flavors danced on my taste buds.

I thought running from Laiden would be liberating. Yet, in this moment I realized it wasn't. Night would soon settle in and we would be cold in the dank landscape. I once had a bed and sheets to wrap myself in. I used to have a family who protected me and I was more than content with life. Now I just wasn't.

Everything was tasteless.

Twenty

Masen

My eyelids were growing heavy and my body craved for sleep. Night was fast approaching and the three of us had just finished a good meal, cleaning off every sliver of meat from the bones. Byrde was already beginning to nod off and it was really just Winslett and me. Well actually just me, because Winslett was keeping to herself. In fact, she hadn't talked much at all after coming back from her hunt.

"Winslett, Mauge got your tongue?" I tried.

She shot me a cold gray look. Hmph.

Minutes past and she still said nothing, so I thought I'd catch some sleep too. As long as she was awake, she could be the lookout.

In what felt like only seconds later, I shuddered awake to Byrde's murmuring. More time must have elapsed because a few stars splattered the navy sky. Winslett no longer was lost in thought. Her stormy eyes were attentive and alive.

"Masen," she spoke hurriedly, "we need to move camp. Now."

My heart dropped to my stomach. What had she seen while I had been out cold?

"What? Why? Was someone here?" My voice shuddered. Underneath the worry, though, lay agitation.

"No. It was nothing I saw..." she trailed off like she had something to hide. Now my concern was only annoyance.

"Wins, I need sleep. I can't be bothered with your paranoia!"

That set her off. "Like any of us have gotten any on this dirt? Listen, you have to trust me on this one!" she shot back. I looked at Byrde. The little girl stirred in sleep.

"Shhh, at least Byrde shouldn't have to be disturbed."

"Please." Her voice was lowered now.

"You tell me to trust you, but give no reason why? Trust works both ways you know." I tried to shoot her the same cold glare she had given me, but to no avail.

She bit her lip, clearly deliberating something important.

"Please," she repeated.

Some odd instinct told me to listen to her no matter how much I had already fought. I sighed once more.

"Well, can we at least wait until morning?"

"No, now."

"Why though?"

"Masen, listen. *Listen* to me. We aren't going far. If what you say is true, that no one is looking for us, then we'll be fine. But changing camps I feel is right, right now. We need to."

Before she let me say anything more, she shook Byrde awake. And without hesitation, Byrde was up on her feet.

"What happened?" she asked in a hurried tone.

"We need to move camp," came Winslett's voice. "Are you up for it?"

"Duh! Are we going now?" Byrde agreed.

"I think nighttime is best," Winslett explained.

"Then let's move," she said cheerfully, rubbing away the sleep in her eyes.

It made me feel guilty I had complained. The nine-year-old had been roughly awoken from a deep peaceful sleep and still readily agreed to make a several mile journey to new grounds. What a loser I was.

"Fine, let's just go," I mumbled, pretending not to notice Winslett's mouth curve into a grin of victory.

Twenty-One

Lennon

"It was nothing. Like I told you for the hundredth time, you need to let it go," I mumbled through gritted teeth.

"I heard you talking to someone! Stop taking this like it's a joke, Lennon. This really is dangerous. That 'thing' you were talking to could be tracking us this minute. For all you know, it could be a spy from the government, then not only will you and I be caught, but so will our only hopes of getting away from—"

"Stop!" I said cutting him off. "Do you know how ridiculous you sound? True, we've been hiding from government officials and hovercrafts, but if I'm asking you to trust me on one thing, I need you to respect that. And by the way, how do I know if you aren't hiding anything?"

Wren glared at me with cold, judgmental eyes. "Are you really questioning my authority?"

"You know what, let's just forget about it, okay?" I mumbled quickly.

Wren gave a slight nod and turned away to tend the fire, the rage still in his eyes. All was quiet.

But as I began to turn away myself, out of the corner of my eye, Wren came sprinting toward where I had been standing, hurling his arm toward my chest and tackling me to the ground.

"What the—?" I panicked, gasping for air under his gripping throttle.

"Don't move," he hissed as he silently stood up, releasing me slowly. He looked out into the direction of where we had come back from.

I watched Wren closely, his fingers curling around the handle of his stun gun from his back pocket. I swiftly pulled myself up off the ground to peer at the disturbance.

It was as surreal as leaving Laiden was. The girl with fiery red hair was leading a boy about the same age with rugged black hair and jaded green eyes as well as a little girl with blonde waves. The girl with the fiery hair quickly looked in my direction. Her eyes widened, and I heard her quietly gasp. I stared back, shocked, with my jaw unlocked. How had she found us? Nonetheless, how had the three of them left Laiden without attracting attention?

Wren began to lift his gun in their direction, and I continued to awe over the mysterious girl. Her eyes of gray, filled to the brim with fear and exhaustion, met mine. A warm feeling swept through my entire body, as if it was some inner sign to not harm the group approaching us. Something told me that they were safe. The boy with jet-black hair moved the small girl behind him with one motion and glared at Wren. I removed my gaze and put my hand on Wren's shoulder, bringing his arm with the gun down to his side.

Wren gave me a look of skepticism.

"You've got to trust me on this, Wren."

He paused, looking between the others and me. And finally, he sighed, released some tension, and gave me a wary glance. I motioned to the girl with fiery hair that it was safe to approach. She took a step forward, only to be pulled back briskly by the boy with the black hair and green eyes. He grabbed the girl's shoulders and whispered a few words into her ear while glaring at Wren and me. The fiery girl shook him off and walked toward us once more. The boy shook his head with a disapproving look, but gave in, following the fiery girl with the little blonde closely behind.

Taking the initiative, I stepped toward the trio, to the girl who had mystified me in the woods. She took another step too.

"Winslett," the boy urged again. I did not appreciate the hostility of his tone.

"It's fine, Masen," she retorted, not looking at him.

"Winslett? It's good to finally put a name with a face," I said, half amused. This Masen gave Winslett a confused look, glancing furiously between her and me.

Wren spoke to the group after a long five minutes of eyeing one another disapprovingly. "Well it seems like we have a lot to talk about. Why don't you follow me?"

Twenty-Two

Wren

So my already overcrowded two just became five. And I hoped it was the final five. This was never what I wanted. I only wanted to escape the crime I had committed, but if this was the way I was supposed to fix my wrongs, then I was damned. I scanned the new trio in front of me. They all looked different. Different hair colors, eye colors, and skin colors; so being a family was out of the question. The two older ones looked about the same age and the little girl was trying to look tough, but was failing miserably. She tried to hold a shaking gaze with me. I broke it off.

It shook me uncomfortably why Extium hadn't worked on yet another three people. Had I failed? Were there others who remained immune to the pill's effects? Although Iris's problems were no longer my concern, the scientist within me itched to understand the error I had too confidently looked over.

"Did you come from Laiden?" I spat at the newcomers.

"Duh, where else would we come from?" the one that identified himself as "Masen" said in a sarcastic tone. I gave him a bitter glare.

"Do you know what's happening there?" Lennon asked the girl. I had forgotten her name.

"It's hard to explain," she answered. "Everyone is different. They all acted the same, as if they have no mind of their own. My own brother and sister attacked me when I said I wouldn't go to the meeting Prime Minister Iris was holding."

"Tell us more about the meeting," I pressed.

"Iris sounded like he was influencing the crowd to chant exactly what he wanted to hear," she shuddered. "Masen and I met Byrde before we left for the forest." She inspected us again. "We would've never guessed that there were more people out here."

So Extium had worked... well except for the glitch with these four. They were the lucky ones.

"Can you help us understand what's going on? Please?" the redhead asked. Masen looked at her meaningfully as if to say, "stop embarrassing us." I was surprised this time when Lennon spoke.

"It'll be okay," he said and placed a hand on the girl's shoulder. "We all left things behind."

She was startled by his touch, and backed away in response. Lennon awkwardly let his hand fall.

"Listen," the girl said, "you're not going to hurt us or turn us in, are you?"

The young one, Byrde, sniffled when she heard this.

"They can't," Masen interjected. "That would mean they would be turning themselves in too."

"We were never going to do that," Lennon claimed defensively. "And besides, I'm guessing we both hate the government."

Masen hesitated, but nodded in agreement.

I mulled over my options. This new group had complicated my original intentions. Any plan I had before had been destroyed. Nevertheless, they were here now, and I saw only one choice that would lead us all to some other indefinite safety. We needed to join forces, to stick together until we could figure things out, or at least until I could figure things out.

The girl whose name I still couldn't recall let out a huff. "Do you need anything else from us since it's been pretty clear that you're not going to kill us, Wren?"

She put a protective arm around Byrde while Masen shot me a cold glare. Lennon raised an eyebrow, searching my face for answers. I knew what he wanted, but he was leaving the decision up to me. I met his stare and nodded.

I tried to delude myself into thinking that this move would be more beneficial to Lennon and myself. But in reality, to let these three kids wander in the woods alone would be horribly immoral. There I went again, I was no father! I sounded like one though, rather than the young twenty-one-year-old I left behind at the government laboratories.

"Listen, there is a better way. Why don't we combine our groups?" Lennon smiled, but there was no response, just surprise.

"It would be best for survival," I added.

Masen spoke up first. "No! No way!" he voiced angrily. "Sorry, but we've known each other for a good ten minutes.

I think it's about time we leave, and pretend this never happened."

He turned his back to us and began to walk away.

"Masen, listen to me. This could be good for us," the sensible other said. "We aren't doing too well on our own. Admit it."

He turned his head where we could see only his profile. "Winslett," he started.

Oh that was her name.

"I don't know what's gotten into you. Yesterday you were perfectly happy with this 'new' family. Why ruin it?"

I could hear his bitterness.

Winslett looked at Lennon and said, "Give us a minute. We need to discuss this ourselves."

He nodded, and they wandered off a little into the distance, behind an aged, uprooted tree.

I could only make out muffled whispers. I heard Byrde's high voice now and again, but she seemed to side with Winslett's fervent desire to join with Lennon and me.

I turned to Lennon. "What do you think?"

"An alliance..." he persisted with caution. "We might benefit from them too."

"True, but I can't figure out how the Cure didn't affect them either…"

"Do you think they know the truth?"

"They've definitely guessed at parts, Lennon. As to whether they know all that we know, I can't be sure."

He nodded. "You know we'll have to tell them everything, right?"

"Yes, but we can wait until they've settled in."

"You already know they're going to join us?"

I shrugged. "Just a feeling."

Lennon turned to grin at me. "Thanks for trusting me on this one."

I sighed. "Thank me when this is all over."

I turned to look at the three kids off in conversation. With crossed arms, Masen hung his head slightly and set himself free from the huddle.

Winslett straightened from her hunched-over position and spoke, "We need to find out more about each other. We want to know all that you know."

I felt a strange sensation that she would hold very true to her word, that she *would* find out everything. But for now, I didn't want to think about it all, the big picture—the real truth. I would take this small victory.

"So will you join us?" I asked, though I was already sure of their answer.

Masen slowly shifted his gaze to meet my impassive one. His combatant-like green eyes told me a war would stir, that his apparent problem with joining Lennon and me was far from over. When our gazes finally evened out, he spoke the word I searched for.

"Yes."

PART 2: Exposure

Twenty-Three

Byrde

I'll admit it. Winslett and Masen really didn't give me a chance to say much about joining Wren and Lennon. But, I *am* glad that Masen finally gave in after Winslett yelled at him. Lennon and Wren have been really good to us.

Nights were still cold, but I've gotten a little used to it. Sleeping in a tent was also a nice change from the cold floor of the forest. But Masen was still angry as usual. He never left the extra tent Wren had given him, and I knew Wren was trying not to be mad when Masen only fed Winslett and me. It took almost a week before Masen really began to start coming out of his tent. I'm guessing that was Winslett's doing too.

I was drawing the dots to one of my favorite constellations in the dirt. Daddy showed me them in the sky once. Wren walked over and asked me what it was.

"It's the constellation, Perseus," I said.

"Ah, Perseus. The hero."

“You know it?”

Wren chuckled and knelt down to sit next to me.

“Yes, I used to study the stars. I’ve learned that as time changes, people change and places change, but the sky has been the one thing that has remained constant in every history. It’s nice to hold onto that. Perseus was actually a favorite hero of mine. He managed to slay the universe’s most evil creatures and still get home in time for dinner. Did you know that Perseus was one of the only ancient Greek heroes to not die a tragic death?” He smiled. “Anyway, I came to ask if you wanted to come hunting with me. We’re running low on herbs and everyone’s getting pretty hungry. Maybe we can snag a Bavine.”

“Yup, sure thing, Wren.” I looked down at the hero that belonged in the sky, and smudged him away with my foot.

Wren and I walked deeper into the woods, until he stopped at a shrub with another kind of berry I’d never seen. It was still strange for me to taste a new flavor with everything I tried. The forest seemed to have a never-ending supply of what we needed. Wren bent down and picked off a handful of the five-pointed, turquoise colored fruit.

“Have you seen these before, Byrde?” Wren asked like a professor would.

I shook my head no.

“They’re called starberries. I have to say that they’re my personal favorite.” He laughed and put a whole one in his mouth. Then he held one out to me.

I took it excitedly and bit it in half, but spat it right back out. On the inside, it was orange—the ugly kind too. “Yuck! That’s your favorite? Gross!” I laughed as I spit again, trying to get the disgusting flavor out of my mouth.

Wren laughed too. "Well, I guess we all have different tastes."

We talked a little longer and kept walking. Now and again, Wren would grab some leaves he called herbs. We didn't come across any Bavines, but Wren caught a Mauge. Every time Wren taught me something new, he reminded me of Daddy.

I could tell all of the older kids tried to look after me, because of my age. But I've always been tough on the inside and I would never show all of my sadness. I knew that they all have families too that they miss, but Mommy and Daddy really feel gone to me. Each day my grasp on their faces slip more and more away. Especially Daddy— who's now in the sky with Perseus. It made me sad to think about the stars and Daddy. He loved them so much.

It was a hot summer night when Daddy took me to the window of his bedroom. That was the night he promised to show me his favorite constellation. Perseus, he said it was called, the hero. Daddy said I was a little hero too. We looked at the stars for a long time together before Mommy came in and said it was time for both of us to go to bed. Mommy kissed my forehead and Daddy's cheek, and then she left.

Daddy had tucked me into bed, and I began to nod off as he told me the poem he always did. He said it was the poem his grandfather told to his father when he couldn't fall asleep, the poem his father told to him, and the poem he would tell to me. Daddy had such a sweet voice.

The hero will always be the guide
Direction and protection to break the great divide

His bravery will unite all
If not, even the stars above may fall

Twinkling above they lead the way west
Following a pattern will show you the rest
Shining with more than beauty
Showing the path is their sole duty

Three points to form a gate
They are the holders of our fate
Connecting the dots just isn't a game
Three will free- Two will open- One will point you in the right direction

So come, the stars are waiting
Enemies forever fading
And hold onto this night sky
But take caution, my child, for the key you seek rests in the looming eye

I was asleep. I didn't even hear Daddy's footsteps as he left.

"Byrde?" Wren called from a short distance away though I couldn't see him. I quickly pushed my way through some shrubs to meet him, not realizing I had fallen behind.

"I don't want to head back to camp just yet. There are a lot more of us now, and I'm not sure just this Mauge will do. He's kind of scrawny anyway." Wren smiled. "Keep your eyes peeled for any movement."

I hummed Daddy's song in my head while we waited.

Suddenly, I heard a soft rustle to my left, and quickly turned to the direction of the noise.

"Over there, Wren! I think it's another Mauge."

"Yeah, it is," he said calmly. Handing me a sharp rock, he asked, "Want to go for it?" There was a challenge in his eye.

"Sure," I said, trying not to sound as shocked as I felt. I wanted to show him that I could be brave too. I chased the Mauge into a bush and threw the stone as hard as I could. Sometimes I didn't feel like a child at all.

Twenty-Four

Winslett

"Let's not do this now." I sighed.

"Do what?" Masen snapped back. "You were the one who started to make things weird between us in the first place."

I shook out a blanket in an effort to clean the tent somewhat. "Masen, we've been friends since who knows how long, and I don't want this constant bickering to ruin it."

"You make it sound like this is my fault, that I'm always the one who's to blame. I guess it's just something I'm used to."

"Masen, you know I didn't mean it like that."

Our gap of silence was filled with the crackles of the campfire Lennon was tending to outside of the tent. I could feel a warmth rush up to my cheeks. Stop it, I told myself.

"What?" Masen demanded, interrupting my thoughts. He had noticed my brief hesitation.

“Nothing.” The doors of our tent unzipped and Lennon’s golden-flaked eyes were inches away from mine.

Stop it, I told myself again, but unknowingly said it aloud.

“Stop what?” Lennon looked amused with a crooked grin. Masen looked confused and aggravated at me.

“Sorry, it was nothing. I was just thinking to myself again.” I was positive my cheeks had turned a bright red.

“Hey, want to help me with the fire?”

I shrugged my shoulders. “Sure, why not.” I stepped out of the tent and quickly glanced at Masen as he gave me a hardened, disapproving glare.

I quickly shook it off, wanting to stay away from Masen until he cooled down. Averting my eyes away from the tent, I followed Lennon toward the campfire.

“Looks like you’ve got the fire all taken care of,” I observed.

He shrugged his shoulders. “Yeah, pretty much. I guess I just wanted the company.”

I turned away slightly as my heart skipped a beat. His small gesture gave me this weird, fuzzy feeling on the inside, a feeling I certainly wasn’t used to. Not knowing what else to do, I chuckled nervously.

“So, is it just me, or do you miss home back in Laiden?” Lennon asked softly.

I sighed. “I thought it was just me, and to be honest, I almost want to go back. I know Iris manipulated everything, but if things could change back to the way it once was, where I could see Evelyn and… Culver.” I choked on Culver’s name.

"Who's Culver? Your boyfriend?" Lennon questioned, kicking a rock into the fire.

I gave him a small, sad smile. "No, he's my older brother. I miss Evelyn and Culver so much. But things suddenly got crazy, before I left. I—I don't know if things could ever go back to what they once were. I even doubt if I will see them ever again."

"What happened?"

I chuckled, looking into the fire, my voice dry with no humor. "They attacked me when I had refused to go to the meeting. That's how my wrist was hurt. But it's not their fault. It was Iris's doing. I know it," I muttered clenching my fist. "I love and miss them so much, it's just hard, you know?"

"Of course I know," he replied. "I ran as soon as I thought something seemed wrong. Thankfully, I ran into Wren or I would've probably been dead by now."

The sparks from the fire simmered in front of us, and I could see Lennon's eyes reflect off of the fiery blaze, coming alive. The wisps of smoke towered above us.

Lennon reached out to put his arm around my shoulder, in an attempt to comfort the both of us. I felt the heat of his side next to mine, swallowed my impulsive tension to run, and settled my head into the groove of his shoulder.

"You know," he whispered, "when I had first seen you in the woods a few days ago, I thought, that girl with the fire hair could've taken down even a six-foot Rawk."

"Really?" I grinned weakly, thinking about the towering black and gray beast. "Even when I was in a face plant, after tripping over a twig?"

Masen's voice snuck behind me. "Oh really, Winslett? So that's what you were doing while I was taking care of Byrde and the rest of camp, you were falling on your face and talking about game?"

I quickly faced him, eyeing the bitter and hurt expression he wore. I chuckled nervously.

"Masen…" I began.

"Winslett…" he replied in a mocking tone. "There's really no need to apologize. It's whatever."

Tears filled my eyes, as he backed up into the darkness, away from the fire, away from Lennon, and away from me. A pang of frustration and misery hammered its way into the pit of my stomach. I turned back around to see Lennon's face and my cheeks warmed. The happiness that arose from the heat of the fire, the sparks of the red flames, and the encircling patterns of smoke above, only made me want to look away.

Twenty-Five

Wren

Byrde was dozing off and I was afraid I'd have to carry her. I really took her hunting for too long, but it was necessary. Our supply would've been completely depleted if we hadn't caught some meager game. Arriving back at camp, the strewn canteens and worn blankets proved my point. We were running dangerously low on everything.

I walked over to the tent closest to our small fire. Gently opening the flap door, I settled Byrde between a sleeping Winslett and Masen. She stirred softly, and I froze, waiting silently. Byrde turned to her left and clung to Winslett's back and began a rhythm of gentle snores. I backed away from the tent and closed the flap behind me.

Then it occurred to me. This was the opportunity I had been waiting for. I grabbed my pack and went out of the tent to sit by the flickering light of the flames.

I unzipped my duffle, and took out four manila folders from the government. In my last flee from the laboratory I had grabbed a few confidential folders. I didn't know what information could possibly be held in them, but I couldn't just look at them anytime without the others suspecting who I really was. I pulled out the first folder and sifted through it in a few swift motions. Nothing. Absolutely nothing. It was filled with insignificant purchase numbers. I shoved it back in the bag and roughly grabbed the second folder.

I heard the light pitter-patter of steps, and spun around.

Two big doe eyes stared at me. Byrde.

She rubbed her eyes. "Wren?"

"Byrde what are you doing up? I thought you were asleep?" I shuffled the papers back into my bag franticly.

She yawned. "I can't fall asleep."

"Why not?"

"What are you doing?"

With the papers safely hidden beneath my dirty clothes, I stood up, walked over to Byrde, and ruffled her blonde head.

"Nothing, Byrde. Go back to bed. It's really late."

"My daddy used to tell me a song," Byrde said.

Ugh, I was no father.

"Umm… I…" I stuttered.

"Can you tell it to me?"

How could I say no? "What's it called?"

"The Hero's Calling."

"I don't know that one…"

"That's because Daddy made it up himself." Byrde grinned. "I can show you how it goes."

Byrde began to recite her song, and she actually had a sweet voice. It was soft and light and flowed through me. It was a little melodic and almost more like a nursery rhyme.

"Back to the tent, Byrde. I'll tell it for you."

She yawned and laid down. I began to retell it and soon Byrde was asleep. I crept out of the tent and back to my bag, back to the files.

I sat next to my dirty laundry and pulled out the stack of papers, eager to read through them. The next folder was yet another dead-end. It was filled with information on Extium. Of course I already knew all that information; I was even quoted a few times.

The third folder was yet another disappointment. It was simply the workers assignments on Distribution Day. Sour disappointment began to creep into any hope I had for the fourth and last file.

Instead, it took me by surprise. Like all the others it read confidential, but I opened it to a familiar name. It read "Reina Faleman." She was my friend, or well I was at least friendly with her, and as friendly as I'd ever be with someone who was a part of the government. I dug further and found a photo of her stapled to a letter. I cast it aside and read her information page.

Most of the information I already knew. She was widowed and had one child. A girl, if I remembered correctly, though I couldn't recall her name. Reina seemed different from other workers; maybe that's what merited her a "confidential file." A few sheets dealt with recent purchases and records of her daughter. Never in my life did I see anyone monitored this closely, especially as high in the government ranks as she was. She was a shoo-in for next year's election for Under Secretary to the Minister. I had to admit I was intrigued. Was Reina really who she had said she was?

I leafed through the flimsy papers, and finally found a report update. "Reina Faleman: Potential Threat to the

Well-Being of Laiden." I read on, and learned Reina was presumed to be in cahoots with something or someone they called the "Outlanders." I mean, of course, as a child I was told the tall tales of the Outlanders, the psycho people the government cast across the barrier, never to be seen again. But if I knew anything at all, I knew they didn't exist. They couldn't. For one, the government denied their existence, but if they were real then Iris would undoubtedly have entrusted his innermost circle with the information. I was part of that circle. He would have told me!

My mind was racing. The document was stamped with the official emblem of Laiden. It wouldn't contain false information. I couldn't deal with this on top of everything else. If there were a way to escape from Laiden, I would be the first to want to know. Wouldn't have Reina known that?

"Wren!" Reina waved me over. She was quite a few years older than me, and it was nice she was as accepting as she was.

"Good morning, Reina." I smiled as I sauntered over.

"One week until the big day, eh?" she said with, in retrospect, a halfhearted smile.

"Yup!" I beamed.

"Wren... you have thought this one through, haven't you? The implications, and what this means for everyone else?"

"Of course. And the government wouldn't warrant something they thought would be detrimental to the well-being of Laiden, now would they?" I asked cheerily.

"Right..." she muttered. "Well, I best be off then." She turned her back to me.

"Our offices are both this way," I interjected.

"Yes, well I forgot there are a few things I left unfinished."
"Umm, okay. I'll see you later then."

Looking back on this one moment in time I now saw things a different way. Reina never liked the idea of Extium. As soon as I had told her my opinion, she left. Maybe she was going to tell me what she knew. How different would things have been?

I laughed a cold dark laugh. Nothing was funny about this situation. I was mad at myself. I was mad at Reina. I was mad at Iris. And I was mad at the four other kids that lay sleeping whilst I tried to put the pieces of our existence together. I fell back onto the soil. Ouch. Something jabbed into my shoulder. Not even for one moment could I relax. I sat back up. It was the paper clip that held the picture of Reina to a letter. I was just about to lift it into the embers when I saw the name the letter was addressed to. How could I have missed it? Byrde.

Memories rushed back. Reina had a daughter. Her daughter was nine. Her daughter was named Byrde. Could it be the same Byrde? The similarities were there. Blonde hair and brown eyes. Byrde had no father; Reina was widowed. It had to be.

I tore open the letter not meant for my eyes and held it to the light of the raging fire.

Byrde,

I'm sorry for everything that has happened to you in your short life. But you are a hero, my child. Sometimes heroes make it back home. I know that in one way or another you will get back to me for however short a time. I need you to know that I have told you lies. First, I know that I have always dodged the questions concerning your father because I wanted to hide you from the truth. He and I were part of something called the Resistance. We dealt with the people the government never intended us to know about, the Outlanders. Your father was caught contacting one. Of course, they couldn't let him live. They murdered him for treason, making an example of what happens to those who disobey Iris, a public display. That's why I work inside the government. They watch me. Know also that it is not only me who spoke lies to you, but our society as well. Laiden is by no means the only place left in this world. I don't know what exactly lies beyond these barriers that ensnare us. I just know there is some other place, maybe better than this one, and it is waiting for you. Find it, my Byrde. There are others out there. Remember especially the things your father had taught you. Remember Perseus and remember the stories. All of them. They may hold more of the truth then you had ever thought possible. Did your father ever tell you why ancient people loved the stars? It's because they can lead you in the direction you are intended to go. Look to the stars Byrde, and know I am looking at the same ones.

With love,
Your mother

I had no words after reading this. The letter filled all the gaps in my reasoning. Things fit together as smoothly as anything possibly could. It made sense now why she had a folder. She was one of them— the Resistance.

It made sense now that Byrde had memory… she hadn't taken Extium! But more importantly... I had a better grasp of the bigger picture. Three things were certain. There was someplace outside of Laiden. There were people outside of Laiden. And, Byrde apparently knew much more then she had let on.

Twenty-Six

Masen

A morning fog lay over our camp as I unzipped the tent. It was early and the sun was just beginning to rise. I rubbed my eyes open with the end of my shirt. It smelled like ash from a campfire. Half awake, half asleep, my thoughts drifted to how I lashed out at Winslett last night. In retrospect, I could've been nicer.

It was just the way she looked at Lennon that irritated me. I had recognized that look; it was the same one she used to give to me. My stomach turned into knots every time I saw the two exchange a glance that made her blush and him show off a cocky smile. Jealousy was a funny thing. You could either let it crush you into pieces, or it could force you to accept the fate of it all. I refused to let it do either.

Nonetheless, it was time for the group to move on and make a change. Although I had pitched this idea to Wren several times, he always seemed so distant, never fully understanding what I had to say, as if he was figuring things out in his own separate world.

I breathed in the cool, misty air and closed my eyes. Doing my best to not let my thoughts escape me, they protested and began to float away in the early morning wind. My thoughts now circled back to home, home in Laiden. I took small steps to the brink of camp. The residue of the campfire crunched under my feet as I stretched my legs. I looked out to the tall evergreens below and the miniscule outlines of houses back in Laiden. My eyes roamed back to House 37. It had only been a couple weeks ago that I was walking to school with Winslett, passing the rows of houses from numbers thirty to forty, then forty to fifty, and so on. Winslett would walk with Culver and Evelyn, Evelyn always clutching on to Culver's left wrist. Before Winslett's mother and father died, they would watch us leave and I would look back to House 37 with some small hope my father would be waiting outside, waving and smiling too. I was let down every time.

It was a rarity in Laiden to not have both parental figures living. I was one out of the thousands who had no mother. Lucky me. But from what I had remembered, she was loving and warm. So was my father at the time. My mother used to tell me her precious stories of mystical creatures, always saying she was born in the wrong time period and that she was meant to live within a fantasy world. My mother had always held a secret hatred against the ideals and practices of the government, especially Iris, although she never voiced her opinion in public. It was no coincidence when my mother had been invited to Iris's laboratory seven years ago, chosen as a test subject for some sort of vague medication that she never came back.

From then on, my father became emotionally detached from the world. In replace of his loving self, he became cold and demeaning to anyone daring enough to approach him. He was a workaholic and couldn't stand being at home for it reminded him of his long lost wife. My family had been ripped from me at an early age, and it was the medication's fault.

A gust of wind swept my shaggy hair back, and I was struck by where I was. I moved my hands along the rocky ground and sighed. Tents began to unzip back at camp, and I heard Wren's yawn from a distance away. Soon after, the others began to arise from their slumber. Not in the mood to deal with the drama of camp, I hustled back to my tent and zippered the door closed from all other thoughts except for my own.

Twenty-Seven

Wren

Have you ever had one of those moments when you suddenly realize that everything you thought you knew wasn't right at all? That's how I felt, as if I was just a puppet and someone above was pulling my strings like a marionette. I went through the motions that felt right, because some hand was always guiding me that way. It was comfortable to not have to move on my own, to never fall down. I snapped my strings the day I left the government.

I was shaken from the privacy of my own thoughts when Byrde accidentally rammed into me.

"Sorry, Wren!" she shouted and ran back to the game of "Kick the Rock" that Winslett was now in on. I mumbled that it was okay and told everyone I would get the next supply of water. I needed time alone, in the woods, with no distractions to gather my thoughts.

Most things were clear to me now. Reina's note confirmed my predictions of existing life beyond the barrier. She seemed to have indicated that there was a loophole, a way we could escape. Perhaps Byrde knew it. I was sure she did. The key was something about her father, something she would know because of her father…

And that's when I, too, knew it.

The song. Byrde's song. The one her father told her, who's father told him, and back and back and back.

Stars.

A hero.

I knew what had to be done.

I practically sprinted back to camp. I had no water, but it didn't matter. The stone was still being kicked around and Masen had come out from under his rock to half-heartedly join in. I couldn't have been gone longer than ten minutes.

"Everyone!" I called. "Get over here!"

"What is it, Wren?" asked my favorite blondie.

"I have something I need to talk to you all about. It's serious."

Lennon looked at Winslett who frowned and gave Masen a worried glance, but came and sat next to the spot where at night a fire would usually be burning.

"You know we can't stay in the forest forever," I began.

"But it isn't like we can just walk back into Laiden. Iris turned them into robots," Winslett interjected.

"That's not what I'm suggesting."

"Then what?' said Lennon. "There isn't anywhere else to go. This is all there is. Laiden and the forest. Our only choice is to stay here in the coverage of the woods! Unless, we're going to plan a siege… because if we are, I'm all in!" He smiled as Masen rolled his eyes.

"I agree—" Winslett began.

Whatever she was going to say was dissolved in the wind when Masen said, "Just let the guy talk."

"Thank you, Masen," I huffed. "Listen, everyone. I have recently pieced some things together and think you all need to hear." I looked around to see if I was finally commanding their attention and it seemed that I had. "We have always been told that this was it. That long ago, something happened in the world and our lone society was all that was left. It was the barrier that protected us from the dying world and all of its diseases. I don't think this is the truth anymore." I closed my eyes. "In fact, I think it's the barrier that's been keeping us from a prospering world. I think there is somewhere outside of Laiden that is not dead." Just those few words alone could have resulted in my execution if I was still under the watchful eyes of Iris. I swallowed my innate anxiety. "Not only that though… I think there are people from the outside who will help us. I think we should try to get to them." I looked up to be met with wide-eyed stares of disbelief.

No, it wasn't disbelief. Perhaps it was more of a blend of emotions, even emotions that normally wouldn't be seen together. I saw, in the eyes of the youth, concern, skepticism, doubt, worry, but also some hope.

Winslett spoke up first. "Wren, the government is wrong in a lot of ways, but do you think they'd really lie about that? This is all a little farfetched if you ask me…" She trailed off, lost in her own thought.

Maybe she was thinking about her family, holding onto the dash of hope that maybe she could help them escape as well.

Lennon looked apprehensive but said, "I believe what Wren is saying. We are blocked in, but maybe right beyond the barrier are people, villages, and creatures. They might even be living a better life than we are." Lennon sat back down, probably contemplating his thoughts even further.

I could count on him to know what I was saying. It would be the others I needed to convince.

"Okay, suppose there are places outside of this hell-hole. What I want to know is why you brought this up now, Wren. Why even think of it?" Masen asked.

That one threw me for a loop. Of course I knew the answer, but that would involve telling everything. It would involve letting these four people know who I really was. What I've really done and what I've done to them. But not only that, it would mean involving Byrde. I couldn't involve Byrde without telling them everything. In response, I shamefully reverted back to my old ways. I chose to lie.

"Thanks for asking, Masen," I said. "I brought this up now because I have just been doing a lot of thinking. The hovercrafts will come and they will come soon. I don't know about all of you, but I'm tired of waiting around." There. That was good. I had basically avoided the whole question altogether.

"Agreed," said Lennon.

Masen and Winslett exchanged a smirk and I knew my answer for action surpassed any need for more questions. My eyes wandered over to Byrde, who continued to gawk at me.

"I need to do a little more thinking," I told them. "We will regroup tomorrow. Our first order of business is sharing anything we know." I made a pointed look at Byrde and continued. "We need to find a way to bring down that barrier, even for a short while in order for us to cross."

With that, I got up and went back to the tent. My lies were bought for now. After all, did it really matter how I came by the knowledge? My only concern was to get Byrde to piece together her mother and father's riddle.

Her father.

Remember all your father taught you, Byrde.

My previous thoughts had to be right. Byrde just became the most valuable person in this whole mess of a place. All I needed now was for her to tell me everything.

Twenty-Eight

Byrde

That day went faster than any in my whole life. But I said nothing. I had tried to hold a blank face as they talked about revolt and the Outlanders. In the end, Wren would make up his mind on his own. Lennon and Winslett would follow, Masen would somehow be convinced, and I would be dragged around like a pet.

People think I'm little, and I am, but I also listen. Mommy didn't think I did. She would talk to friends and even sometimes Prime Minister Iris. I gazed at the sky, but really I listened. He smiled down at me sometimes with black eyes that looked like beetles. He told me one day I could be just like him. Only I didn't want to be. Never.

I had a feeling that Wren had a secret. He kept staring at me when he said we needed to tell everyone everything. But what could he know about me?

I once again started to draw Perseus in the dirt. There wasn't much to do anymore out here in the forest. I was bored. Maybe it was time to do something. Mommy wouldn't like it though. Wren came over and knelt down beside me and I smiled.

"Hey, Byrde," he said with a horrible grin I didn't like. "Would you do me a favor, kiddo?"

Not wanting to make a big deal I said, "I guess so."

"Remember that rhyme you told me yesterday?"

"Mhmm! A Hero's Calling!"

"Yes that's the one!" he said. "Will you tell it to me again?"

"Yeah, sure!" And I did. His tone then changed completely. He had a spark in his eye I'd never seen.

"What does it mean, Byrde?"

"It's just a poem my Daddy made, Wren."

"That won't fool me, kid."

"I don't know what you're talking about!" I stepped back nervously. And no matter how hard I fought it, tears streamed down my face. They were silent at first. This was a Wren I didn't know and didn't like.

"I put it together Byrde, Byrde Faleman. I know all about you and your mother! I know who your father was! I know that this song is a guide for us! It tells us how to leave this godforsaken place!"

"How do you know any of that, Wren?" I tried to ask in a commanding voice that came out as a whimper.

"All I know is that you are the key, Byrde. You know more than any of us! What are the stars, Byrde? Who is the hero? Have you met the Outlanders?"

He was huffing by the end. I had no idea what to say, so I didn't.

"Prime Minister Iris, he has to be the eye you spoke of. But the stars are our guides? How? Your mother said to remember all your father told you. What has he told you?"

I said nothing. How would he know this? It didn't make sense.

"SPEAK up kid!" he yelled.

"I—I don't know!"

"Yes, you do! You do know!" he pressed.

Wren's eyes reminded me of all the people I ever hated. He reminded me of the ones who killed my father and of Iris himself. It made me think Wren was the bad guy. This was crazy. Shouldn't I want to tell Wren all I knew? Why had I hid some of my knowledge from all these people? Not saying I did know much, but I knew a bit. I knew there was something more than Laiden and I knew somehow my parents were part of something greater than this. I knew heroes mattered. I also knew I couldn't stay here any longer.

All I really wanted now was Mommy. I wanted away from Wren and Lennon. I wanted away from lovesick Winslett and bitter Masen.

"The hero, Wren!" I screamed. "After all this, you can't remember my favorite constellation? We've talked about the stars!"

I ran then. I ran away from Wren, back through the forest. I was not at all like the hero Daddy thought I could be.

I had planned to not look back until I tripped and fell. I looked back then because I heard Wren calling me. I heard his heavy footsteps breaking twigs in the forest. But I knew I was about to break through. I would take whatever was waiting. Somehow they would bring me back to where I needed to go. I hopped back up and raced forward once more, but Wren was gaining on me.

This wasn't good.

"Byrde!" came the same voice, yet it was now much closer. Just a few more paces I thought.

I fell to the ground again. Wren had tackled me.

He still had the mad sort of sparkle in his eyes, but it wasn't the same one. He was mad about saving me as well.

I wriggled out a bit and looked up. Two large men were standing over us. It seemed like Wren had been too late.

Twenty-Nine

Lennon

My thoughts of finally fulfilling a siege, after Wren's baffling announcement, were interrupted by a faint scream. Stifled, but clearly a scream. I whipped my head around and scanned the woods, squinting my eyes for any sign of life. Winslett and Masen poked their heads outside of the tent, just as I quickly stood up to see what was going on.

"What's happening, Lennon? Did you hear it too?" Winslett asked frantically.

"I'm not sure…" I trailed off.

"Argh!" The scream was muffled once again.

Silence. None of us knew what to do, how to approach the situation. We were paralyzed by the worst fears of our imagination.

"Lennon…" Winslett began. "Where are Byrde and Wren?"

I searched her face and our eyes met. Hers widened slowly.

With no time to waste, I immediately dashed in the direction I had heard the call for help, dodging under thick branches and swiping away shrubbery. My heart beat faster with every leap I took as I flew through the woods. I glanced briefly behind me to see Masen and Winslett right on my tail.

Stumbling upon a large, open field, I halted immediately. Nearly twenty feet from where I stood, a hovercraft was planted in the center, its engine whirring. Masen and Winslett had both run into my back.

Masen groaned, but quickly stood. I helped Winslett onto her feet, ignoring Masen's annoyed stare.

"Guys," I said, calling their attention toward the hovercraft.

They looked up to where I had motioned and the color quickly drained from their faces.

"What are you waiting around for?" Winslett hissed. "Let's go!"

"No, wait!" Masen whispered furiously.

I turned my direction back to field and to the hovercraft, searching for signs of Byrde or Wren. My heart pumped louder and louder, dreading the possibility of catching sight of them.

I prayed silently. Please don't let them be here. Please don't… my prayers were short lived.

There was Wren, struggling to fight his way out of the arms of two burly men. The two officials were holding Wren in some sort of arm lock that must have been painful, judging by the reaction on his face. They were dragging him into the hovercraft.

Winslett began to lurch forward, but Masen grabbed her in time, before we would all be caught. It was clear that Wren could see us, and the officials most likely knew it too, but their goal was clear. They had come for Wren. Not for us. I looked back up to see Wren's face. His expression clearly read, "stay back," and I curtly nodded once, herding the group behind some foliage. I still kept my guard up, because I knew that whatever was about to go down was going to be one hell of a nightmare.

Thirty

Winslett

It was surreal. It was like all of us had been in this bubble. For the last week or so there hadn't been any other world besides our own. Now the very people we had worked so hard to hide from, were here in the flesh. They had found us. My heart sank.

Byrde hurriedly brushed herself off of the ground, and bolted toward Masen. He waved furiously toward her, and she ran with an impossible amount of adrenaline. Curiously enough, the officials ignored her.

"Get off!" Wren cried and threw a left hook at one of the men. He missed and the other official grabbed him in a headlock. Wren wrestled his way out and this time his foot made contact with the dark-haired man's chest. The wind was knocked out of him, but the two officials worked together like Wren's capture was choreographed. They were too quick for Wren. They grabbed both his arms this time and rendered them useless. Both men smirked.

"Isn't this interesting?" said the one man who I had dubbed "Stubby" in my mind because of his ugly, stout figure.

"Wren Casterra, coming back to where he belongs."

"Knock it off!" Wren snarled, pulling at the official's arms with no success.

I eyed Masen and mouthed, "What are they talking about?"

He didn't respond.

Stubby then said slyly, "Your experiment has been a big success. You should be proud."

Wren spit in his face and that set the two men off even further. They pushed him to the ground and Wren yelped in pain, but his struggling had ceased now. He looked ashamed.

Byrde had made it back to Lennon, and Lennon looked at the officials with distaste. Masen looked impassive as always. My best friend was so guarded I had no idea what was racing through his mind.

The forest was no longer safe. I was lost. We were lost.

I still had yet to grasp how Wren had let this happen. Yes, I blamed him. What would we do now? He was the unspoken leader amongst us.

"Wren…" I choked in a very unattractive sob. He was leaving me.

His eyes connected with mine and I saw that tears had begun to leak across his cheek. His eyes spoke his soul and I knew he held regrets. Wren was good, I told myself. He had chosen the safety of Byrde over his.

Almost subconsciously, the four of us who remained slowly began to back away from him, not wanting to share the same fate. The officials heaved Wren up higher and started off in the opposite way. I wondered why none of us tried to save him, so I stepped forward only to find a firm hand holding me back. Masen looked me straight in the eyes and merely shook his head. I stayed where I was.

"This is bigger than us now, Winslett. It's time to let it go," Masen comforted.

I knew exactly what he meant, but it made me sad.

Wren was becoming a little less visible. The two officials dragged him like a rag doll, not caring what he hit.

We all remained silent. Minutes, hours, or days could've passed by. Time had stopped for a while.

"Hero's Point!" I heard Wren call as he shook himself from one of the official's hands grabbing him uncomfortably.

I jolted from my trance and shook my head. What did he say?

"Hero's Point!" Wren cried again. "Byrde will know!" One of the official's fists went whirling toward his head. From what I could tell he spit blood out of his mouth.

Then he was gone and the four of us were alone. We exchanged no words and slowly and much too silently walked away.

Thirty-One

Masen

The scene replayed through my head over and over again. Hovercrafts. Officials. Wren. Hero's Point. Gone. But nothing seemed to bother me more than one question. Why? Why had they only taken Wren? And what the hell was Hero's Point? My thoughts had been interrupted by a quiet sob. Byrde had been crying and stumbling along the walk back to camp, and Winslett looked like she would break down too. Lennon donned a brooding face. It still hadn't sunk in for me yet that our five had whittled down to a four.

We reached our grounds and Lennon snapped back to reality.

"Everyone, pack your stuff. We're leaving." Lennon commanded, already gathering some of our belongings resting along the fire pit.

This would not fly.

"Since when did you become the new alpha? You don't get to make that decision," I said curtly.

Lennon ignored me and began packing away the tents.

"When was the coronation? I must have missed it," I snapped.

Winslett, gathering her bearings, said, "Masen, it isn't safe here anymore. Those two officials know we're here in the woods too. There's a good chance they might be able to torture information out of Wren about us."

I sighed, outnumbered once again. The others had already started moving on without me. Lennon and Winslett both had their things saddled up to go. Winslett, I assumed, had my few belongings bundled along with her own. I stared blankly, and then crinkled my eyebrows.

"Do any of you even know where Hero's Point is?" I accused.

"Wren said Byrde would know," Lennon replied.

We all turned to look at our littlest member who until now, I had forgotten about.

Hunched over Wren's things, Byrde's hopelessly milky brown eyes blinked away tears and she shook her head. "I don't know."

Lennon groaned and Byrde changed the subject. "What about Wren's things?" She referred solely to the duffle bag since Lennon had already gathered the useful things they shared.

"We may as well leave them, I suppose," Lennon said.

"Let's get going soon," said Winslett. "It's almost dark. We should pack up and start heading out before night. Where to, Byrde?"

Winslett was quick to agree since no better plan was available. I nodded my head, unfortunately, because the options were few.

"Byrde?" Lennon asked impatiently.

Byrde wasn't listening again. Instead, she had opened Wren's duffle. It was a small bag that contained a change of clothes, a knife, some weird pair of glasses, and his long empty canteen of water.

"What are you doing, Byrde?" Winslett probed.

Byrde was in some kind of a trance. With no words spoken, she lifted one last thing out of the bag, manila folders. She handed them to Winslett.

"What are those?" I wondered out loud.

"Let me take a look," Lennon demanded.

Winslett handed them over willingly. I didn't blame her. I wouldn't have wanted to been the first one to look in those files.

Lennon whipped out the first folder, flipping through pages of meaningless numbers.

"Its nothing," he sighed. "We're wasting time!"

"You need to keep looking," Byrde said.

Lennon opened the second folder, which contained the government's official work schedules for Distribution Day, the day we received the Cure, the Cure that was far from a healing kind. It dawned on Lennon a second before I had recognized what it meant on my own.

"These folders are from the government."

"Why would Wren have them then?" I asked, my head spinning. It didn't make sense.

Lennon flipped open the third folder, and I saw Winslett cringe as he read out the title of the official government document.

"Extium," Lennon read sullenly.

Extium? What a strange word.

"Read on," I said with an honest curiosity. He did, and I soon regretted it. The document was pointedly written to explain the Cure, how all citizens were made to bend to Iris's will, how he molded their minds and cut off all senses of feeling, compassion, and rebellion.

I couldn't bring myself to think of it. Yet, I knew Lennon had. A look of betrayal encompassed his face, but he continued.

I didn't want to jump to any conclusions yet, I told myself. For the sake of Wren's honor I wouldn't. It took me a moment to realize Lennon had stopped reading. His face went pale.

"What is it, Lennon? What does it say?" questioned Winslett.

"Guys," Lennon addressed the two of us, "Wren created Extium. He did this."

The statement was so profound I almost didn't believe it. But I couldn't dispute it after I ripped the document from his hands and read the next line of the article myself. I read it aloud for Winslett who had now buried her face in her hands.

"'Extium is everything I wished it to be. I think the Prime Minister, too, will find it very satisfactory.' The young creator of Extium, Wren Casterra, was quoted in the earlier stages of the development processes."

My skin crawled.

"He did this to us?" Winslett queried.

"It just doesn't add up," Lennon said frustrated, throwing down the book of files. "If he was a part of the government… how and why was he out here hiding like us? He made the damn thing!"

I almost felt sorry for Lennon. He had known and trusted Wren the longest. The blow must have been twice as worse for him.

Winslett whispered softly, "Maybe he had a change of heart or maybe he had cold feet. Think of all he's done to help us! We would've been caught and probably would've been dead by now if not for him."

She was right, but I couldn't swallow the clump of betrayal any easier. I had let down my guard and let him lead us. Wren was the next person I trusted after Winslett. But he had let me, and the rest of our group, down. He had lied about his identity and pretended he had no knowledge of these blasted Extium pills, the Cure, whatever you wanted to call it. He destroyed Laiden. He destroyed the lives of everyone in Laiden.

"I just don't get it!" Lennon roared.

He struck a tree with his fist. I think it hurt him more than the tree. He sunk down in defeat.

I moved to sit next to Winslett, but she scooted over to the files. She picked one off the ground and flipped through pages of documents. The rest of us sat in silence, staring at the dirt. My eyes drifted to Byrde. Something had gone down this morning. Something between Wren and Byrde that had driven them to the forest. It was time we asked Byrde what it was. After all, Wren may have betrayed us, but he believed Byrde held answers.

I was about to open my mouth to ask, when I saw there was still one more folder in Byrde's hands. She was hugging it tightly.

"What's in there, Byrde?" I questioned. At the sound of my voice, Lennon and Winslett became engaged again. They hadn't noticed the final folder either.

Byrde finally addressed us directly and said, "It's my mom. This folder is all about Mommy."

"What do you mean, Byrde? Was your mother a part of the government?" Lennon asked skeptically.

"Mhm, they are after her. It's all in here. Mommy told me to run on that last day. She must have known they were coming," she responded, speaking more to herself.

"I'm sure she's alright. If she worked for the government she must be a smart lady," Winslett soothed, trying to smile.

"Only she knew too much," Byrde muttered. "She and Daddy had known all about it."

"All about what?" Lennon asked.

"The Outlanders. The Resistance. How to break the barrier."

I stood quickly in response and strode over to Byrde. Winslett and Lennon joined me. Byrde wasn't just a nine-year-old kid. Right now, she was the most important one out of all us. So it seemed Wren wasn't a complete liar after all. Byrde did have the answers. Her statement put me into shock. The life Wren had believed existed outside of Laiden, and yes it was hard to believe so much had happened in one day, I had so wanted to believe in. Yet, I didn't know if I could. Byrde said it without a shred of doubt.

"You know how to break the barrier?" I repeated slowly.

She shook her head. "No. I only know some things Daddy said, but it could help us maybe," she said in a regretful tone. "Maybe I should've told Wren before or he might never have been captured."

"Don't regret not telling him something. He is back where he was meant to be after all. The more you told him, the more he could have used against us," Lennon said quickly.

"Well, there was one more thing in the files I found," Winslett said, "but I'm not sure if it's anything worth paying attention to."

Lennon turned away, not in the mood to hear anything else about Wren.

I stepped toward Winslett, and she pulled out a single sheet from the folders, one with the meaningless numbers.

"I had looked over it before, but look at the margins," she said handing it to me.

I turned the paper and started to read aloud.

"All it says is west," I said, shrugging. I turned to give the sheet back to her, but she shook her head.

"Look down at the bottom of the page."

I faced the page again and squinted at more of Wren's scrawled notes.

"Twinkling above they lead the way west?" I asked. "That sounds like a part of a song."

Byrde butted into our conversation abruptly.

"Masen, what did you just say?"

"Uhhh, that sounds like part of a song?" I repeated slowly.

She rolled her eyes. "Before that."

I looked back to the bottom of the page and repeated Wren's words again.

"Twinkling above they lead the way west."

Byrde gasped. “That is part of a song— my Daddy’s song.”

I raised an eyebrow and Lennon had turned back around to face us.

“That must have been what Wren meant, to listen to you, Byrde,” Winslett said. “Will you tell the song to us too?”

Byrde cleared her throat and began to recite. Her voice, sweet and clear, carried a sad melody.

“When did Wren hear this song?” I asked her when she was finished.

“I told him... right before he was taken away.”

Byrde looked down at her feet and kicked a small stone. The guilt was written all over her face.

“Can you repeat the line about something west?” Winslett asked.

Byrde nodded. “Twinkling above they lead the way west. Following a pattern will show you the rest. Shining with more than beauty, showing the path is their sole duty.”

“Don’t you all see?” Lennon finally spoke up. “Wren is manipulating us again. I bet ‘west’ leads straight to a trap. Don’t trust him.”

“Lennon, I know it seems like Wren is a traitor now, but this is our last shred of hope for any sense of what we should be doing to open the barrier, even if we do make it to Hero’s Point,” Winslett replied.

“I—” Lennon started.

Winslett didn’t let him finish. “And if there are people who live outside the barrier, that’s where we need to go. There’s no hope for us in Laiden anymore and I don’t plan to live in the woods for the rest of my life.”

“Here, here!” I exclaimed.

Lennon gave us a pained look, but nodded reluctantly after realizing this fight was three to one.

I grinned. Alpha dog no more.

"One more thing," Byrde spoke up again, "I think we need to follow Perseus."

"Wait—who's Perseus? I thought we were talking about stars?" asked Lennon.

"Perseus was Daddy's favorite constellation, mine too." Byrde replied.

"Oh, but this helps us how?" His voice was strained.

"Another part of the story said 'the hero will always be the guide.' Perseus means hero. And Daddy and Mommy both said we need to follow the stars."

"But it's not like some ancient Greek guy is going to fall from the sky and come help us," Lennon protested.

I ignored him. "If the stars lead us to Perseus, shouldn't Perseus be in the West?"

"Are you saying Hero's Point is near the constellation, Perseus?"

"Or it could be directly under. Couldn't this song be telling us that the stars are our map to find Hero's Point?" I suggested.

"Isn't that a bit far-fetched?" Lennon said bitterly.

"Direction and protection to break the great divide is the next line," Byrde continued. "That should help us."

"Let's think," I replied. "Direction and protection should mean that the hero, Perseus, is trying to lead us somewhere, to Hero's Point."

"Yes, but we haven't been able to figure out its significance," Lennon interrupted.

"To break the great divide," Winslett pondered out loud.

We kept walking, weaving in and out among the trees. Nobody spoke. Everyone was in deep thought.

"Ah, of course!" Winslett finally exclaimed.

We all looked at her, waiting for her to speak.

"The divide is the barrier!"

I shrugged my shoulders, and Lennon scrunched his face disapprovingly.

"Why not?" she pressed, excited now. "All along, haven't we always been traveling toward the barrier? Hasn't Wren always pushed us to keep moving farther and farther away from Laiden? Wren had been convinced there was an outside world too, outside of Laiden, outside of the barrier. Everything lines up to what Byrde is trying to tell us." Winslett turned to face me. "I think you're right, Masen. Perseus is directly above Hero's Point, and a break in the divide, the barrier, is Hero's Point. It's our way out of Laiden!"

I couldn't help but smile at Winslett's enthusiasm, and also at the fact that she said I had been right over Lennon, who was having trouble hiding his misery.

I ignored him, grabbed some of the supplies from under Winslett's arm, and walked up to Byrde.

"Let's follow the stars then!"

Her little fingers pointed toward the stars that aligned across the western sky. She smiled at me.

"After you," I said to the shorty.

As queer as it was, it felt good to finally get some answers.

Thirty-Two

Winslett

I leaned against the bark of a fir tree as I stopped to catch my breath. Delusional from dehydration, my fingers fumbled in an attempt to open the cap of Wren's canteen. My shaking hands brought the cold bottle up to my dry lips, the persistent sun beating down on me. A mere dribble of water fell from the nozzle. Shaking the canteen was hopeless, but I couldn't be any more desperate. I let out a groan and sunk into the earthy floor. My hands guarded my eyes from the bright sun as I looked up.

Our flight from the camp that we once called home was only a memory now. It had to be almost three days since we left, and the amount of exhaustion we all felt at the end of the day left us too tired to complain. The nights weren't easy either. The four of us would stay up to the late hours, trying to chart Perseus. If it were a cloudy night, the stars would be impossible to see. But on the clear nights, Byrde patiently pointed out Perseus for us each of the many times we asked her. I couldn't help but feel that the constellation didn't want us to catch up with it, that it moved further away each time we looked.

However, it was useless to delay our journey, even to rest. We all knew the cost if the hovercrafts were to ever locate our whereabouts. Having a similar fate to Wren was something none of us wanted to risk.

Beads of sweat dripped from my forehead and I lifted my forearm to wipe them away. I pulled myself up off the ground and shook the dirt off my pants. Maybe I could look for something to eat before our ten-minute break was over. I pondered over my limited options. Well, game was out of the question. We hadn't seen any signs of real meat the closer we moved toward Hero's Point. My stomach grumbled embarrassingly in response to my frustration.

Hunger was something none of us had experienced, and I hated it. It left an empty feeling of craving in my stomach, resulting in a severe amount of impatience between the four of us. I missed the gray mush we called food in Laiden. It was tasteless, but it filled us. Now, we had to ration away our food a lot more carefully until we could find another source. If only Wren was here, he could help us. He was our best hunter, our best leader, our best everything. And we lost him. Even trying to find a water source was tricky, maybe even harder than trying to hunt.

Out of the corner of my eye, I saw Lennon walking over to me with a pile of dirty clothes. I felt my cheeks grow warm, but I couldn't tell if it was just the heat of the sun. Lennon teasingly bumped his shoulder against mine, his way of saying hello. He had begun to return to his normal self a few miserable days after finding out the truth about

Wren. I sheepishly looked up and welcomed him with a smile.

"Mind helping me with some laundry?" he asked casually.

"Sure, no problem." Any time spent with Lennon was better than hanging around camp.

He laughed in reply. "Come on, let's go! I have to show you something!"

"What is it?" I searched his face for answers.

"It's a surprise!"

I had no choice but to follow him.

Thirty-Three

Byrde

Silence was a sound I heard a lot lately. I thought it was because of a mix of a lot of things. Wren was gone, and that topic was still touchy. Lennon would be in a bad mood if anyone brought up Wren, and he only eased up if he was watching Winslett. Masen watched Winslett too. I didn't understand. Boys and girls were really strange. I had been meaning to ask Winslett if she liked either of them. But like I said, we all usually stayed silent unless it was when the big kids needed help finding Perseus. I liked those nights when I could help them figure out the clues to Daddy's song. I wasn't just a kid anymore. I was a leader.

We had been walking for a couple of days and the journey wasn't over yet. Perseus was making this harder than it needed to be. I just wanted all the tension to stop. Lennon and Winslett had gone off to do who knew what. Masen and I were left alone.

I was okay with that, because Masen seemed to have warmed up to me a tiny bit. I think we were both happy to finally rest our feet.

I decided to shoot a tired smile at Masen.

He smiled back.

"Masen?"

"Yeah, Byrde?"

"I know you guys haven't been too happy with me."

He paused. "Where'd you get that idea?"

"I heard you guys talking the other night when you thought I was asleep," I said, embarrassed that I had eavesdropped.

"Oh…"

"It's okay. I get it. You guys are confused about me knowing things, and I should've told you everything. But the thing is, before Wren told me so, I hadn't any idea that I held the clues to getting out of Laiden."

"Well, I guess it's because we feel pretty powerless right now. Wren always had an answer. I'll give him that," Masen replied.

"I don't know how he figured it out. One night I told him the song my Daddy used to tell me. He thought it was telling us the way to get out of here."

"How would your father know that, Byrde?" he asked as the muscle in his neck tightened.

I wanted him to understand so I kept talking. "My daddy was the chief of a special research lab specifically for the Minister. He knew all of the government's secrets. He knew so much that if he ever told even a bit of it, the whole society could've gone up in flames. He never thought anyone could guess he was a double agent."

I could tell Masen was really trying to hear me. He wanted to figure out the mystery also.

"What do you mean a double agent?" he questioned. His eyebrows pushed together to form a small crease in the middle of his forehead.

"My grandfather used to be the leader of the Resistance. Wren wasn't lying about it. They're out there, Masen. Believe me."

I knew that he secretly did. He had read Mommy's letter. He had heard Wren proclaim it. He was just denying it because it meant he could've escaped Laiden a long time ago. I could tell Masen hated Laiden. I could tell he was ready to leave.

"Outlanders," he muttered. "It's just a bit weird you know, to think of a place outside of Laiden? I really always thought we were it."

"We never were though," I reminded him.

"So why did no one ever come to help us?"

"They were working on it. Think about it, if we couldn't get the barrier down, then how would they be able to?"

"Yeah, you're right. Byrde, sometimes I forget you're only nine. You seem so much older. You make me look stupid." He grinned at me.

"Ten actually," I corrected him. "My birthday was yesterday."

"What? Why didn't you tell us?"

"No one ever really talks anymore."

"Well, we all need to get over ourselves," he declared.

I smiled faintly, without showing my teeth. Things like birthdays didn't seem like a big deal to me ever since Daddy was taken.

It was my sixth birthday, the last one Daddy was at. I woke up early, alert with excitement. Birthdays were a big deal to a five-year-old. I ran down the stairs as fast as I could and dashed into the kitchen where Daddy waited.

He brought a finger to his lips, going "Shhh."

I giggled. Mommy was still fast asleep, but Daddy woke up early for me.

He had a plate filled with the morning rations, and had arranged the two bland eggs as eyes and shaped the meaningless mush as a smile.

Daddy could always find a way to make things special. "Byrde, I wanted to give you a special present before Mommy wakes up."

"Isn't it from Mommy too though?"

"No, this is just from me, sweetie. And I need you to promise you'll never lose it."

"Okay, Daddy." I stuck out my hand to receive what was mine.

"This is much too important, Byrde, my daughter. But I trust you more than anyone."

"More than Mommy?"

"With this sweetie, yes." He handed me a small pearl-colored box with a thin pink ribbon. It was an odd thing to see in Laiden.

I opened it as carefully as I could.

Inside was a very thin leather string necklace and it was decorated with a spherical orb. The color was a wispy blue. It was beautiful.

Daddy smiled. He must have seen how my eyes lit up at the sight of it.

"Put it on me, Daddy?"

"Of course." He tied it around my neck and let it fall.

I smiled up at him again, unable to hide my joy.

"Treasure it with your life, Byrde. It will help you when you need it most." He smiled back at me. The smile did not quite reach his eyes though.

Mommy's footsteps started to echo down the stairs.

"Tuck it in your shirt, sweetheart," Daddy said quickly.

"Why? I want to show Mommy."

"You can't."

I frowned, still not getting it.

"Mommy wouldn't understand. Just promise me you'll wear it always. You mustn't show anyone."

"Okay, Daddy. It can be our secret." I pressed the pretty speck of midnight to my heart.

"When Wins gets back, I'll tell her about it, okay?" Masen asked. "And err—I guess I'll mention it to Lennon as well." He frowned.

"You don't like Lennon do you?" I questioned.

"No, its just... never mind," he stopped himself short.

An awkward silence fell around us for a few minutes. We weren't used to having to spend this much alone time together, especially since I used to avoid him altogether.

Masen got up and went to shake the long empty canteens. The sun was still burning. I lay down on the dirt, not caring if my tangled blonde hair got dirtier. I'd wait it out and they'd see I was right. I pressed the orb necklace to my heart like I did four years ago. I would have to share my secret soon.

Thirty-Four

Lennon

Most guys my age would say carrying a load of extremely dirty laundry would never classify as romantic. I looked over at Winslett, by my side, who tried hopelessly to tame her wild, fiery hair that had frizzed in the heat. Her fair skin was beginning to turn red from too much exposure to the sun. I shuffled her under the shadow of the trees to hide her from more of the rays. She seemed to turn redder when my hand grazed her shoulder. I smiled to myself. Winslett was different from the other girls in Laiden. I could see that now. She was pure and she was selfless, filled with so much love to give. She didn't like to depend on anyone, and actually refused most help of any kind, especially when it was from Wren and me.

"So where are we taking all this?" she asked as she uncomfortably tried to gesture to a couple shirts she held in her arms.

"You'll have to wait and see," I taunted.

I heard her stomach rumble and quite truthfully I was hungry too. We hadn't had good meat since we left our old camp.

"Hungry?" I playfully poked her stomach.

She turned the shade of red I was so used to seeing. "Maybe a little."

She then frowned, biting her lip, clearly confused as to why I was keeping my surprise hidden for so long.

"I'll show you, Winslett. I promise." I smiled for the millionth time. "It's just that I thought we should finally get ourselves some fresh meat."

"You know we haven't seen any game in days. And what about the others, and what about these clothes?"

"They can wait. Come on, we can try!" I grabbed my handmade weapon, a sharp rock fastened to a branch that I tied to my waist.

I pulled her forward, and she willingly followed my lead as we sauntered quietly into the brink of the woods.

A good half an hour had passed and we had tried all of the few tricks Wren had taught us when it came to hunting. I knew Winslett didn't like to stay in the woods too long to hunt, because it always put her on edge. I could understand her still not being used to the wilderness.

"Let's leave, Lennon," Winslett suggested. "Nothing's here."

Sorely disappointed, I nodded and followed her lead out of the thick woods. She sidestepped a massive tree stump, balancing her weight with an arm against my shoulder. Her foot graced the edge of the stump, but with her other foot, she tripped over a hidden branch, stepping on a nut that had fallen from the tree above. The shell broke against her weight and resulted with an echo throughout the silent woods. I grabbed her waist and held her back, preventing her from a hard fall. She grimaced and almost let out a groan until I saw it out of the corner of my eye. A target. It was a plump-looking thing, its tail wagging furiously behind the tree stump. Scurrying past a few branches, it continued to dig around the leaves absentmindedly. Pressing my finger to her lips, I quickly lurched forward, throwing the spear into the side of a Bavine. Success! I looked back at Winslett and a smile spread across her face.

We soon left the woods, Bavine in hand, back under the tree to retrieve our pile of dirty laundry.

She licked her lips and wiped the sweat sitting on her forehead with the back of her hand.

Patience broken, she pleaded with her gray eyes beaming. "Come on, Lennon!"

"Alright," I broke. "I found a fresh pool of water. I thought we could fill up our canteens and get the dirt off these clothes."

She stopped in her trail.

"You found water, Lennon? Why'd you wait so long?"

She broke into a sprint. I stayed behind.

"Winslett!" I shouted. "You don't even know how to get there!"

"Then what are you waiting for?" She laughed from a few feet in front of me.

I burst after her, catching up within seconds. We ran all the way to the small lake.

It was only a short distance away and it sparkled a light crystal blue. She knelt down next to it, taking in the water's mesmerizing glow. Breathing heavily, I knelt next to her.

She stared at me somewhat mischievously and the next thing I knew, I was in the water.

I didn't mind though. The water was cool and fresh and I bobbed back up to the top, shaking my hair like a wet Jyla. Winslett giggled, guarding her face with her arm from my splashing. Winslett's hair took on a darker shade when wet, a rustic red color that mirrored the creature more than mine did. The lean stature of a Jyla and its supposed cunningness reminded me of her even more. I wondered if we would ever get to see one in these woods.

"Hey, want to help me up now?" I teased, doubling over, laughing.

"Sure," she answered laughing just as much.

But instead, I pulled her gently in, her face in full shock. I was surprised to see her land in the water somewhat gracefully. I laughed to myself when I saw her rise to the surface.

The water reflected off of her fair skin and the sun shone on her eyes. I held my breath, taken aback by her natural beauty. I had never been so close to a girl before. I slowly drew my hand against the side of her face and gently brushed away the drops of water resting on her cheek. Winslett looked up at my touch. My fingers lingered toward her scarlet, wavy hair. I smoothed a stray wisp behind her ear, and I could feel my hands begin to shake. Winslett laughed softly and nervously. Her gray eyes looked so beautiful as she looked up at me curiously. I swallowed the lump of excitement and anxiety forming in the base of my throat and brought her lips gently up to mine. The quiet intensity between the both of us built with each second. There was only one thing clear to me in that moment. I was falling for Winslett. And I had never been surer of anything.

Thirty-Five

Winslett

Lennon's soft lips were pressed against mine. I wanted to smile, but found it hard to do, seeing as my lips were already busy. I inched toward him, putting my hands on his chest. His arms wrapped around my waist. He kissed me gently and I kissed him back. I had been waiting for this and was left with no disappointment.

In the heat of the moment, I pulled away from Lennon. I couldn't explain it, but I had a sudden fear we were being watched. I was right, and I felt my eyes widen.

He was a distance away looking at us, full of bitterness and anguish. Quickly turning around, he tore back in the direction to camp.

I swam to the water's edge. I gasped, almost choking.

"Masen!" I cried, but he was far in the distance by now. I stopped short and watched his figure disappear. Lennon, too, had gotten out of the water. He came up behind me and wrapped his arms around my waist, holding me. Warmth surged through our chilled skin.

"Wanna go back?" Lennon asked. I knew he understood.

"Yeah."

We walked silently back to camp as I eagerly awaited the cold jaded stares Masen was sure to give me.

Thirty-Six

Masen

My eyes stung, though I didn't know why. Who was I kidding, of course I knew. Lennon and Winslett had kissed right in front of me. Did they really think bringing back a Bavine would help their case? Okay, maybe it did a little because no one saw me complaining when I shoved a whole leg in my mouth.

God, I despised Lennon more each day. I mean, everyone had known Wins and I were really close. But come on. We weren't *together*. I wasn't gonna lie and say I had never thought about her in that way. She was just a good friend, a best friend. We both didn't have parental figures, so we helped each other through the good and bad. She always had to take care for Culver and Evelyn, and if there was a way I could contribute, I always would.

I didn't even mind, because it made me happy to help her. The helping went both ways too. At times, when my dad would shirk his parental duties and stop coming home for a week or two, Winslett was always there for me. She kept me from cracking.

Nothing romantic ever came from our late night rendezvous. And I hated myself for thinking it, but maybe I was an idiot. She was there all along. Winslett was mine and not Lennon's. I wanted her too, and not so I could just beat Lennon, but because we were made for each other. Now, the only problem standing in my way was the fact Winslett didn't want to talk to me.

I shot Winslett a sideways glance. Her pale skin was growing slightly red as she leaned against the side of a wide oak tree. Her hair was frizzed out from the day of heat. Her clothes were dirty and her face was tired. She looked good.

I swallowed my pride and went to talk to her.

"Hey," I said, not meeting her eyes.

When she didn't say anything, I knew she was waiting for me to say something more.

"Err, I'm sorry, Wins. I know we've been fighting a lot lately. But I really want to go back to the way things were before we left Laiden. Back to when it was me and you against the world."

Still silence.

"It's just this whole thing," I made a huge gesture with my hands, "freaked me out. I know it freaked you out too. I still have no idea what's happening. It's like my whole life has sucked, but at least I knew what I was doing. Now I don't." I let out a sigh and continued. "As soon as we found a little direction from Wren, he was gone."

"It wasn't his fault you know," she whispered.

"That's not even what I was getting at."

"Isn't it though? This is all just going back to your abandonment issues."

"You never understood as well as I did what it was like!" I retorted.

"Never understood? How dare you! I lost *both* my parents. No matter how flaky of a dad you have, you still had him! Mine is never coming back."

Great. I had just managed to do the opposite of what I had meant to. I wanted to patch things up, not unweave them further. It was too late though. I had let my anger leach out.

"You still had people who loved you! You had Culver and Evelyn. I thought I had you, but it didn't matter because you always had them! Whenever I wasn't enough, whenever I got boring, you had them to support you!" I snapped back.

"They're a responsibility! I was envious of you. Do you think they never were a pain? Did you think it never became too much? So yes, Masen, I had you. With you I could escape everything that kept me up at night. With you I was able to forget about the pain of my parents' deaths. You were always there," she rebutted insincerely, as if I was a burden too.

She was angry, and she was right. I wanted this argument to stop.

"Winslett, I'm so sorry," I sighed heavily, swallowing the apology like a hardened lump in my throat. I told myself to get it together. "I'm just losing it out here. I feel insignificant, like no one would care if I were gone. I see you all the time with Lennon and it's like you've forgotten about me."

That was when her face softened to the one I had always loved. She looked at me like I was the silliest person in the world and it made me feel good.

"I could never forget about you."

She jumped and held me in a tight embrace. Startled, I fell back a step.

"Whoa, okay. Ouch, Wins, you're hurting me!" I laughed as I tried and pulled her off.

The tears threatening to fall from earlier were now actually cascading down her face. She smiled through them.

"Masen, you big baby," she choked through her laughter and tears.

"I missed you," I said bringing her into another embrace, this time softer.

She rested her head against my chest and we stayed like that for quite a while. In that time all that should've been said, was. How we were both childish, how we were afraid, how we never really had anyone to care for us, but somehow here we were even more alone. The understanding we always had for each other seeped back in.

When we eventually did release from our embrace, I smiled at her and grabbed her hand. It fit in mine just as it did those many years ago when we were children. That was the thing about a best friend. You always loved them.

We were a few paces in front of the tents. I stopped Winslett in her tracks. I didn't know if I could let her choose Lennon, especially not without taking my own shot first. She would need to decide whom she couldn't let go of, Lennon or me. Just being friends wasn't going to be good enough.

Adrenalin washed over me as I leaned in to kiss her. I felt her sweet breath on my neck and could smell the rustic scent of her hair.

All too soon, she had pulled away from me.

"Masen…" she said drawing farther and farther away.

"I'm sorry," I mumbled again, scratching the back of my neck.

She looked behind her shoulder to stare at me disapprovingly, before disappearing into the tent.

Thirty-Seven

Lennon

"Three points to form a gate... They are the holders of our fate... Connecting the dots just isn't a game... Three will free— Two will open— One will point you in the right direction," I repeated slowly after Byrde. She stared at me, waiting.

"I still don't think I understand."

I began rubbing the corners of my eyes. I could tell all of us, well, except for maybe Byrde, were beginning to let down all signs of hope. Trudging along the edge of the woods, we kept under the protection of the trees in case the hovercrafts were to make another reappearance. It was risky to even stop to rest. We had a destination to think about. Hero's Point. Hero's Point. Hero's Point. It would be a miracle if we somehow found a way to stumble upon it. If only Wren were here to help us get some answers. NO. I couldn't let myself think like that. Wren was a traitor, nothing but and nothing more than a traitor. All of the lives cost, all of the families torn, especially ours, were all thanks to him. I thought about Winslett. Her parents were killed by the wrath of the government, leaving her and her siblings alone. Extium had only ripped them apart from her too. I glared at the ground and gritted my teeth. I was wasting my energy thinking about Wren.

Winslett had been hiding in the tent all day, but came out to reach for the canteen near Masen's foot. She took a long sip and looked over the rest of us dwindling about.

"I think this might help," replied Byrde.

I watched her as she brushed her mangled, blonde hair behind her shoulders and fished around the front of her shirt for some sort of necklace. Pulling it from underneath the cloth, she held out a delicate blue sphere fastened by a leather string. The jewel seemed to shine a different color each time it slowly spun, suspended in the air.

"It's beautiful," Winslett breathed.

"What is it?" Masen asked, approaching silently from behind me. That guy always seemed to come out of nowhere.

"I call it an orb. Daddy gave it to me for my birthday four years ago. I would've shown you sooner, but I was scared, because he said never to let anyone see it."

"Why are you showing us now?" I asked her.

She shifted in her tree stump seat. "Because I've been thinking about the last line in the poem..."

"But take caution, my child, for the key you seek rests in the looming eye," Winslett recited.

Byrde nodded. "I think this necklace could have something to do with it."

"How?" Masen interrupted.

"Daddy used to say how the orb was a key or how it would help me when I needed it most."

"And what we need most is to get through the barrier," Winslett stated. "It's hard to believe this orb would be able to get us through."

I shook my head. I didn't know either.

"I'm sorry, Byrde. The necklace is nice and everything, but I don't think it really means anything," Winslett said.

"She only thought it could be a theory," Masen snapped back at her.

I ignored the two. "But the last part of the line, the part about the looming eye, you don't think that 'eye' could be the government do you?"

"It's possible," Winslett whispered.

"Well, if this orb is the key the poem talks about, is it so crazy that Iris has the other?"

Nobody answered as Byrde tucked her necklace behind her shirt. We all sat in silence.

Winslett finally spoke. "Do you hear that?" Putting the canteen back on the ground and wiping her upper lip, she looked to Masen.

"Hear what?" he asked, looking around.

I stared at Winslett whipping her head in different directions, trying to track down the invisible noise.

"Winslett, I don't hear anything," Masen replied again.

But then I heard it too, a soft buzzing sound in the silent sky, increasing in volume by the minute. We could all hear it now. The louder the sound became, the more fidgety we all were. What was that noise? Winslett turned to me and gave me a look of anguish. The buzzing had turned into an all too familiar whirring of some sort of motorized engine. I could sense Winslett could tell what it was too. The horrible noise was coming from one of Iris's hovercrafts. I heard Byrde gasp in front of me, and I whipped my head around to see if she had been hurt, but instead she was looking upward into the sky. I followed her gaze. Several hovercrafts loomed above us, suspended in air.

Dirt was flying off the ground, in a whirlwind around us, and we did our best to cover our faces from any debris flying into our eyes. But the noise was incredibly overbearing now, and I saw Byrde covering her ears. Masen turned to grab Byrde, and he tossed her body onto his back like a rag doll.

"Run!" he exclaimed, as loud as his voice would carry over the earsplitting shrills of the hovercraft. He took off sprinting through the woods with Byrde clutched to him.

I grabbed Winslett's hand.

"It'll be ok," I said, trying to convince myself more than her. We ran after Masen and Byrde.

She bit her lip, and kept silent.

Luckily, hovercrafts weren't designed with any intention other than the convenience of transportation. The pilot would need to have some seriously great eyesight to see us down here, but there was still no waste in getting out of its line of sight.

Almost a half an hour had passed of sprinting through tall trees and rough terrain until the whir of the hovercrafts had finally deceased and the sky had begun to darken. Byrde had slid from Masen's back half the time ago and ran behind him.

"Where do you think they went?" I heard her ask Masen.

He shrugged, and looked to Winslett and me, running a few feet to the right of them.

Smack! Panicking again, I searched where the sudden sound had come from. I looked straight ahead and saw only more of the forest. I kept running until *Smack!* I was rapidly repelled, shooting backward several feet.

My back hit the ground first, and crumpled at contact. I let out a groan. My head was spinning. What kind of force had made me propel backward? I turned my head to see where Masen had sprawled across the ground a few feet away from me. He had a bloody nose, and was trying to balance himself steadily by leaning upright on his elbow.

"Lennon, are you alright?"

I looked up to see Byrde standing over me, waving her hand above my eyes, trying to catch my attention. Winslett, who luckily seemed to not walk into the sudden force, was busy tending Masen's nose. She ran over and knelt by me. Voices swarmed over my head and I couldn't concentrate on one thing for too long. Out of the corner of my eye, Masen limped over to see how I was doing, but everything became blurry. Objects were moving. It wasn't helping my headache, and I held out my hand to stop all the movement.

The next thing I remember hearing, I could barely make out. "Uh oh, he's gonna..."

I closed my eyes and blacked out.

Thirty-Eight

Byrde

It was several minutes before Lennon came back around, but I laid down on the dirt next to him anyway.

"What did I just run into?" he groaned.

"The barrier," Masen stated, wiping some dried blood from under his nose.

He sat up quickly and looked at Winslett, kneeling beside him.

"It's the only explanation. I mean we have been heading west for so long, we were bound to run into something sooner or later," she confirmed.

"What is this place anyway?"

I hadn't bothered to look around, but I did now. We laid in a small clearing that didn't look too different from the rest of the forest we had camped in the past few weeks. There were trees and there were rocks and there was dirt. Nothing looked out of place, and I would have never thought that we were actually in arms length of the barrier.

"So now what?" Winslett asked, helping Lennon stand.

"Let's sleep here tonight. It's dark already," Masen suggested.

Lennon nodded and told Winslett he was fine to stand. "I'll set up some of the blankets."

Nobody ever asked me to do anything. It was one of the better, and one of the worse, parts of being the littlest in the group. I leaned one arm against my head and the other went to feel for my necklace behind my shirt. My heartbeat began to slow, and my eyelids were heavy from all of the running. I tried hard to keep them open, and decided to look at the stars to keep them busy.

Perseus, where are you? I searched for the familiar cluster of stars to the west. It wasn't where it usually was, and it was a clear night too. Closing my eyes tight, I prayed. Daddy, if you hear me, please help us.

Peeking through my eyes, I looked up at the night.

This time, I broke into a huge smile.

"Guys," I yelled, pointing up to the sky. "Look!"

They paused folding blankets and organizing rucksacks to turn and follow my eyes and my outstretched arm.

"What are we looking at?" Masen asked.

"It's Perseus!" I exclaimed. "He's right above us!"

The stars shone especially bright tonight. They couldn't miss it.

Winslett was the one to speak after minutes of quiet stargazing. "You know what this means right?"

Masen nodded and smiled for the first time in days. "We finally made it to Hero's Point."

"So now what?" Lennon asked.

I stood back up to look around. I was confused too. I didn't know what I thought would happen when we reached here either. It's not like I thought Daddy would be here telling me what to do.

"Too bad there's no tour guide to Hero's Point, huh?" Masen joked. Nobody laughed.

"We're all too tired. Let's just get some rest, okay?" Winslett suggested, rubbing her eyes. "We'll figure it out tomorrow morning."

Lennon shrugged and spread out a blanket. He smoothed it over and gestured for me to come and lie down. Not like Winslett and the rest of them, I was wide-awake and excited to search for more clues from Daddy. I didn't want to sleep. Maybe Daddy could help me again. I closed my eyes tight. Sometime around the end of my prayer, I fell asleep too.

Thirty-Nine

Winslett

"Winslett, wake up."

A voice hissed my name again, and lightly shook my shoulder.

"Go away, Culver," I murmured instinctively, turning away from the disturbance.

"I'm not leaving."

Ugh. What was so important this early in the morning?

"I don't want to go to school. Leave me alone." I answered.

"No," the voice protested.

"Then you can tell Professor Darys to—"

"Winslett, get up. This isn't funny." A hand shoved the blanket covering my shivering body.

"Hey!" I glared at the intrusive voice, not really seeing a face.

"Yes, hello."

I stared blankly at the figure and rubbed my eyes. I sighed. It was Masen, and this was no emergency.

Crawling out of the bundle of dirt I had slept on, I stretched my arms and smacked my lips. The sun had just risen. The dew on the grass was fresh, and a gentle fog lay in the air.

"You were never a morning bird, were you?" Masen smirked at me. His black hair was wet, indicating he had gotten up early in order to clean himself.

"You were never not annoying," I shot back. Grabbing a half-empty canteen next to my blanket, I poured some water into my mouth and sloshed it around.

"Let's go on a walk now that you're finally up," he said.

I spat the water out onto a small patch of grass. "Is this about a couple of days ago?" I asked, staring for his reaction.

He looked down at his shoes before I could see him turn red.

"Come on," Masen urged. He walked inland, the direction we had run from the hovercrafts, away from the barrier and away from Lennon and Byrde. I jogged to catch up with him, and thought about our unsettling near-kiss.

Lennon was the one on my mind, and I'll admit it, I had been crushing on him for our several chaotic weeks away from Laiden. Then, of course, Masen had to come along and ruin it.

Did he really ruin it though? Something about the way Masen had closed his eyes and leaned into me would've felt so right if only I could've returned the gesture. In many ways, a kiss was long overdue. How many cold winter nights had I grabbed onto his arm and looked up at him with wanting eyes? And every time, it seemed like he never saw me like that. My heart couldn't help but flutter a couple nights ago when he looked at me with the same wanting. I had always seen our futures intertwined. In Laiden we would've earned the right to a job, and probably a good one at that. He would've applied for my hand in marriage and it would have been granted. We would have moved into the branch of houses designed for newlyweds. Our children would look more like Masen. Their skin would be a perfect blend of white and olive. They'd have his shocking green eyes and his charming smile. We'd be happy.

Masen led me through the forest where dirt became less visible and grass grew higher. My clumsy feet stomped across the fallen leaves and broken branches whereas Masen tiptoed around the debris effortlessly.

"Where are we going?"

"Nowhere in particular," he answered.

"Do you go on walks a lot?"

He shrugged, and a gentle breeze blew through my tousled hair. "On good mornings like these."

We had been away from Lennon and Byrde for almost ten minutes before Masen spoke again. "Remember the small hill by the Square we used to go to and watch the clouds?" His voice had the same sweetness I hadn't heard since our time in center-city Laiden. It made my heart ache.

"Yeah," I said simply.

"It seemed like we never had a care in the world. We could spend hours doing nothing and it didn't matter as long as I was with you." I couldn't see his face but I imagined him smiling.

"It was a simpler time," I replied in a melancholy tone.

"Life will never be exactly the same anymore, will it?" He phrased it as a question, but it was a statement.

"Humans are about adapting, Masen."

"Humans are prone to change, but they find a hard time adjusting to it."

"Professor Darys always used to say that," I mused, remembering our tenth year philosophy teacher.

I turned my head over to Masen's direction, stomping on more leaves. He was still watching the passing fog.

"I'm sorry," I said, and I knew he understood what for.

"I know."

"Why aren't you mad at me?" I whispered.

"I don't want to lose you again," he replied earnestly. "If it means that all I can be is your friend, then that's what I'll be in order to keep you."

"My best friend." And that's the best I could give him, hoping things could fall back into place.

He smiled and stopped walking to look at me. I knew then that Masen and I would be all right. As all right as two people could be when one of them was in love with the other. I couldn't say for sure what I felt for Masen, but I only knew right now my desire for Lennon overpowered whatever it was.

"You know how important you are to me," he said.

I couldn't help but cringe.

"You're important to me too," I responded. My words were true even though they held a much different meaning.

He took me by the hand, and leaned against a tall rock covered with vines and moss.

"Oh, and Wins?"

"Yeah?" I asked hesitantly.

"Don't mistake this for me giving up on us."

He let my hand fall, and I looked down at it, not wanting to face his creased brows and focused eyes waiting for an answer.

I stayed silent and he leaned against the oddly slanted rock.

I walked over to him, and dared to search his face. He simply leaned back, smoothing his arm against the rock. Masen brushed a couple strands of vines away, aimlessly toying with its leaves. I ignored a smirk, and turned to head back to our makeshift camp.

"Ow!" Masen yelped.

Turning quickly, I watched him hold up his arm, and eyed a trickle of redness.

"What is it?" I asked, hurrying over to him.

"I hit my arm on something sharp..."

"You'll be fine, Masen. You probably scraped yourself on one of the rock's edges."

"I don't think so," he began, swiping more of the vines away.

"Then what could it be?" I was getting annoyed and it was getting later into the morning.

"It felt like metal."

I turned away. "Let's go. You're being a baby."

"No, Winslett! Look, I told you!"

"You didn't tell me—" I stopped my thought and gaped at Masen.

No freaking way.

Forty

Lennon

It only took a rough shake of my shoulders and a call of my name to make me rush out of bed and onto my feet.

"Get up, Lennon," Masen urged.

Winslett was gently shaking Byrde awake too.

"What is it? What's going on?" I panicked.

"There's something we need to show you!" Winslett exclaimed, rushing over to Masen and me.

"What is it?" I repeated.

"We're not exactly sure," Masen started, "but it's something else..."

"What about our stuff?" I asked, looking back to the strewn blankets and canteens.

"Leave them. We can come back later," Masen ordered.

I began to protest, but Winslett gripped my forearm and pulled me toward the direction we had come to Hero's Point from. Masen had Byrde holding his hand and jogging alongside of him.

Masen wiggled out of Byrde's grip and ran over to what looked like a large, slanted rock, covered with vines and moss. Waving some of the vines away, he felt around the rock's surface.

"What are you looking for?" I asked.

"A handle," he replied. "Here it is!"

Winslett stepped over to Masen to help him clear away more of the leaves covering the... I looked at the rock closely. It was no rock. This was a door— a large set of dark wooden double doors with an iron bar set over its entrance. It leaned against another strong piece of wood at a forty-five degree angle. Masen tossed the iron bar to the side and grabbed the door's smooth handles. Balancing one foot on its ledge, he ripped them open and they fell to either side with a loud *bang*. A cloud of dust arose and Winslett waved it away.

I stepped forward to peer inside. I couldn't see much, only a hazy outline of a set of steep stairs and its railings.

"Whoa," Byrde awed.

"Yeah, I know," Winslett agreed.

"I think I've seen this before," I thought aloud.

"You have?" Masen and Winslett both asked in shock.

"I mean, not this exact one, but Wren pointed one out to me once. They're supposed to be scattered all over the forest."

"But what are they?" Masen questioned.

"Wren called them shafts. He told me that before any Resistance group had formed, people used to live out here. It wasn't always trees and dirt. There were actually small communities living far from the center-city. And within each community, the government had a shaft built as an easier means of transportation."

"What kind of transportation?" Winslett demanded.

"Well, inside each shaft is a set of stairs leading to an underground shuttle station. They were incredibly fast and used to transport people and goods. But after the Resistance, Iris wanted a more defined centralized government. People were banned from living out here and since then, the shuttles and its shafts were closed down."

"That's amazing," Winslett breathed, peering into the shaft's darkness.

"Where did you say these people and goods were coming from... or going toward?"

I nodded, understanding Masen's question. "They lead straight inside the government building."

His jaw dropped. "Seriously? Like the government building outside the South Gate?"

"Yes, the only government building we have," I replied.

Masen rolled his eyes.

"And you're sure they're not being used anymore?" Winslett asked.

"Well that's what Wren said, but I wouldn't be so sure."

"Can I see inside too?" Byrde asked from behind me.

I turned around and easily picked up her lightweight body. "Of course you can!"

As I leaned in with her to look into the shaft, a thin beam of blue light pierced through the dark cellar. I whipped my head around to look for the source.

"Byrde, your necklace!" Winslett breathed.

I bent my head to look down at Byrde and nearly dropped her. The orb fastened around her neck, tucked behind her shirt, radiated effervescently.

Forty-One

Byrde

"Uh, Byrde," Masen said staring. "You're glowing."

I was glowing. Well not exactly me as a whole, more my neck. My necklace.

"Take it off, Byrde!" cried Winslett.

Lennon set me down and I unfastened the leather rope, letting the orb fall to the ground. What had Daddy given me?

The glowing stopped.

Lennon swiped the orb off the ground, and it began to glow a pretty blue color again. I could tell the thin piece of orb light pointed down the shaft, as if Daddy was leading us where to go.

"Let me see it?" Winslett asked, holding out her hand.

He tossed my precious jewel to her. But as quickly as the light came, it died in midair.

Winslett caught it, but it didn't spark to life at her touch.

"Hmm..." she murmured.

She walked over to where Lennon and I leaned against the door of the shaft. It sparked to life again.

"Byrde, a couple of days ago you were saying how you thought the orb was the key to your father's poem?" Winslett recalled. She twirled my orb between her fingers and held it up against the sun, watching different lights reflect off of it.

I nodded. Of course, why else would Daddy tell me the necklace was so important? He had given me everything I needed to succeed on this mission. How had he known that one day I might find myself in this situation? Had he? Somehow my orb unlocked whatever was here in Hero's Point.

"Three will free. Two will open. One will point you in the right direction," Lennon recited.

They nodded their heads, remembering.

"And it's pointing down the shaft, straight to the government building, which leads to Iris," Lennon reminded us. "Who we thought could represent the looming eye."

I breathed a sigh of relief. They were finally beginning to understand.

"Yeah, I guess that makes sense now," Masen agreed.

"So there are two more out there!" said Lennon.

"We need all three," I whispered.

"Well, we know where one is, right?" Masen asked.

Lennon nodded, but didn't seem pleased at all. He looked down the deep, dark shaft.

"Yeah, through there."

"Looks like you're getting the siege you've always wanted," said Masen.

Forty-Two

Masen

After discovering the insanely random secret shaft, we went back near the barrier to organize the few supplies we had. I looked around at my two and a half friends. Lennon barely counted. We had all lost a little weight since Wren left because we no longer knew which western berries were safe to eat, and it was clear to all of us that we didn't have the same knack for hunting. I looked over at Winslett sitting on a tree stump. She had just finished braiding her hair and now was braiding Byrde's. Lennon had ripped out Wren's knife and was stabbing a tree repeatedly, trying to master the technique. That guy was making me nervous.

But what really had me worried was our lack of organization. We were nothing but talk. As far as I knew, our plan was to knock on the front door of the government building and offer Iris some cookies as we let ourselves in like welcomed guests. I figured I'd let the "siege extraordinaire" take the reigns on this one.

"I think it'd be a pretty good idea to use the rest of the day to prepare for the trip to the government building. We'll leave at night," Lennon decided without consent, per usual.

"Can we run over our plan?" Winslett asked.

"We wing it," I suggested.

"Not helping," Lennon grunted.

"Well, that is our plan, right? To go into the government building and get the orb from Iris, along with any other information we can find? That's a goal, not a plan of action."

"Don't be seen and don't get caught," Byrde added from Lennon's words to us earlier.

"This is a suicide mission," Winslett stated.

"What other choice do we have? Like you said, I don't plan to live in the woods the rest of my life either, and Byrde really believes there's life outside of the barriers. If these orbs are our best shot at finding our way out, I'm going to take it. And although we all hate Wren for betraying us now, there have been good reasons to believe him."

Byrde nodded. "I think Wren had figured out some of Daddy's song. When we go into the government building, we don't have to rescue him."

The kid made a good point.

"I hate to ask this Byrde, but since your mother worked for the government, do you know anything about the layout?" Lennon inquired.

Byrde nodded her head. "Mommy always used to bring me to work with her."

Lennon tried to coax more information from her. "So what did it look like? Were there a lot of guards?"

"Oh sure," Byrde said. "Everyone in there is like a guard and they all have stunners. I've seen it before when Mommy took me to work once."

"Stunners?" gulped Winslett.

Lennon sighed. "We don't have access to anything."

"We have Wren's knife, right?"

"Yeah," I replied, "but it's not like any of us have been actually trained in hand-to-hand combat."

"Better than nothing," she said defensively.

"What do I get to use?" Byrde chimed.

I stared at Winslett; neither of us wanted the ten-year-old to wield a weapon.

"Well, Byrde," Winslett cooed, "we don't have enough good weapons for any of us really."

Byrde pouted, but remained quiet.

"Wren had a stunner," Lennon said quietly.

"Oh, right." I laughed. "Didn't you get shot with it?"

Lennon glowered. "Cut it out. I scared the guy. You're lucky I stepped in and saved you. Otherwise, he was going to shoot you with it too."

He turned on his heel and walked away, deeper into the forest with Byrde, searching for some stones and probably some time away from me.

Winslett remained behind. She was used to tolerating my unique nature.

"Do you think this will all work out?" I asked, walking over to put my arm around her.

"Truthfully, I don't know. It's just so risky. So many things are bound to go wrong," she answered.

I nodded in understanding.

"Yeah," I said, "I know Byrde is strong and everything, but I'm worried about her for this part."

"Me too. But we couldn't leave her behind."

"That's true. I only wish it weren't."

Winslett then shrugged out of my arm, and I knew why. Byrde was back carrying four almost-sharp stones. Lennon was by her side carrying the same amount of spear-sized sticks.

"Got the stuff," Lennon told us.

Winslett and I eyed each other again. Four sticks. Lennon was really going to give Byrde a weapon.

Byrde happily set down the stones and Winslett told her to match each one to a stick. She then sauntered over to Lennon and I followed.

Winslett whispered to Lennon, "Are you sure it's the best idea to give her a weapon?"

"She's just a kid," I added.

"We're all just kids," Lennon said gravely. "She needs to be able to defend herself."

It was sad, but true. If we did have to take Byrde into a fight, we couldn't leave her unable to protect herself if the rest of us were preoccupied. This wasn't some babysitting job, no matter how much I cared for her.

I whipped out Wren's knife I kept in my pocket and began whittling the sticks and filing the stones.

It was tiring work and nothing came out perfect. I never claimed to be an expert whittler, and it wasn't like these sticks were going to save us anyway.

Forty-Three

Winslett

I breathed in the crisp air and opened my eyes. Masen's handmade spear was at my throat.

He grinned a devilish smile.

"Gotcha!" he said pulling away the spear.

I muttered curses under my breath. Masen was merciless.

Lennon had us all practicing this mock fighting for hours at a time. It served as a way to let out our stress and frustration of the day's events, while of course helping us prepare for whatever was to come.

"My turn with her." Lennon winked.

He swiftly swapped spots with Masen.

Our steps turned into a dance as we blocked back and forth blow after blow. Lennon's movements were stealthy and sure. He lunged at me and we twisted and turned in choreographed movements.

Out of the corner of my eye, I saw Byrde watching with a wide-eyed stare of glee. Masen's face, on the other hand, was stone.

Lennon kept circling me until my clumsy feet got in his way. He tripped on them and fell back. I, of course, took this opportunity to beat someone, and aimed my spear at his chest.

He laughed. "You win, Winslett."

Byrde and Masen snickered and I blushed.

"Sorry, Lennon." I sighed, helping him up. "You were going to win anyway."

He smiled, accepting my outstretched hand that lifted him up.

"I had intended to let you win. Your foot interfered," he teased.

"*Let* me win?" I said in mock disgust.

He came over and kissed me on the forehead.

"My turn, my turn!" piped Byrde.

"Come here then!" challenged Lennon. He was really good with Byrde and it made me happy to see her flutter over to him.

I went over to Masen and watched them "fight."

"She's a little monster, isn't she?" Masen mused in reference to Byrde.

The little tyke was relentless. She pounced at Lennon without holding back.

"Yeah she is." I smiled at the youngest of us. "Go, Byrde! Get him!"

Masen shot me a stare.

"What?" I asked.

"Nothing," he said and went back to his brooding.

I withdrew my look of suspicion and turned my attention back to the fight. Byrde skidded to the ground and dodged Lennon's attacks effortlessly. We were all impressed, even if

Lennon had been holding back. She jabbed the back of his knees, enough to knock him to the ground.

Masen and I cheered.

"You got me!" Lennon acceded, wiping away sweat that didn't exist.

"Sure did!" Byrde said with pride.

After that round, Masen and I both had a go at Byrde. Masen, too, let her win. It was good for the little girl's self-esteem. I would like to say I let her win as well, but the reality was she could've beaten me fair and square.

Byrde skipped over to give Masen and Lennon a high five, and I followed her. Then it dawned on me that Masen and Lennon were the only ones who had yet to fight. They sized each other up and went over to where the rest of the mock fights had taken place.

The intense looks in the boys' eyes were alarming. Their spears were at the ready and they lunged at each other like one would lunge at a prey. This fight was much better matched than the others had been. I was strangely worried for both of them. They came at each other again and again, but neither could seem to gain the upper hand. It was hard for me to watch, but I couldn't tear my eyes away.

Masen's movements were more agile, while Lennon stayed stronger with his blows. It seemed to go on forever.

"Guys, we have a shuttle to catch and a government building to invade. Let's not take any longer," I joked, knowing the match might never end.

Their eyes darted to me and they straightened up, though they remained on edge, as if the other would have used this opportunity to strike.

Byrde whined, "Aww, Winslett, it was just getting good!"

"Guess it's a draw now," said Lennon, extending his hand.

It was clear to me Masen wasn't happy, but he reluctantly shook the hand offered.

"Guess so," Masen replied.

I felt the slightest remorse that I had ended what I guessed was their "fun." But if I was being honest, I was afraid Masen would hurt Lennon. Not because Lennon wasn't more than capable of fending for himself, he wouldn't have wanted to hurt Masen. It made my stomach lurch.

Seeing them fight like that made me realize where we were actually going. Four kids? With minimal resources and a lack of food and water? We weren't ready, I kept telling Masen. But this, they had both surprisingly agreed on, was no time to wait. We were as ready as we could get.

The best-case scenario? Don't be seen and don't get caught, Lennon told us all. We would have to search for an orb, if Iris even had one at all. Ugh. What a disaster. If it turned out there was no orb, our efforts would be futile.

I shook my head at the thought. We were all aware of the risks. This mission could cost us our lives.

Forty-Four

Lennon

Ten minutes... Masen, Winslett, and I had agreed when we would finally leave. It was dark by now and Winslett and I had headed toward the shaft, before Masen and Byrde, to talk in private.

I tried to meet her eyes, but they continually flickered away.

"What is it?" I asked, turning toward her and running my fingers over her tangled hair.

In response, she inched closer to me, allowing her head to rest on my chest. I wrapped my arms around her petite frame, pulling her close to me. I felt a part of my shirt dampen and looked down at Winslett and my shirt, which was now soaked with her tears. Pulling away from my sudden movement, she looked at the dark, sodden spot she had rested on and hid her face in her hands.

"I'm sorry. I didn't mean to ruin your shirt," Winslett said, clearly frustrated, briskly brushing away the tears remaining on her face. However, the tears continued to stream. I held her face in my hands, moving my thumb across her cheek to gently wipe away her tears. She grasped my wrists in protest, but I continued to stroke her face and calm both of our nerves.

"Shhh," I soothed, smoothing her hair once again.

"Lennon," Winslett began again. There was a pleading behind her voice. "We can't go down there. What if we never make it out?"

"I know, I know," I reassured her. "I don't know what would happen if you were to get hurt."

It killed me to see her this way.

And just then, I kissed her. I guided her full lips toward mine, reaching behind her warm neck. I felt her face redden as she tried to object, but I only pulled her closer. I felt the wetness of her tears against my cheek, and tasted the saltiness on her lips.

No matter, I couldn't pretend reality would simply wish away with a kiss. Our mission hadn't disappeared. It pounded against the back of my head unbearably, a responsibility, urging me to get up and go.

I felt her fingers curl into fists against my chest, her eyes still closed as I reluctantly pulled away. She blinked her eyes open and I gave her a halfhearted smile.

"It's time?" Winslett asked, already knowing the answer.

I tucked the loose strand of fire behind with the rest of her hair and stood up, lending my hand out to her.

She clutched it, and briskly pulled her pack on. I stood next to her, soaking the darkness in, breathing in the cool fresh air. She looked at me with a fierce expression.

"Winslett?" I heard Masen call from deep into the trees.

She cleared her voice and took a deep breath. "We're over here."

Minutes later, Masen approached with Byrde, empty canteens, and blankets. He looked curiously at Winslett and walked over to where we stood, next to the door of the shaft.

Masen pulled the doors of the shaft open and on cue, the light from Byrde's orb produced a shimmering blue beam.

"Ready?" he asked, looking back to all of us.

"Ready," I answered, waiting for Masen, Winslett, and Byrde to find the first step of the stairs. Winslett looked up at me anxiously.

"Don't worry, we'll be back," I told her.

I climbed in after them and closed the door of the shaft with less confidence, leaving our chapter in the forest behind.

PART 3: Invasion

Forty-Five

Wren

I woke to the sound of water dripping next to my ear, echoing through the walls of my hollow cell. Lying on the cold damp floor, a chill shot up my spine. I peered around at my surroundings, eyes half open. A dim beam of morning light shone from a small crack in the ceiling. It reflected onto my hand and I pretended to clench it, as if the thin stream of light was a truly tangible thing.

I had been forced into another life. The wooded surroundings I had lived in only a short week ago had been changed drastically to the musty basement cell I was held captive in now. I couldn't tell exactly where the government officials had shoved me in, but the last thing I recalled before being knocked out and forced into the hovercraft was Lennon, Winslett, Masen, and Byrde watching me, horrified. I moved my fingers, playing with the light. They were bound to figure out the truth about me somehow, most likely through the files I mistakenly left out, unguarded. I had no doubt they thought I was a traitor, a liar.

Looking over to where the drops of water had created a decent sized puddle in my undersized cell, I scrambled over to scoop up a couple sips. My hands shook as I lifted the remaining drops. Such water couldn't be wasted.

The liquid met my lips and I swallowed it down. My eyelids fluttered and I quickly bent down to drink some more, until I caught my reflection. I hadn't had the chance to look at myself since I had been captured. I hadn't eaten either for that matter. The head official, Fahad, demanded that I was to be starved until I started spitting out some information. I turned my head and examined the swollen bruise on my collarbone he had given me after talking back to him, when his "torture session" hadn't worked. The bruises showed that time had indeed progressed; it was already yellowing. These "torture sessions" existed of a three-hour period where I underwent some sort of gruesome beating or electrocuting, whatever Fahad felt in the mood for that day. They were an attempt to pry information out of me. What did I know about the Resistance? Why had I run away before Distribution Day? Who had I helped along the way? Where were the others going? The questions were shot at me again and again. With each one I refused to answer, the severity of the beatings intensified.

I stroked the lines of my bruise and a sharp pain shot throughout the area. Inspecting the rest of my body, I gnawed at my lips and saw that my cheeks had hollowed immensely. Leaning over the puddle, my arms began to shake due to the lack of food in my body and the lack of energy I could hold. I was growing weaker every day now, and if I didn't get some sort of food into my system, it would cause my entire body to break down. A few sips of water weren't going to cut it.

My attention shifted to a ricochet of several pairs of footsteps that boomed through the hallways, stalking straight toward me, until finally an expensive pair of leather shoes stopped directly in front my cell, inches away from my face. I despised them all— the shoes and their owners.

"Wren," the all too familiar voice acknowledged icily. Iris.

In disgust, I spit on the well-shined soles.

In turn, I was answered with an expected kick to the mouth by some other government official, I presumed. Clambering back, I turned away from the Prime Minister in disgust, spewing blood over the cell's filthy floors. I kept myself upright by balancing my weight on my forearm.

The official accompanying him threatened in a fury, shaking the bars of my cell. "Another kick in the head would do you good! You ought to be taught a few—"

"Now, now. Let's not get ourselves off track here. We don't want any of that," Iris toyed. "We wouldn't want to *hurt* our friend here, not when he still is so much use to us."

I chuckled to myself, still not looking up to meet Iris's face. "You haven't learned, have you?" I fought harder, raising my voice. "I'm not revealing anything. No matter what kind of torturing your officials give me. No matter what you threaten to do. Nothing will break me."

Suddenly, a tight, cold hand gripped my face. Iris knelt down and pulled my chin to the bars of the cell. Squirming desperately, I struggled to pull my face out of his crushing grip.

"You may still have a sliver of life left due to the mercy of my officials, but you've seemed to let one little detail slip away." He gestured with his hand.

Breathing heavily, I was choking from the pressure of his clench that was moving dangerously toward my throat.

He forced my head upward to look into his black, flickering eyes.

"What's that?" I spat.

"You haven't felt pain until you've dealt with me," Iris shot fiercely, his temper lost, for the first time I had ever seen in the years I had know him.

Iris stood back up and inhaled a curt breath, smoothing his hair over again with his fingers. I glanced up, with a flicker of curiosity running through my eyes.

He waved his fingers for the official to come over and collect me. My cell door was opened and I was peeled off the floor, covered in sweat and dried blood.

"*Such* a disappointing future, for *such* a promising individual." Iris tisked.

For the first time, I was scared, truly scared, because whatever Iris had in store for me would be unquestionably terrifying. In pure desperation, I swung my elbow back into the throat of the official, hard, causing him to gag and drop me to the ground. Seeing Iris in front of me, I kicked his chest with all of the force I could muster, making him stumble backward. I lunged toward him to strike again seeing I had the advantage, but was suddenly pulled back and grappled at the waist with an electrical band, a weapon of my own invention. The official had strapped the band and locked it tight. Knowing fully well the power it contained, I stopped fighting immediately. Beads of sweat dripped down my face, and a huge force knocked me cold at the back of my neck.

"Hmmm," Iris mused, getting up now. "It would seem that our little runaway does need a few lessons taught to him."

Peering blearily through my bruised eyes, I cringed as I saw Iris take the beating stick from the other man. The light from earlier had since been gone and I was consumed by blackness. I let it overtake me as I prepared my worn body to endure the coming blows.

Forty-Six

Masen

"Byrde, when you touch the ground, could you shine the orb to the bottom of the steps?" My voice echoed off the walls.

"I'm nodding, Masen," said Byrde.

My sweaty palms clutched the railings of the stairs as I stiffly walked alongside what I could make out to be Lennon and Winslett.

"These are some long stairs," I thought aloud. I heard the shake in my own voice.

"We've been walking for a while," Winslett agreed. "They should end soon."

"Ahhh!" I heard Byrde scream.

She wasn't too far in front of me... what could she have run into?

"Byrde!" Winslett panicked.

"What happened? Are you okay?" I questioned.

We were answered with a soft whimper. "Ow."

"Byrde, what's going on down there?" Lennon tested.

"I just hit my knee on the bottom of the stairs. I didn't know where they ended," she whispered back. "But... something is hitting me behind my back."

"Byrde, can you put the orb at the bottom of the stairs?" I asked again.

Byrde's hazy outline unfastened the leather rope around her neck and pulled out the glowing sphere, still pointing straight forward.

"Thanks," I murmured, rushing down to the bottom.

I kneeled beside her and she clutched her knee tightly to her chest. I swiped the orb from the step and shone it on the wound. Fresh with blood, the gash looked bad, but it wasn't deep. I breathed a sigh of relief, and moved to lift Byrde off of the cold ground. I felt Lennon and Winslett hurry beside me.

"Is she okay?" I heard Lennon ask.

"Yeah," I replied. "She cut her knee, but it's not too bad."

"Yes, it is," Byrde protested.

"Okay, Byrde."

"Lennon? Can you look over where I was sitting?" she asked. "Something was poking my back."

He shifted positions to investigate where the blondie had fallen as I moved her out of his way.

"Hand me the orb?" Lennon asked.

I did, and he shone its light toward a metal box.

"Don't fear, Byrde. It's only a box with sharp corners."

"Wait, take a look at this," Winslett spoke up.

We shifted our focus back to the box, and Winslett gasped.

"Masen! We learned about these at the Institute!"

I stared at her blankly. I couldn't have imagined it being any more than that: a gray box.

She rolled her eyes. "Oh, that's right, you never paid attention in Professor Kott's class."

"A History of Laiden's Purpose and Function? That class?"

She nodded, and I quickly agreed. "Oh yeah, I hated Kott."

"You took that class? I had to take it my previous year at the Institute," Lennon recalled.

"Can we get back to the box, Winslett?" asked Byrde.

"Yes," she continued, clearing her throat. "Haven't you heard of power boxes kept in the government building to maintain all of the homes in Laiden?"

"No?"

"Well, they have them, and the boxes run something called electricity which can control light and power and—"

"Why is this important now?" I interrupted.

"Well, if it helps us see out of this underground pit, it might be useful."

I reached toward the sharp corner of the box where there was a slight indentation. "Can you open it from here?"

I pulled the small door of the box and the latch swung open.

"Shine the orb over here?" asked Winslett.

Inside the gray box was beginning to look familiar. Maybe I hadn't totally slept through Kott's class. Multiple colored wires strung across the inside of the box loosely, plugged into random compartments and outlets.

"How do you find anything in this mess?" asked Winslett, pushing some of the red wires aside.

"Is that a switch?" asked Lennon, peering above Winslett's shoulder and scooting closer to her. Ugh. He was blocking my view.

"Yeah, it is," replied Winslett slowly.

"Well, what are you waiting for?" I asked, grabbing for the switch between the two lovebirds. I pulled it toward me.

It didn't budge.

"I think you're supposed to pull it upward," stated Lennon.

"Oh, right."

"Here, let me," said Winslett, flicking the switch.

We waited in silence for some sort of miracle. But nothing came. No lights. Nada.

"Well, that wasn't a waste of time or anything," I sighed.

"How much were you expecting? This has been shut down for years," said Lennon.

I gave him the death stare.

Winslett stood up slowly and brushed some dust from her knees. "Let's go then. We have a long way to go and we can't expect that the orb will point us in the right direction forever."

"Look!" cried Byrde.

We whipped our heads around to face blinding white beams. A shuttle, monstrous in size, stood several feet from where we were.

I heard Winslett gasp behind me.

"The power box turned on the shuttle, not the lights!" she breathed.

I nodded. The shuttle, headlights shining, was made of a rusted silver metal complete with glass doors and small windows. It wasn't huge, but must have been big enough to fit a good fifty people.

"Wow, it's incredible," Lennon gawked.

"Thank you, Daddy," whispered Byrde from beside me. I was starting to really worry about the blondie. She was relying on her dead father a lot recently.

Forty-Seven

Winslett

The glass shuttle door slid open with a *ding*.

"Please take caution of the sliding door," a female voice chimed.

I jolted at the sound of the voice, not because I hadn't expected to hear anyone talking way underground, but because it was the first voice other than the four of ours I had heard in a long while. Taking Byrde's hand, I hesitantly walked into the shuttle with her and gaped at its interior. Inside the shuttle was just as impressive as its exterior. Everything was the color of silver steel, the walls and the floors.

"Wren mentioned that they had modeled these shuttles from the old world. He said that this was one of the few useful inventions they had come up with," said Lennon.

Seats carved from the same steel were placed along the perimeter of the vehicle. I sat down in one, and shivered. The seat was like ice. Masen, Lennon, and Byrde sat down on the seats next to me.

"Shuttle F will be leaving from Terminal F in a few short minutes. Please stay seated until we have arrived," the cool female voice spoke again.

Besides Byrde's bleeding knee, she seemed so content. How?

The shuttle lurched to start and we all jerked forward. It began at a slower pace, but eventually picked up a much quicker speed.

"Everything's black," Byrde pointed out. She was referring to the underground path outside the walls of the shuttle. Through small windows, we could see more darkness moving past us with the occasional red blinker.

"Wins, you're shaking the entire bench," said Masen.

"What?" I asked, startled.

He pointed to my knee. I had been bouncing it up and down subconsciously. With a frustrated sigh, I stopped my shaking and twiddled with my thumbs instead, continuing to look out the windows of nothing.

It dawned on me then, how terrible it would be to be caught. Maybe we'd become lab subjects to cruel scientists. If we didn't die in the process then surely we would be executed soon after. Our future didn't seem great.

So it seemed the only option would be to not get caught— easiest thing in the world, right? Break into the government, us kids, and not be seen by the thousands of workers who were lucky enough to be high enough in rank to not take Extium? Yeah, sounded easy.

Only a few minutes after, I looked away from the window, seeing enough.

Forty-Eight

Lennon

The shuttle screamed to a halt and we bounded off of our seats.

"Ow," Byrde groaned. She had fallen off onto her knee again.

Masen gently reached to help her up as we exited the shuttle.

"Enjoy the rest of your day!" the female voice of the vehicle cheered.

"Byrde?" I called to her, about to ask her for the orb's direction.

Its shimmering beam of light answered me, pointing down a dark tunnel.

"Great, more darkness," Masen grumbled. "I swear the next time I see light, I'll have a seizure."

The lights from the shuttle dimmed as we entered the darkness. I instinctively reached out to interlock Winslett's fingers in mine. Winslett grabbed Masen's hand, and Byrde clutched onto Masen's back as we hesitantly took our first steps down the echoing tunnel. I moved the palm of my hand along what felt like a cold steel wall, to help guide the four of us. Byrde's delicate orb necklace hung around her equally delicate body, glowing brightly enough where I could see the blood dripping off of her scraped knee and onto the metal floor. It was the only sound we heard besides our own footsteps. It had seemed we were walking for miles again, feeling the edges of the narrow tunnel, making sure to not bump into anything. But this time it was worse; the road ahead was more dangerous than a walk through the woods. Although it was harder to tell where we were in the woods, we all knew this tunnel led straight to Iris and his headquarters. With one thought of the official from my bedroom, I shuddered.

The farther we traveled, the more distinct Byrde's groans began to become as well.

Exasperated, I let out an irritated sigh and suggested, "Byrde, do you think it would be better if we were to let you rest here and then come back for you?"

Byrde shook her head. "It's dark and cold."

"It is, so you'd be braver than all of us put together," I tried again.

"I guess..." she contemplated. "But what if someone bad finds me?"

"They won't," I replied confidently. "We won't be gone long, and we'll come straight back for you as soon as possible."

"But don't you need my help?" she whispered.

Masen glanced over at me. "Lennon, this may not be such a good idea."

"It's dark. Nobody would find her," I said, frustrated.

Masen put Byrde down next to where Winslett was standing and pulled me aside.

"Lennon," he began again.

"Look, Masen, we're running out of time, and Byrde might give us away," I fiercely whispered. "She's slowing us down and we need to do this on our own. She's too young."

Masen glared at me.

"If we had a better choice, I wouldn't want to do this either, but this seems like the best option right now."

"Fine, but we have to be quick," Masen said, defeated.

We walked back to the others and Masen knelt to comfort Byrde. We tended her wound the best we could before leaving. I laid her spear on her lap in case she was to need it.

"Come on, Masen," I urged.

We kept walking, our fingers brushing along the walls, until suddenly, they did no longer. I tried feeling for the wall next to me, but nothing was there. Winslett must've been doing the same, but instead flung her hand into Masen's face.

"Really?" he said annoyed.

"Sorry," she answered curtly.

"Guys, where are we? I don't feel the wall anymore," I spoke up.

I took another step forward and as if on cue, lights in a dark, steel room flickered on. I blinked. Laid out in this huge room were hundreds and hundreds of weapons. My jaw dropped as I gazed at the cases of stun guns. My eyes then fluttered over to the endless rows of silver knives glinting miraculously off the walls. I stood there staring for what felt like hours.

My paralyzing moment was over when Masen burst into a run to inspect the guns in a corner of the room. I ran over to the rows of knives. Out of the corner of my eye, I saw Winslett run to the section of Farspects.

Brushing my fingers along the back of each smooth blade, I inspected each weapon's durability, sharpness, and beauty. I lifted up a weapon that caught my attention, a wicked bronze dagger, with patterns engraved on the side of the blade that read "katar." I spun it in my hands, intrigued, and to my surprise, two smaller, but just as deadly, blades popped out from the black leather handle alongside the main dagger. I stared at the knife in awe; it resembled the claws of a Rawk. I twirled it again, and the blades went just as easily back into its handle. I glanced behind me to see Winslett staring at both the knife and me. In a sly attempt to impress her, I spotted a target several feet away and I flung the knife, aiming straight for the bullseye. To my humiliation, the knife clattered to the floor, inches away from the target. I felt my face grow red as I heard Winslett and Masen, behind me, both guffaw. Masen walked toward the knife and slowly picked it up, studying the katar with interest. He spun it in his hands and the two blades appeared once again, as he walked back to me. He then, unexpectedly, hurled the knife to the spot I tried to aim for at the wall, and succeeded with great accuracy, striking the center of the target.

"Whoa! Where'd you learn to do that, Masen?" Winslett asked.

I didn't try to hide my jealousy.

"Just some practice." He shrugged, like it was nothing. "Wanna try it again?"

I backed away from it, putting my hands in front of me in defeat. "I… better not."

More laughter came from the two of them.

"Okay, so we all know that I am not the best knife thrower Laiden has ever seen," I said, laughing to myself now. "I think it's best if I just stick with the stun gun."

I walked over to the glass case of stunners and pulled one out.

"Hey, toss me one too," Winslett, who was inspecting the row of electric belts, exclaimed from the back of the room.

I pulled another out of the case and tossed it to her. She then put it in her pack, carefully placing the electric belt with it.

Winslett looked up, realizing the room had gone silent, to see Masen and me both eyeing the electric belt in her bag.

Masen spoke before me, wanting her to stop too. "Winslett, that may not be such a—"

"I can take care myself, okay?" she said calmly, cutting him off. "I promise I'll be careful, and you never know when it may come in handy."

"But you don't know how to use it, none of us do," I pointed out.

She shrugged. "Maybe Wren will know how."

Although I remained skeptical, Masen gave up with a shrug of his shoulders and turned to go retrieve the katar from the wall.

Realizing I was still holding onto the flimsy spear I had made earlier, I tossed it casually onto the floor, not needing it any longer. Masen and Winslett did the same after they saw me. I saw Winslett toss her spear over to the direction of the center of the room. I looked over curiously to where the spear had landed. It lay on top of the center of a very familiar sketch of an eye, an eye similar to the ones etched onto each of the government uniforms. I walked over to it and leaned over, calling Masen and Winslett to come join me. I noticed a black handle coming off the floor, lying closely to the eye.

"It looks like some sort of basement cellar, doesn't it?" I asked, puzzled. The three of our heads bent over the mysterious ground door. "Do you think it leads somewhere?"

"What could be further down than this?" Winslett asked.

"Well, there's only one way to find out, huh?" Masen replied.

I lifted the handle of the door on the floor and looked around in an effort to spot something that could help us, and to my relief, I did. "Hey guys, see that ladder over there?"

Winslett and Masen stuck their heads in further to see. We peered into the dark, damp cellar and a stench that smelled like something dead filled our nostrils. Masen only responded by hacking profusely as he jerked his head up, out of the door.

"Ow!" Winslett yelped.

Masen had clunked heads with her on the way up.

"Isn't there another way out?" Winslett mumbled, rubbing her forehead desperately.

"I'll double check," Masen said, quickly getting off of his knees.

"Hey, unfortunately, this may be our best way to get up to the real floors of this building," I said, disappointed. "It looks like the least obvious. I can't imagine too many of Iris's guards would want to be down here."

Winslett responded with a sigh and a nod of the head. "Masen, we're leaving. Come on."

Masen appeared behind a row of practice targets. "I didn't see any other doors anyway," he muttered, kneeling down next to the ground door again. He eyed us hesitantly and unwillingly.

I turned and set my foot on the rung of the ladder. I tested it by shaking my foot. "Hold your nose, people."

Winslett groaned and followed after me. I climbed down a short distance to the dirt floor and jumped off of the ladder. I held my hand out to Winslett and she took it, jumping off the ladder too. Masen climbed down next, stiffly, and I offered him some help, while he held his breath.

"Need a hand, Masen?" I joked.

Masen slapped my hand away and I chuckled to myself. He grabbed the handle of the lid and pulled it toward us, shutting ourselves from the outside world once again, and back into the darkness.

"Can we get a light in here?" I heard Masen call.

"Yeah, I brought a flashlight from the arsenal upstairs," I added, rummaging through my pack, while walking. "Here it is!"

I grabbed the light and turned it on. I looked down. We were no longer walking on the dirt ground, but back on the steel flooring. Huh. That was strange. I looked up, shining my flashlight, looking for a direction to turn to.

But instead, the flashlight glinted on an object that made me do a double take. I heard Winslett gasp behind me, knowing she saw it too. We were looking into the eyes of Wren Casterra.

Forty-Nine

Wren

Time didn't seem to mean much anymore. So when I saw the faces of Masen, Winslett, and Lennon, I hadn't known if it had been weeks or days. I couldn't help but break into a manic smile at the sight of the three familiar faces so different from those of the officials.

I couldn't believe they had come back for me. Wait, of course I could. I had been their fearless leader, the guy with all the answers. All my hopeless thoughts dissipated from my bruised skin.

I was dazed to see that Lennon wore a look of repugnance. Was it asking too much they discounted the fact I created Extium?

Suddenly, through the bars, Lennon grabbed my ragged and stained shirt. He held a stunner to my throat. At that proximity, I knew the blow could kill me.

My voice came out hoarse. "Lennon, what are you doing here?"

His eyes were the most unwelcoming that I'd ever seen them. He held me in that uncomfortable position for several moments longer, sizing me up. Surely he would see my hollowed cheeks, sunken eyes, and yellowed teeth. He would smell my putrid breath.

I saw his lip twitch as his gaze softened, but it was still guarded. Perhaps the sight of my mangled body made him pity me.

"You're in no position to be the one asking the question, Wren."

I laughed. How much he sounded like Iris and the guards! As if there were any ways left to try and break me!

Lennon looked back at his two friends. I saw Masen hovering about a foot in front of Winslett. He looked at her and she shook her head. Lennon let his hand fall. Why were they looking at me like I was someone to be feared?

I let the light go out of my eyes.

"Why didn't you tell us?" asked Lennon. He no longer spoke in a threatening way, but in a longing way, a way that really begged for the answer.

I chose to ignore him though. "Did you follow my directions?" I questioned instead.

Then Winslett spoke. "We figured you had tried to piece together Byrde's song. But we also found out that Hero's Point means nothing if you didn't have the orbs."

I looked at her, not bothering to hide my hopelessly confused expression.

"What orbs are you talking about?"

She lowered her voice and shifted her eyes back and forth a few times before continuing. "We believe they're the key to getting us across the divide. The barrier."

Masen added, "Byrde has one that her father had passed onto her. And in the song it said, 'Three will free— Two will open— One will point you in the right direction.' Byrde's orb led us to the secret shaft that took us here."

"The shafts I told you about when we first met?" I probed.

Lennon looked away.

I pressed on, "And what's your plan now?"

"We think Iris has another orb, so we've been planning to take it from him," Winslett answered.

I rolled my eyes at their naivety. "You can't expect it to be that easy. What if he doesn't have it?"

"Iris is the most likely suspect to have the orb. The song even mentions an eye. Hello! Eye is Iris!" Winslett shook her head. "We don't expect this to be easy, but maybe you'd like to help us."

How clever they had become without me. Indeed.

Lennon looked back at Winslett. He wasn't pleased with her remark.

"Not too happy, Lennon?" I asked with a twitch.

His brow creased. "We can't trust you with this kind of information."

Winslett's face turned to stone. Masen couldn't even meet my eyes.

Lennon's face was still unmoving.

"Come on, Lennon. Do you really believe that I betrayed you?" I asked.

"You work for the government. The government is our enemy, which makes you an enemy," he said stiffly.

I cackled. Masen and Winslett exchanged concerned looks. "Does it look like I work for the government at the moment?"

"Whatever," he spat. "You still worked for the government. You never thought to tell us about Extium?"

"Yes. I did think about it, but I knew how it would look. I left Laiden for a reason. I didn't want that to be my life anymore."

"Well that sucks, because it will always be a part of your life. Wren Casterra, the great inventor of Extium." He gestured in the air at the sound of my name. "Extium will never leave you, and it will never leave our lives either. You destroyed whatever we had. I'm not saying we had much, but you had no right!" Lennon was screaming by now. "You had no right to claim ownership over what was ours! Masen had his father. Winslett had her brother and sister. Byrde had a mother." I backed away from the door of the cell. Lennon's nostrils were flared. "Aren't you too old to run away from things that don't appeal to you, Wren? When you ran away from your life you destroyed mine."

"Your life? What life. You had no life worth living, Lennon," I said coldly.

Masen and Winslett stared at me again like I was a stranger. I was losing them.

"Where's Byrde?" I suddenly asked.

"Somewhere safe," said Masen.

I nodded. "The guards will be coming for a nightly check soon. I assume you have a plan?"

They exchanged nervous glances.

"Like I would've thought, you still need me," I stated.

Winslett looked to Lennon meaningfully, as if to tell him it was time to let things go. He approached me again.

"Look," I said, "I may have not been entirely truthful. But do you think that if I agreed with the government I would've left? I saw the wrongs I had done. I hate myself for it. But when I think of the four of you, I have hope again. You were supposed to be like the rest of them... but you aren't. I live to discover things and to create things with the mind I have. There's no doubt the scientist within me will disappear, but it gives me a reason to live." I turned to Winslett and aimed an apology toward her. "I'm sorry for the pain I caused you and your siblings. I had never known about Iris's full intentions for the pill until very late in the Extium trials. I'll do everything in my power to return them to you, even if it takes a lifetime of work."

She nodded once, and actually smiled at my apology.

Lennon soaked in my words. "The problem is, Wren, we didn't ask for this. We never got a choice."

"And sometimes the very thing you don't ask for is the thing you end up needing the most," I countered.

"Time's running out, Lennon," Winslett whispered. "We need his help."

Lennon sighed and looked at me. He didn't need to say it. I knew he was giving me permission to lead them again. A little bit of purpose returned to me. Next to Iris, I knew the ins and outs of this place better than anyone.

"We are now on the clock. I'm not sure what you mean about the orb, but if anything of value is to be found here, it will be in Iris's office. Winslett, I suggest you go up and find a way to breach it. It isn't going to be easy, just do whatever you have to. If the orb can really break the barrier and get us to the Outlanders, then that's what the priority is. Taking down Iris will come later, when we have the upper hand."

"Whoa," said Lennon. "Why her? She can't go alone."

"I'll be fine. Don't get too worried," she replied through gritted teeth.

"It's dangerous," Lennon said protectively.

I raised my eyebrows at this one.

"Okay then, go with her if you must. The government building can be confusing to maneuver if you're visiting for the first time. Everything is white and the hallways are long. It's very easy to get lost. Right beyond the end of this hallway there'll be a steel door and a set of stairs, and a couple more doors after that, leading to the main floor of government headquarters. The first time you see officials alone, attack them and take their uniforms. Also, you're going to have to take an elevator. It'll take you right up to Iris's office if you ask it too. But I'm warning you, don't attract too much attention to yourselves. Play dumb if anyone approaches you. Don't trust anyone. Except for Reina, Byrde's mother. She is safe."

Masen spoke next. "What about me?"

"Someone has to stay behind and get me out of here, right?" I voiced.

"Where'd you get that idea, Wren?" Lennon smirked. "You're still more use to us behind the bars right now."

I snarled, but Masen spoke before I had the chance to make a nasty remark. "It's fine. I'll stay behind and make sure no one comes along to kill him. Lennon, trade me your stunner."

I smiled for the first time in a while. "Not a bad idea, Masen. It could make this whole thing a lot easier."

Winslett held up her stunner and they both nodded. Lennon reluctantly took Masen's katar in return. He spun it in his hand, uncomfortably.

"Good luck," Masen said to Winslett and Lennon.

"To you too," they replied in unison.

Tension hung in the air, but no one added anything else. They wanted to believe all of us would make it out alive. How naïve they all still were. This was the government, where everyone was a prisoner.

Fifty

Winslett

We turned a corner in the prison chambers. Lennon and I had left Byrde behind first, and now we left Masen with a questionably sane Wren. With us separated, it would be easier for the government to pick us apart, one by one. I gnawed on my lower lip with growing anxiety at the thought, until a trickle of blood swelled my taste buds.

Lennon and I had made it to the end of the long prison passageway and were greeted with another door made of a burnt-colored steel. With my left hand buried into my back pocket, gripping the stun gun from the arsenal, I stuck out my right hand to push the door forward to a winding set of stairs. A coolness rushed past my face and through my hair as Lennon and I begun the ascent. One step in front of the other, I thought. The stairway seemed to become steeper the further we climbed.

I was expected to break into Iris's office. And now that I thought about it, why hadn't Wren approached the idea as more of a challenge? Did a lot of people have access to it?

Or was there an eye scanner, where there was no chance at all I could get in? Why didn't I ask these questions? I glanced at Lennon again, willing to distract myself with anything in order to avoid the clamor of my own thoughts. Surely, these were Lennon's thoughts now too.

After what felt like a lifetime of climbing, another door with a small window, labeled Level One, came into view. I hurried to crouch underneath the window as Lennon leaned over me to peer through.

"There are three officials, two guys and one girl," he whispered. "Two are guarding the door at the end of the hallway."

"And the third?" I hissed back.

"The other is around the hall. Oh, look, he left. Come on, Winslett, we can take them. You can stun them as soon as we barge in." He offered his hand to help me up.

I nodded and exhaled a shaky breath. He had his katar at the ready and I had my stunner. Lennon opened the door this time, but things didn't go as smoothly.

Alarms rang the moment we stepped into the room, its shrill reverberating against my eardrums. I scanned the hallway, in search of the alarm's source. A familiar gray power box sat on the wall out of the corner of my left eye. I turned my gaze back to the officials, and saw the girl official elbow the other man, jerking her head toward our direction.

"Lennon, turn the alarm off," I murmured.

"What?" he shouted over the noise.

"Find out how to turn the alarms off," I repeated, louder this time. "There's a gray power box to my left."

He swiveled his head around, searching for the power source.

"What about you?" he asked hurriedly.

"I'll stun them when they get closer. Just go!"

I saw him run toward the gray box and hastily slash its lock with the katar. The door and its hinge fell to the ground.

"Which wire?" he shouted.

I kept my eyes focused on the two officials running toward me. "Any wire!" I screamed over my shoulder.

Not a second later, the fluorescent lights flickered and shut off. Darkness surrounded everything, and I blinked my eyes to readjust them. The alarms still screeched in my ears.

"Not that one!" he yelled.

The lights flashed back on.

"Hurry up!"

"I am trying, Winslett!"

The girl official led the pair, sprinting toward me now. In response, I held out the stunner an arms length in front of my chest, squinted one eye, and pulled the trigger. She dodged effortlessly out of the way, and I waited for her to come closer before I aimed another stun dart. This time it hit the side of her neck. She fell to the floor instantly.

The second official gawked at his unconscious partner, and I aimed my stunner, closed one eye, and pressed the trigger. He fell too.

"Gotcha," Lennon yelled. I turned to look at him as he pulled a lime green plug harshly from its socket. The alarms died quickly.

"Nice," I muttered shakily.

Lennon came to join me, but paused, suddenly frozen. Before I could ask, he grabbed my shoulder and furiously pushed me down. My knees buckled beneath me, and I grabbed his upper arm for a supported fall.

Behind us, the glass of the door's window broke with an erupting *crack*, its shards falling onto the floor from what I could only assume to be a bullet. I scrambled out of Lennon's grip and stood up, looking for the bullet's source.

"Winslett, behind you!"

I whipped around to see another man running out of a room and toward us at an impossible speed. I had forgotten about the third guard. And he had a gun, not a stunner. By the time I mentally processed that I should stun the official, Lennon was already running toward him. They met in a horrid crash, and the official had somehow already knocked the katar out of Lennon's hand, and now had him in a chokehold. I was stuck between a rock and a hard place. If I shot my stunner, he would shoot the gun. I would die and Lennon would live. Lennon was losing air. The burly guard sneered at me. So many thoughts ran through my head. I knew he wasn't going to kill me if I was a valuable source of information. He also couldn't alert anyone else at the moment. He was alone. I wasn't.

"Just shoot!" Lennon said, wheezing.

"Stop moving, then!" I cried.

I looked at Lennon, whose face was turning both red and blue. He clawed at the official's forearm pressed against his esophagus. Struggling with his legs, Lennon kicked the official in the shin with the back of his heel. Underneath his right foot, the katar lay only a foot or so under him. But I knew he would never reach it.

"Hey!" I shouted wildly, pointing at Lennon's foot. "Don't do it!"

"Wha—" the guard started to say as he too, turned to look at the katar. Lennon's face read shock.

They had halted momentarily; this was my only opportunity. My hands shook this time as I pulled the trigger and the stun dart fired from its hold. It lodged itself into the neck of the official and he tumbled to the ground. Lennon quickly escaped his newly loosened hold and jumped to my side just in time to see the man land on his katar. It pierced through his side near his kidneys. I dropped the stunner on the floor.

I had killed someone.

"Look away," Lennon whispered in my ear.

I kept my eyes trained on the pool of blood seeping from underneath him. The official stared back at me haughtily, his mouth ajar. I imagined the man had a family, with a pretty wife and two lively children— a little boy and girl maybe. "I killed him, didn't I?"

"It wasn't your fault, Wins. It was going to be me if you hadn't."

"I know, but he didn't have to die. You can't justify that."

"Nothing is fair anymore. It never was. At least if we continue on we have a chance to help people."

I took a deep breath. There would be time to mourn later. "Okay."

"Let's keep up with the plan."

We had to take the uniforms, that's right.

I took hold of the uniform of the first woman I stunned, prying my eyes away from her sculpted face and curved chin. She was much taller than me, but it was the best available. Lennon obtained his uniform from the muscular guard that lay beside her. It was a bit awkward stripping the woman to her undershirt, but it had to be done. I also was a tad shy about stripping down to my own undershirt in front of Lennon, so I did it quickly while his head was turned.

When we were both finished he called me over and fixed the shirt that was still a little loose on me. On him, I saw that the dark jumpsuit fit like another skin. He looked effortlessly good, and it made me wonder if Lennon's life, without Extium, would've brought him here as a real guard. It was crazy thinking about how our lives could have, should have, and would have been if Distribution Day had never occurred. I looked down at Lennon's calloused hands, fumbling with the zippers across my uniform's chocking neckline. I shoved his hands away. My uniform would never fit me as well, and we were wasting time we didn't have.

We were no longer encompassed by steel. In fact, these walls were made of bright tiles. A lot of the place was a clear blinding white, a stark contrast to the all black we were both wearing. I still found the symbol on the jacket pocket a little unsettling. It was a plain eye with a red iris.

"Which way?" I whispered to Lennon.

"Left," I stated surely. It was the complete opposite direction of the man that lay bleeding to death.

Lennon nodded and we continued to walk until we reached the end of yet another door. I looked up at Lennon for his familiar nod of reassurance and he smiled. Resting his hand next to mine, palms both pressed against icy steel, we pushed the swinging door open with force.

We were welcomed with an organized chaos, contained in one hallway. Papers lay strewn across hundreds of desks. Phones rang in multiple places and government officials, guards, scientists, and advisors to Iris alike, teemed the area. I glanced along the walls of the white-tiled hallway and saw glass doors opening to more glass rooms. These rooms filled with even more life: laboratories, health offices, and storage, with government workers passing through all with an eye scanner. The back of my neck tingled as I waited for someone, anyone, to notice us. However, no one looked our way and no one peered over and saw the scene behind us. Safe from watchful eyes, due to the security of our uniforms, the two of us walked in an official, stiff-like manner. We disappeared into the life the government workers led, becoming more invisible with each step.

Fifty-One

Byrde

Daddy and Mommy always left a night light on. I wasn't used to the dark, especially not this kind: the kind that was everywhere, the kind that was so dark you couldn't even see your hand when you put it in front of your face.

Now I was alone in this tunnel. Winslett, Lennon, and Masen had left me here for safekeeping. If something bad happened to them I would never know and I'd be left here to die. I sat down against the cold steel walls I was stuck in. I couldn't see my knee anymore but when I felt it, the blood was sticky and dry in some places. The gash had been large, but the worst was over.

It felt like hours had gone by since they left me, although I knew that wasn't the case. I tried counting to pass the time. I got to two hundred thirteen before it became boring. Next, I started singing softly. It was so soft I knew no one could hear, but the singing didn't stop my voice from shaking.

I felt for the spear they left me to use as protection. I tightened it in my hand and stood up. I thought back to earlier in the night, or morning, whatever it was. I didn't have any idea what time it was… just that it was dark. Anyway, I pretended to spear people again. "Yahah!" I whispered. I jabbed away at the invisible people, killing them off one by one. Maybe the gang really should've taken me with them. I smiled. Surely I could've taken down a few guards that they couldn't have.

I kept swinging. I brought the stick above my head and twirled it some more, ready for one final deathblow. That was when things went wrong. The spear began spinning wildly out of control. I had to let go, and the stone spear part clattered against the steel wall with a boom.

I panicked. There was an echo in this hallway. I wouldn't have been surprised if everyone in Laiden had heard the noise. A sickening feeling was in my stomach. Someone would surely be coming for me now.

I quickly felt for the spear again and sunk down once more onto the cold floor. I wrapped my arms around my knees and rocked back and forth. I was given one job. Stay put, stay safe, and they'd be back for me. I couldn't even do that. No wonder why the big kids didn't want me to come along. I choked back tears, but what did it matter now? Someone would find me. Would they kill me? Would they make me rat out the others? I needed Mommy and I needed Daddy! They weren't coming though. No one was. My breathing became heavy.

I looked around, but that was silly of me. I was still in darkness. I realized the darkness was better, until the lights started to come.

I saw a tiny yellow beam in the distance, but it became bigger and bigger as the minutes passed by. The bright light scanned all over the tunnel, trying to follow me. I scooted away each time. At first, I was too quick. I ran away trying to find more darkness. But, suddenly the light was coming too fast and I was running away too slowly. I looked back and saw a small face glinting above the brightness of the light beam. Breathing quickly, I rammed myself into the side of the tunnel and shut my eyes tight.

It wasn't long before the lights had touched me completely, and I could see the person's face now. It was just one man. His features were clear under the glow, and he was only a few feet away from me. His big face was red, his eyebrows were dark, and his teeth were sharp. I closed my eyes to go back to the darkness. I had never known darkness could be so safe.

Suddenly, I had an idea. My spear. I realized I hadn't let go of it. I opened my eyes and jabbed it at the man running toward me, but he was too strong. He grabbed the top of the stick, right under the stone and he snapped it. He snapped my weapon in half.

"You foolish, foolish girl," he jeered. "You believed this could save you?" He gestured to my mangled weapon. "Answer me, darling."

I recognized his government uniform. Uh, oh.

I answered with a kick to the part Mommy once told me really hurt guys.

He grunted and I ran away. Again, I was not quick enough and he grabbed me by my hair. I shrieked. He yanked me in closer and I kept screaming as tears began to leak out of my eyes.

"Darling," he cooed as he stroked my face. "There is no one here to hear you."

He must have sensed my next move, which was to scratch his face until it bled, but he quickly grabbed my wrists and twisted them until they burned. I collapsed onto my injured knee.

"I have some important people to introduce you to," the man told me casually as he untied a piece of cloth wrapped around his waist. People? Why did anyone need or want to see me? The evil man spun me around roughly and wrapped the piece of cloth tightly against my eyes.

"Ow, you're hurting me!" I yelped.

"It's for when we get out," he explained. "Can't have you seeing around anywhere, can we now?"

Then, I felt my wrists being tied together by a similar cloth. Before I could protest at the man again, he hoisted me onto his shoulders. Now, the only part of my body I could control was my mouth. I put it to good use, and I began to scream.

I couldn't see his face, but I heard the evil man sigh.

"Haven't we been over this?" he asked. "No one can hear you and as soon as we get out of the tunnel, no one will care. However, if you continue to scream, I'm sure someone will politely ask me to stun you so you shut up. And you know what? I'll be more than happy to oblige."

I stopped then because I knew that was probably true, and I needed to be alert for whatever was to come.

"Isn't that better now, darling?"

"My name is Byrde, not darling," I grumbled and he chuckled.

"Whatever you say, darling. You know what the funniest thing about all this is? You led me here yourself."

I snapped. "What do you mean? No I didn't."

"So it wasn't your blood all over the floor?"

I thought about my knee and it's dripping blood. Oh, no.

"Now, of course, we would've found you anyway, but you sure did make it a bit quicker."

I thought of the others. Where were they? Did they make it? Did this man know they were with me? I had to keep my mouth shut... I prayed to Daddy that he thought I was here alone.

He started talking again. "Now it will only be a matter of time before your little friends are found too. Then we can all have a nice reunion."

"What friends? I'm here alone."

He laughed at me. "I'm not stupid, child."

We eventually reached a stop, and I stayed silent. The official would talk to me from time to time, but I had nothing to say to him. I hadn't given up. I was just waiting for whatever was coming my way, and hopefully it was coming soon. This was starting to seem longer than the time I had spent in the tunnel—but I'm glad it felt long. More time meant a better chance for the others to get out, hopefully.

I felt a jolt, and recognized the feeling of moving in an elevator. We were in the elevator for more than ten minutes before I heard another two doors click open. Then the man stopped again. Suddenly, I was coming down from his shoulders.

"Darling, I want you to see this," he told me.

He untied the blindfold, but kept my hands bound.

I opened my eyes and I was not impressed. It was a pretty bland and narrow hallway. I recognized where we were. Mommy had taken me here hundreds of times on her way to work. The man entered a room through a sliding door, scanning his eye on the way in.

A voice spoke. "Welcome, Felix. Proceed with business and have a lovely day."

Felix? What kind of name was Felix?

We then walked in and I quickly shut my eyes from being blinded by white. I hated this room.

"Open your eyes," Felix commanded.

I hesitated, but blinked my eyes open, too curious to know any better. White tiles lined the floor and the walls were covered with white cases, cases of pills. White tables filled the room. We were in Mommy's laboratory. Two people with white lab coats were in the back of the long room facing away from us, discussing things in indoor voices.

Felix shoved me forward and I fell. The sound echoed. I stayed down behind the table and looked up to Felix. He laughed.

"Who's there?" called a voice that everyone in Laiden would know. Prime Minister Iris.

"Ah, Felix!" he called again. I heard his heavy footsteps and another lighter pair. They crept closer. "It's rather early to see you around these parts, is it not?"

"Well, I had some fairly important business to take care of. Come closer and see for yourself."

I stayed curled up. I didn't want to see Iris.

Then chimed a voice that made my heart jump.

“Felix, we are going to have to ask you to go. The Prime Minister and I have some important business of our own to take care of,” the voice said.

“Of course,” Felix responded coolly.

Iris and the other person came closer. I turned to face them. I was met with a full-toothed grin from Iris, and the bright familiar eyes of my mother.

Fifty-Two

Masen

I really took in the state of the jail. It was old and run-down, not nearly as hi-tech as the other parts of Laiden. The dark steel walls and floors were smeared with dirt and dried blood. Puddles of water formed in different places of the large, dark room from leaks in the ceiling. And the holding cells, the bars that kept Wren captive, were rusted and worn. To top it off, the stench of the room was almost as unbearable as the sight of Wren.

His bruised face, hollowed cheeks, and sunken eyes were grotesque enough to give me the *hibijibies.* Granted, I probably wouldn't have been picture perfect either if I had been starved or beaten for a week.

A cold shiver went down my spine. This place was as un-Laidenesque as I could imagine.

I yawned, leaned my back against the bars of Wren's cell, and slumped down next to him. Wren may have been slightly crazed when we all first saw him, but he was steadily regaining his senses, not that that was a good thing.

The other Wren in the woods was at least a bit more exciting. The Wren in the holding cell was just as boring as my father. He kept going on and on about the different facilities located on what floor and blah, blah, blah, yeah I stopped listening too.

I felt some remorse though; I knew it had been a while since he had anyone to talk to. Still, why'd it have to be me that stayed behind?

"Wren?" I interrupted.

He halted his train of thought on the modern day uses of simulations and cleared his throat, waiting for me to speak.

"What's up with this place? Why is it so dingy?"

He seemed bemused by this. "It's a jail, Masen."

"Yeah I know, but still, it looks so… I don't know... ancient? Before technology."

"And perhaps it was, or perhaps it's for the fact they want criminals to feel so distant from society, from civilization."

"Not a bad theory."

"Trust me, it worked." I swore he gave a slight shudder. Whatever Wren went through down here must have been really bad. After all, out of the five of us, Wren was surely able to withstand the most.

There was a silence that I felt the need to fill.

"He'll forgive you, you know," I said, referring to Lennon.

"I made a mistake." He grunted after some more silence.

"Everyone makes some mistakes," I said in my awkward way of comforting.

This conversation was getting uncomfortably deep.

"I know."

I murmured the next part under my breath. "Some bigger than others..."

"I shouldn't have though. I'm a scientist and I thrive off the truth. I wanted that bit of truth from Byrde too much," he grumbled.

"Well, we have it now. Byrde is no traitor, and you've paid for your mistake enough already," I told him. The last part was meant to show him I knew whatever he went through was not easy. I wanted to let him know even though I had never been too fond of him, I cared enough that I didn't exactly want him to suffer.

He nodded his head solemnly, and let out a sigh.

I turned to face Wren. "Let's be clear that I'm not forgiving you about creating Extium. I might be able to understand why you lied, but don't think it was any less of a deceiving move."

He turned his head slowly to look at me, grimacing at the pain, but all I saw were his eyes, widening. He wasn't staring at me.

"Masen, behind you!"

I turned around just in time, and by just in time I mean not in time at all to stop my attacker. I felt a pair of hands grab my waist and strap a black band around it. My head went numb at the thought of the electric belt.

"Get off!" I screamed, trying to wretch the pair of hands away.

I lunged toward the official, ready to tackle the person to the ground. Grabbing for the official's shoulders, I was met with a flood of electrical shocks. I gasped, whipped my hands off the shoulders, and glared at the official.

This one was a woman and she sneered at me. "In a bind there, boy?"

She stepped closer, and I could see her features now. She couldn't have been that much older than me. Nineteen maybe? Twenty? Her cheekbones were high and her dark blonde hair was tied back in a tight long braid. Her skin was rosy and her eyes were clear blue. She didn't look like the typical official. Even the uniform of a guard, if that's what she was, was different. It was hinting more toward burgundy than black and the collar split into a defiant "V." The ensemble was slimmer fitting to her figure as well, rather than the typical jumpsuit. There was something about her that was downright intimidating.

She grabbed my arm and pulled me close to her face. Her eyes glowed in a way that the other officials' didn't. As strange as it sounded, she looked like she had life in her, some sort of goodness deep inside her that I couldn't grasp.

She yanked my arm up and pressed some sort of control that could only be meant for the belt. An impressive shock ran through my body and seared through my veins, targeting every bone and muscle in me. I gasped at the pain, but bit down a scream.

I took back what I thought was goodness in her.

She smirked, not totally impressed with my lack of emotion, but it was clear she had originally pegged me as weakling. Grabbing my arm, she twisted it and jerked it wildly around. I worked so hard to keep my legs stiff, but I couldn't afford any more shocks. The pain was intolerable now. I wanted so badly to buckle my knees, to lie down on the floor, to stop trying.

"You're stronger than I thought you'd be," the dark blonde haired girl snickered.

It sickened me that she could get enjoyment out of this pointless torture.

I grunted in response.

"Didn't your Mommy ever teach you to answer people when they talk to you?" she asked, kicking me sharply in the gut.

That was it.

I threw my body full force at her and screamed, "My mom is dead because of you and everyone else in this stupid place!"

She met me with a rapid fire of shocks right in the stomach.

My body broke down in pain and the screams finally came out of my mouth. My vision blurred in and out, my ears ringing loudly.

I swore she was laughing.

We had fallen to the ground, but my strength left me. The shocks were still defiant, but my screams were now agonizing moans.

She threw my body off of her. Which of course set off another round of jolts. I sank against Wren's cell bars. My vision was black by then and I begged for all that was good in Laiden to let me go unconscious. The official had the mercy then to come sit me up and switch the belt to off, I think. My body twitched unnervingly at even the slightest movement, and I could taste the distinct saltiness of tears. The pain had become so much I had actually cried. Thank god no one important was here to see it.

"I think he'll be out for a while," a girl somewhere spoke.

"Don't punish him for what I deserve," another voice echoed a distance away. Was that Wren talking?

My vision blurred to see the bars of the cell, and I squinted through my watery eyes to see Wren. He was glaring at me, as if to say "get your lazy butt off the ground and find us a way out of here."

I thought out a reply. I can't, Wren. I think I'll just die here, in this disgusting sewage water. I shifted with extreme effort to lay completely on my back, only to be in more discomfort. A sharp object was prodding the small of my back. I groaned and attempted to shift my position again.

I saw the girl look over at me and roll her eyes. I returned her nasty look with a glare of my own. If only I had my stunner, she could be the one lying on the floor. My stunner!

It must have slipped from my back pocket, and under my back when I fell. I was lying on top of the stun gun. This could be our way out. The girl hadn't even thought to see if I had been armed. I willed myself to move, but found my arm couldn't move.

With a click of a communication gadget, the girl turned her back from Wren and me, and held the device up to her lips.

"It all checks out fine here. Send them along when the rest are collected."

I didn't have the energy to decipher what she had been referring to. Instead, I blinked over to where Wren knelt, clutching the bars of the cell.

"Wren," I whispered. The girl hadn't heard me.

"Wren!" I hissed his name again.

He glanced down at me, refusing to take his focus off the girl. Slowly rolling my eyes toward the back pocket of my pants, I looked back up at him and mouthed "stunner."

I had Wren's attention now. He widened his eyes and quickly glanced between my back pocket and the girl official almost a dozen times. Nodding, he reached his arm out of the cell and grasped for the sleeve of my shirt. The cloth bundled beneath his fingers, and I was surprised at the strength of his grip.

He dragged me closer to the bars of his cell, staring at the girl the entire time. Her back was still turned, hunched over her communication gadget. Wren felt around for the handle of the stun gun, around my back pocket, and I mentally cringed. I felt violated, funny enough, even though I couldn't feel my legs, chest, and arms. Patting the area around my lower back, he finally gripped the metal and whipped it from beneath me, just as the girl turned around.

"What are you—" she started.

She was interrupted by the shot of the stunner, now pinned to her chest. I heard a thump to the floor.

The girl would be truly unconscious for a while, not drifting in and out of consciousness like me. We were safe, at least for now.

Wren roughly shook me.

"Masen, you're not in a full state of comatose. I need to get out of this cell, and you need to get her keys."

He motioned toward the ring around her belt loop.

I gurgled something like "herply derp."

"Come on, it's life and death here. Choose life. Get up."

I knew he was right. It was just so much easier to be swallowed up. I flipped myself over and army-crawled to her limp body.

"That's it!" encouraged Wren. "You can do it."

I blinked my eyes opened a few seconds at a time. It was all still too painful. Her keys were in her jumpsuit breast pocket, which I had checked first. I blindly crawled back to the cell and slipped Wren the keys before sinking back to the dirt floor. I heard Wren clamor to his feet, and swing the jail cell open, along with moving my body. He didn't approach me though; he took the girl by her ankles and dragged her into the cell that was his prison only moments ago. He inserted the keys back in and locked it, confining her.

I tried to say "nice job Wren" but it may have come out as more murmured gibberish.

Wren approached me for real this time and hovered over me. I could feel his presence, if not see his face. Then a searing pain came back. Wren had slapped me across the face.

"Ouch!" I bellowed.

"Good, feeling is starting to return."

"What? How could any good come from slapping me! Did you not see what she did to me?"

"Ah, and verbal speech is coming back too I see."

"How is your sight and hearing?"

"Still foggy."

"How many fingers am I holding up?"

I only saw blotchy blackness. "I can't see anything."

"Hmmm, well let's stand you up."

Wren hoisted me up onto my legs, but they felt like mush. I sunk right back to the floor. My legs couldn't support my body.

"It's worse than I thought," Wren mumbled to himself.

I still knew only pain and wondered if my body would ever function again.

"I choose death, Wren," I muttered with an irritated sigh.

"Don't be ridiculous," he muttered.

A recognizable crackle of a communication gadget came from the girl behind the bars.

"Arrivals will be there shortly," a new voice sounded from a distance away.

"What does that mean?" I mumbled.

"I don't know; but this time, we must be ready for whatever it is."

"How can we be ready if my body isn't even working?"

Wren became serious. "You'll have to get it to."

He wasn't joking around, and I so badly wanted to stand on my own if my limbs would allow it.

Wren hoisted me up, gripping underneath my arms, and told me to hold onto the cell's bars. We quickly found out that my arms clearly lacked the strength as well. After a good five minutes of pure struggle, we decided to stand me up against the wall to the left of the cell. I slumped back to the cold, damp ground.

"I'll keep hold of the stunner for now," Wren said, awkwardly trying to hold me up again.

Wren took the odd spasm of my head as a nod. The two of us were alone with one round of stun bullets left. I was unable to move and Wren had been starving for a week. It was a joke to even act like we stood a chance against any potential arrivals. I was just hoping the others were faring better than us.

Fifty-Three

Lennon

We were two specks of ink, traveling in disguise along the white halls of Iris's territory. Completely lost. The layout of the government building was as intricate as it was confusing. Wren was right. Everything was white and it was impossible to keep track of each floor, because the farther you walked, the more everything seemed to blend together. It was an endless maze.

Winslett glanced down at her watch. 17:04. An hour and a half had already flown by. Yikes.

"We're running out of time. We should've been back to Masen and Wren by now. I'll try looking along that hallway," she whispered, beckoning to her far left. "And you check one more time in these two rooms."

"I don't think it's a good idea if we split up," I replied, shaking my head.

I looked up to see that she had already walked to the far end of the corridor.

She peered over her shoulder and stared as I wildly motioned for her to come back.

"What a baby," she joked and briskly turned to enter the hallway.

I hid a smile and ran to the nearest door. The small glass window lay inches below my chin, and I uncomfortably positioned myself to peer through it. My eyes glanced from lab coat to lab coat as they simply walked back and forth, holding test tubes. Most of them sat at lab tables and studied some small subject. I leaned in closer to the window to see what was so interesting.

"Hey! What are you doing?" a voice boomed from behind me.

I immediately stood up, whipped my head around and was greeted with a cold stare from a monstrous official looming nearly a foot over me.

"I—I— uhhh, was just umm." My voice shook inside my throat.

"Spit it out."

I answered quickly, "I'm a bit lost, and I need to head up to Prime Minister Iris's office right away. So if you could just point me in the right direction, nobody gets in trouble."

He squinted at me. "What do you need to do in Iris's office?"

"Minister's orders. Strictly confidential," I answered, my eyes flickering around the hallway, attempting to avoid his gaze, and met with Winslett's instead.

I saw her glance at the official and immediately shrink back into the hallway she had come from.

"What's that supposed to mean? I may be new here, but whatever your little errand for Iris is, you can answer to me," he challenged back fiercely, suddenly raising his voice.

"Whoa, slow down there. It's nothing personal, just some stupid errand I was forced to run, probably not worth your time, umm, official… sir."

"Level twenty-six, three doors down," he grunted, still glowering at me.

After an awkward couple of minutes of stare-downs, the official mumbled something inaudible and turned the direction he came and began walking away. I watched until he disappeared out of sight.

"Over here!" I called to Winslett in a hushed tone.

She peered over to where I had been standing and sauntered over, hiking up her sagging trousers.

"What was that all about?" she asked nervously.

"Luckily, nothing, for now. But I don't want to be caught like that again. I thought I was done for." I wiped my sweat filled brow that had formed while being interrogated. "He seemed suspicious, but eventually gave into giving me the directions to Iris's office."

I moved at a swift speed toward the end of the corridor, trying to find an exit in this godforsaken place.

"So where did he tell you to go?" Winslett asked, falling into my pace.

"Twenty-sixth floor, three doors down," I said in reply. "We need to move."

She nodded curtly, pulling my arm around the corner. "I think I saw the elevators at the end of the hallway."

Our brisk walk came to a halt as we stared at the empty space that should have continued the hallway in front of us. The space was a form of a clear cylinder that protruded stretched out tubes, going in every which direction.

"I swear I just saw it five minutes ago. Where did it go?" Winslett panicked.

"Please step forward and take caution of the sliding door," answered a cool female voice.

Winslett raised her eyebrows at me and I answered with a shrug of the shoulders. I looked down at the floor and stepped forward, not knowing what to expect.

Whoosh. A clear contraption rose from out of the ground and through the clear tubes to a level right in front of us. Its cylinder-shaped doors slid open, welcoming us to walk through them.

"You don't know how to work one of these things by any chance, do you?" I leaned over to ask Winslett.

"Nope." She continued to gape at the elevator in awe.

"Five… Four… Three…" came the cool female voice.

"Hurry!" I panicked, grabbing Winslett's hand and running into the elevator.

The clear door slid right behind her. The entire elevator resembled a human-sized soup can, and couldn't have fit any more than four people. There were no complicated buttons, but instead, two handlebars dangled from the roof of the elevator.

I looked up at them when the voice started, "Please state your desired destination."

"Ummm, level twenty-six, I guess," Winslett replied.

The number twenty-six appeared, blinking in red over the sliding door. The entire elevator then began to shake.

"Whoa!" Winslett yelped, and I nodded in agreement. We shot up a quick three or so floors, and were then rocketed to the left.

I heard Winslett smack against the glass and I followed her lead.

"Uhhh," Winslett groaned, pressing her hand to her temple. "That was my head."

"Here, hold onto this!" I yelled, trying to steady myself, and yanked down on the handlebar hanging from the ceiling closest to Winslett.

She grabbed it and we continued to jerk back and forth, left and right.

"When is this going to stop?" she moaned.

I turned to see her face drain into an impressive shade of white. I moved toward her and wrapped my one arm around her shoulder, my other arm still gripping the metal handlebar, as we zoomed forward. The government building was filled with moving people, endless amounts of white rooms and more white hallways. Each floor we passed was a blur and with each lurch that threw us against the walls, my stomach tightened.

The elevator finally glided to a halt and its doors slid open once more. Glad to be rid of the contraption, we scrambled out, and the elevator flew back down.

"Okay, now remember to stay calm," I said slowly, trying to keep my voice from shaking.

We swiftly passed door one.

"You're telling me?" she said, raising her eyebrow.

"Har-har."

We swiftly passed door two.

"Come on!" she exclaimed, breaking out into a run for the third door.

We reached the door and stood in front of it. A thin green beam of light pierced its way through the door and scanned the eye on each of our uniforms.

"Access approved," stated the cool, female voice.

"Ughhh, it's her again." Winslett chuckled, rolling her eyes. I noticed how her fists clenched and her posture stiffened. Her attempt to lighten the mood failed, because I knew we were both trembling on the inside. But there was no time to contemplate about turning back now. The door opened and we slipped in.

Iris's office was dark and cold, and a chill ran through my body. All of a sudden, an incredible jolt shook my insides, as if I had just landed after falling fifty feet in the air. I was brought back to the real world by a clatter on the floor and a groan from Winslett.

"Winslett! Are you ok?" I exclaimed in a hushed tone. "Where are you?"

"I'm fine, I'm fine. Stop worrying," she answered in almost a whisper, "Did you feel that too?"

"Yeah, I have no idea what that was though," I said, shaking my head.

"Here, help me up," Winslett said softly.

I reached for her arm and the lights flickered on. I glanced up and my eyes widened. Iris's office was unbelievable. I helped Winslett off the ground and we began to walk around the room in a state of awe. The office was surprisingly simple, white like the rest, but the star of the room laid in the center: a huge panel of screens surrounding one computer that created a huge hologram hovering in mid air. The hologram flickered as it gave a revolving view of Laiden. I hovered my fingers over the computer's keys, almost afraid to invade such perfection. Instead, I sat in Iris's office chair, overlooking the countless number of monitors, able to do millions of tasks at a simple command. Out of the corner of my eye, Winslett messed with a screen to my far left that controlled the hologram.

"Come on," I called over. "We need to hurry."

She looked over and left the screen reluctantly. "You're right."

I ran my fingers across the keyboard and was welcomed with an incredible number of separate computer folders.

"What are all of these files?" I pressed, furrowing my brows together, scrolling through the endless pages of Iris's records.

"Wait, look over here." Winslett pointed to "Recent Files" on the computer's touch screen and the hologram in front of us changed again. The Resistance… Wren Casterra… Reina Faleman… Here! Lennon, look at this!"

I squinted at the hologram and made out the file Winslett had pointed at. "Orb: Status: Unknown." My eyes widened as I double-clicked on the file on the computer screen and an immediate replica of the orb spun in a three-sixty view.

"That's it!" I exclaimed.

The excitement loosened the tension in my palms and I smiled. Finally, we had done something right. We were on the brink of discovering something useful. I stared intently at the hologram, pouring out hundreds of documents and archives. Scrolling up and down the display, I clicked on a file that interested me, a list of possible locations where other orbs would be. The document opened and words and pictures poured out onto the screen. I gaped at them, trying to make a sense of what they meant, but my vision was suddenly failing me. The words blurred back and forth, right and left, as if they had taken the same elevator ride Winslett and I had been shaken up on. I leaned forward as the black letters flickered on the hologram spilled out, literally spilled out onto the floor and underneath my feet. My mouth lay ajar, in shock, as I turned to Winslett. The ink from the words spread across my feet, against my legs, and on my hands from the computer screen. She gave me a petrified look as a horrible jolt shook my insides once again. The spilled ink ran like fear, through our body and into our veins.

Fifty-Four

Winslett

I opened my eyes to an alarmingly familiar sound. My body, huddled in a ball, refused to move in fear of finding out where I was. I ignored the hesitation and lifted my head out of my arms. In turn, I slowly eyed the entire room, still not getting up. I recognized the dull room I was in now. It was my bedroom from back in Laiden. The walls were an untouched gray and the floors remained unchanged, the same dark hardwood boards. A single light swung silently above my head. I looked ahead and then glanced at the frail desk where I used to complete my schoolwork. The feeble table leaned for support against the wall next to the meek, gangly closet where my so few clothes hung in. I took another quick spin around the room and my eyes met with the only thing that was different before I had left: a music box. I felt a twinge of resentment. Sounds of a lullaby tinkered its way out of the small, intricate box, lying on top of my wooden bureau. It was a delicate, glass instrument, with a small songbird etched on the lid. I knew well of the cage and the bird held captive in it. It belonged to me, or at least it had belonged to me.

I strode over to the glass box, still in disbelief. This shouldn't have been here, and not just in Laiden, but in this bedroom altogether. The memory was as clear as the box I held in my hands, and recalling it was like stepping into a pool of ice. The last time I had laid eyes on it was when I had smashed it onto the floor the day my parents had been taken by the officials. It was a device that didn't belong in Laiden. In fact, it was banned. It was classified as a frivolous trinket, but my mother and father had given it to me anyway. They had given a twelve-year-old girl some illegal piece of junk. Running my fingers through the carved lines, I stared at its beauty with distaste. It didn't deserve to be here. I didn't deserve to be here. I screamed words in my head as I felt the lullaby screeching in my ears now. I hated this stupid music box. I hated the stupid bird. I hated my stupid parents for leaving us, keeping us trapped in this stupid society. In an impulse of sudden rage, I lunged forward and threw the beautiful, glass box with all the strength I could muster into the wall next to my bed. The screeching lullaby stopped and silence hung in the air.

I straightened myself, taking in deep breaths as I watched the songbird shatter into millions of jagged pieces. At least it was free now. The glass crunched underneath my feet as I walked closer to where I had thrown the music box, but halted immediately when the impossible had happened.

"Winslett?" an all too familiar voice whispered in my ear. "Are you all right?"

It couldn't be. I whipped my head around immediately and was met with big, frosty gray eyes, the spitting image of mine. "Evelyn?"

She gazed at me and cocked her head slightly to the side in response.

"You're b-back!" I stuttered, my knees immediately collapsing to the floor, embracing my arms around her.

"Back from where, Wins?" Evelyn sang in a clear, innocent voice, although it rang of slight confusion.

I searched her face to see if she was pulling one of her tricks, but was only greeted with a wide, toothy grin.

I smoothed over the back of Evelyn's hair and met her eyes.

"It doesn't matter now. We're safe. There's nothing to worry about," I told her.

"I know," she replied with as much sureness.

A knock made me swivel around again.

"Culver!" I gasped. He leaned against the door, his arms crossed, staring at Evelyn and me.

"Hey, kiddo," he grinned. "Am I interrupting something here?"

"Nope," Evelyn piped up.

"Good, because you don't want to skip out on breakfast right?" he teased, rolling his eyes. "Don't wanna miss out on that delicious bowl of hot goop."

Evelyn giggled and I chimed in, knowing fully well that Laiden's idea of food was as drab and tasteless as the gray paint on my walls. I looked from Evelyn to Culver, Culver to Evelyn. My eyes watered at the joy of being reunited, even if they didn't know it. I had missed them. I had missed this, when it was just the three of us. It was a struggle to be away from them both, separating our impenetrable bond. I realized my arms were still wrapped around Evelyn, and I squeezed her close. This time, I was determined to not let go.

I looked at her face again and her beautiful gray eyes began to swell black, as if someone had poured ink into them.

"W-what's happening, Culver?" I stuttered, in shock.

I looked up at Culver and saw as the ink began to take control of his eyes as well.

"No! Make it stop!" I shrieked, but knew no one could hear me. Because what I had feared was coming true, Extium was sinking into Culver and Evelyn, just as it had before.

A faint, panicked voice whispered in my ear. "It's not real, Winslett. It's not real."

"It is!" I screamed back at the voice, keeping my arms wrapped around Evelyn.

Her eyes were now completely black, not an inch of misty gray left. My mind shouted at me to run, to get out of here, but my body remained paralyzed, still searching Evelyn's face for the angel I knew her to be.

"You have to let her go," the voice urged once more.

I recognized the voice now, but I struggled to find the name.

"Winslett," the voice began again, calmly this time. "Listen to my voice."

I was pounded with such sudden realization, as if buckets of water splashed onto my face. This world I was in was fake. I needed to focus on the present and separate my fantasy from reality, not the mirage that took the forms of my siblings. Our mission. We couldn't give up on it.

"Lennon?" I sputtered, stunned.

"Listen to my voice. Come back to me. This isn't real. The orb is real. Masen, Wren, Byrde, and I are real. They're waiting for us."

I nodded. It was time to go. I stood up.

"Don't move, #454027," a voice of a robotic child echoed out of Evelyn, pulling at my arm.

I tore myself away from Evelyn. "I have to leave."

Hesitation tugged at me too. It took everything from me to not scoop her back up and tell her everything would be all right.

I faced Culver at the door and he glared at me.

"No, #454027," he barked.

"Culver," I pleaded.

"No, you're not leaving," demanded Culver, raising his voice.

"Yes, she is. We both are."

I felt a familiar squeeze at my shoulder and looked behind me to see Lennon glaring at my brother.

I was so blinded by my desires that I couldn't see two feet in front of me, if it hadn't been for the person that brought me back to earth and grounded me. The black ink of Culver and Evelyn's eyes began to swell my entire room, and their figures turned to dust. The only thing that held me back from screaming was the sliver of hope that my real brother and sister were out in Laiden somewhere, and that I would be back for them. I hid my face in the crook of Lennon's shoulder, tears rolling silently down my face. Another horrible jolt took over me, tying my stomach into a knot as I collided with the ground.

Fifty-Five

Wren

It quickly became apparent to both Masen and I that the supposed arrivals wouldn't be coming anytime soon. Even leaning against the slanted wall caused pain for Masen. I dropped my guard and helped him sink to the ground.

A soft sigh escaped his mouth.

I felt a bit guilty. Even though Masen was there to guard me, as the adult, I felt it somehow my obligation to protect him. I was powerless behind bars, but surely I could've warned him a few seconds earlier. The seconds would've made the difference. I knew what an electric belt felt like. However, I knew it could have been worse. These things have left stronger men dead.

The thing that prevented me from shouting my warning was because of whom I saw. The clear blue eyes lighter than the sky had stared at me. Those eyes were a contrast to her lethal personality. Those eyes were the ones I had become so familiar with, but now, were the ones I was so distant from. I had never thought I'd see those eyes again. And while she was performing a mild form of torture, her eyes had never looked my way. They stared at Masen, her victim.

Maybe it was my hallowed look? My brown hair fell a little lower over my eye line than it ever did before, and scruff was building on my face. I wasn't the smooth-faced man she had known. Yes, I knew this girl who attacked Masen. And I couldn't even look. I turned away in shame. Was Laiden and Iris sucking out the good that I knew was buried inside of her?

I turned my attention back to the boy and away to the unconscious young woman I had thrown in my prison cell.

"Ugh, I hate this," Masen mumbled.

"You can endure it," I told him.

Masen glanced over to the girl. "Why is her uniform so different from the other officials?"

It was deceiving for one who did not know the specific attire for government workers. Black jumpsuits were worn by anyone who was an official or guard of some sort and lab coats were worn by the scientists. However, her slender burgundy fitting jumpsuit suggested she had risen in rank since I had last seen her. It was a uniform given only to the highest-ranking officials. The uniforms suggested a sense of unspoken hierarchy. For instance, my white lab coat collar was lined with a black trim, indicating my higher status.

"It means she's the head or co-head official," I answered.

"Oh, but she's so young."

"She's a year younger than me."

"You knew her?" Masen asked with a twinge of anger.

I wanted to brush away his accusation. The truth was, I knew the girl very well. Or, I thought I had. "I knew just about everyone in the government, or at least the people higher up in rank. Like I said, she's one of them."

"How'd she get such a position? I mean I get you were a brilliant genius and whatnot so you had a high rank, but what makes her so special?"

What made her so special? The way she had her own independence, her strength, her integrity. Her ruthlessness.

My real answer was much flatter. "I guess Iris thought she had what it took to be a strong leader."

"If his idea of a strong leader is someone not afraid to kill innocent people, then I never want to be one."

Somehow this made me angry. Sure, maybe no one in the government would have qualms over killing someone, but she was no killer.

"She's skillful, quick, and cunning," I added.

"So you knew her well, then?"

"I know that all heads of the government have to be that way."

"Who is she?" he persisted.

Our conversation abruptly stopped when we heard a groan from inside the cell. The girl flipped over and pieces of her dark blonde hair slipped out of her braid. I so badly wanted to lie next to her and brush the loose strands from her face.

"Looks like the stun is wearing off," Masen said.

"I wouldn't be surprised if she's almost fully conscious," I replied. "In fact, she can probably hear us," I replied.

"You locked it, right?"

"Of course I locked it, Masen. If I hadn't, it would have defeated the purpose of putting her in the cell to begin with."

I could tell Masen was tense. He was afraid of her.

Her hand grappled around the floor. Maybe she thought she still had her communication device. I twirled the gadget in my hand. She then swept the piece of hair dangling in front of her face away.

She sat herself up. Her eyes were open, this time connecting with mine. "Clever, Wren, trapping me here."

Masen cocked his eyebrow and shot me a serious look.

"You attacked us," I stated plainly.

"No, I attacked him," she said gesturing to Masen who was masking his pain. It was clear he wanted to act as if she hadn't hurt him.

"Can't move still? Shame, legs are darn useful," she said with an air of arrogance.

"Don't," I hushed.

"Don't what, Wren? You know what it's like here. I'm doing my job. Not all of us can just drop everything and leave it all behind."

She was targeting the words at me. Her life was here at the government like mine had been. And yes, maybe it was less complicated for me to just go, but I wasn't going to pretend I didn't have to make sacrifices.

Right on cue, Masen cleared his throat. "Knew you knew her! You're not gonna introduce me to the girl that nearly shocked me to death?"

I feared that my face turned scarlet. She smirked, but not at me, at Masen. This was the kind of behavior she liked.

"I'm Masen, by the way. Thanks for this," Masen joked in reference to his still limp body.

"You mean Wren hasn't told you?" she gawked mockingly.

"You know, I tried, but he was very evasive. Classic, Wren, of course."

"Yeah, doesn't surprise me much," she responded. Their smooth conversation didn't set right with me. They talked as if they had known each other for years rather than minutes, and as if she hadn't electrically shocked him. No one minded poking fun at me.

They both were waiting for me to speak. She clearly wasn't going to introduce herself. I bit my tongue, not wanting to talk. If I said her name, I would be the one to admit that I was wrong for leaving into the forest while she had stayed behind in the government. I hadn't planned on ever seeing her again, the girl I had once loved.

I closed my eyes and released my tongue. "This is Carra."

"That wasn't so hard now, was it?" she mocked.

"Nice to meet you, Carra, or well, be introduced. I think we had a pretty intense meeting," Masen said with a wink.

My face grew dark. Moments ago, Masen was livid about his electrocution. I wanted him to show defiance. I wanted him to hate Carra. Not joke with her, not *befriend* her. Carra and the whole government needed to be held accountable for every terrible thing they had done. That didn't exclude me, but at least I was trying to change things.

"That we did." Carra smiled. "You seem annoyed, Wren."

"You seem different, that's all," I said simply.

"My hair got longer." She smiled again. But this time the smile was softer, the one I knew outside of work hours.

Carra was different from anyone else who worked in the government. That was what had drawn me to her. It was early this past spring. She had been an intern; I hadn't known the government did that sort of thing. At the time, she was trying her luck at each part of the government facilities. I met her on her laboratory rotation.

Spring was in the air, and I was resolving some of the explosive kinks in the pill. I was holding a tray of test tubes and turned around only to be inches away from a girl's face. She was holding out the pen I usually kept behind my ear. I nearly dropped the test tubes.

"You dropped this," she said bashfully. I hadn't known then that she was anything but shy.

"Thanks," I said as she tucked the pen behind my ear. How did she know?

"I'm Carra."

"Wren."

"Yes, I know. I've heard a lot about you."

"Oh? I only just got promoted last month."

"My father speaks very fondly about you."

I was surprised. "That's nice of him."

"I have to go, but I hope to see you around, Wren."

She was still inches from my face. It was then that I noticed the sprinkling of freckles across her nose. One would only notice if you were this close to her. It was cute.

She turned and left. I watched her as she went.

"Not just the hair, Carra," I said sadly. She stayed quiet. I so wished our reunion was in a different setting. Not me in a decomposing state, not her behind bars, and not Masen awkwardly listening to our every word.

I felt uncomfortable. "Err—well you look good."

"You too," she mumbled.

Masen cut in. "You think so? I don't know, to me he still looks a bit too thin. You know, because Iris starved him and all."

Carra's pale skin grew darker in anger.

"Whatever," she grumbled, brushing the insult off.

"Really? That's all you're going to say?" Masen asked harshly. "It's obvious to anyone with ears you two have some sort of past."

"I didn't know he was down here!" she shot back.

That surprised me somehow.

"Even if you did, you wouldn't have done anything," stated Masen.

"What would you suggest I do? Not everyone can just go around defying the government, defying Iris."

"Why not? Wren did. Wren was close to Iris."

"I'm not Wren. I made different choices than he did. I pledged a duty to Laiden, and I take my job seriously," she said with a tone of finality.

"Whatever. If that's what helps you sleep at night then by all means have that be your story," Masen scoffed.

"That's enough, Masen," I told him. "Carra is doing her job. I've made it clear how I feel about the practices. But three months ago? I can't say for certain I wouldn't have done the exact same thing she did. It's what you learn here."

I was staring at Masen, but I imagined Carra smirking. This was more like the Wren I'm sure she knew.

I stood up and moved closer to the cell. Carra stood up too. Masen looked away, giving us as much privacy as possible. We held each other's gaze. So many unspoken words, so many conversations unfinished.

"I'm sorry this happened to you," she said quietly.

"It's in the past. According to the government, I'm a traitor. They took the right protocol."

"They always do."

I chanced saying a risky thing. "I've missed you, Carra."

"Wren, I..." she trailed off.

"I know. Just thought I'd tell you..." I murmured.

Masen interrupted us once more. "Wren, the thing you took from Carra is buzzing."

"It's a call from the other head of officials," Carra said.

"What happens if it doesn't get answered?" I asked.

"They'll either be very upset, or they'll come here thinking something went wrong. Maybe both. And for sure they will be armed."

"We can't let it go unanswered, Wren," Masen said in urgency.

"Well, it's not like we can answer it without giving ourselves away," I pointed out.

"Give it to me," said Carra firmly.

"No, way!" cried Masen. "You'll just tell them we've trapped you!"

"No, I won't." She didn't say it in an answer to Masen, but as an apology to me. It was a gift.

"We can't trust her, Wren!" Masen warned.

"Yes, we can," I demanded. Yet, I too hadn't directed my reply to Masen. I spoke to Carra.

I took the phone from Masen and handed it to the girl behind bars. Carra pushed a button and it came to life.

She held it to her ear as an unknown voice spoke. The other side was softer, but I could just make out the words.

It sounded like the voice of a man, very gruff sounding. "*I was worried you weren't picking up there for a second,*" he told Carra.

"It's all fine here. It took some time, but both prisoners are now gated behind the cell bars."

"*Good job. Now you just have to keep them there. They are rounding up the others as we speak. It shouldn't be long now. Prime Minister has some games planned for the rest.*"

"Wonderful. It should be quite a show."

"*Sorry I won't be able to make it.*"

"I'll fill you in with the details later."

"*Thanks, doll. See you later.*" The device clicked off.

"Wow, thanks," uttered Masen, astonished.

I went and took the device back.

"You did hear what he said, right?" she spat. "They've got your friends."

That was true. I had heard that. Lennon and Winslett had failed, or were failing. Masen and I had succeeded, but that came with its own losses. We were divided. Our poorly constructed plan was now crumbling all around us. Soon, it would fall and we would suffocate. I was sure Carra wouldn't protect our backs from the rest of the falling debris then. It was time to build something better out of the rubble.

Fifty-Six

Byrde

"Hello there, child!" Iris beamed. He held his hand out to me. I guess he wanted me to shake it.

"Shake his hand, sweetie," Mommy whispered with a smile. Something was off about it. It wasn't Mommy's usual smile.

I stretched out my hand and he clasped it in his. Mine was much smaller. His hand was cold and it didn't make me feel good.

"Well, Felix, where did you find Reina's little cherub?" Iris asked like he knew.

"She was in the tunnel near the prison, sir," Felix answered.

Iris directed his attention to Mommy. "You must be very relieved, Reina, that she has been found..."

"Yes, yes of course!" she exclaimed. "It was very irresponsible to run away like that, Byrde. I thought I taught you better."

Run away? She was the one who told me to run!

"But, Mommy—" I started.

She cut me off nervously. "Byrde, you know the officials are nothing to be scared of. Mommy works with them everyday." She added to Iris, "She was a little apprehensive when they came knocking on the door. The next thing I knew, she was gone!"

I was so confused. This was not what happened at all. Was Mommy lying?

Iris seemed slightly amused. "You are aware, Reina, that I have heard several other reports that you did not want Byrde to take the pill. Some of your co-workers, I won't name names, think that this is simply some cover story. Some people even say they saw Byrde in the Square on Distribution Day."

Felix smiled evilly.

"If Byrde was only afraid of the officials," Iris continued, "why has she only turned up now? Surely a ten-year-old girl can identify her own home. She shouldn't have strayed far. Wouldn't you think, Felix?"

"Most certainly, sir," Felix said.

Oh, no. I saw Mommy's face freeze. I had to help her, even though Daddy told me to never lie!

I murmured softly, "I didn't want to come back..."

"What's this now?" said Iris as he arched an eyebrow.

"Mommy was mad at me and I ran away when I saw the officials. I thought they were coming to arrest me because Mommy said I had been bad. So I ran away and was never going to come back! I didn't want to go to jail!"

Mommy said nothing. I wasn't sure we had convinced him. It seemed Iris already knew for sure that this all was a lie. He was waiting for just the right moment to catch us in our web.

"Jail? Where would you get such an idea?" Iris asked. "Reina, you wouldn't tell Byrde about such wives tales?"

"She must have picked it up from another child at school, Prime Minister," she responded quietly.

"Another child. So please explain why she wouldn't return to her home, school, or get buzzed through the main entrance. How is it she ended up in the tunnel chambers?" Iris cooed.

Felix stifled a laugh and Mommy opened her mouth several times before closing it again.

"I was just afraid Mommy would be mad, that's all," I said.

"So you decided to come through dark tunnels? That sounds reasonable," Iris scorned.

"I was, uh, exploring."

"And all the other times you were here with Mommy, you never felt this need to explore? I'm sure your mother has always told you how respectful you had to behave in the government building. Isn't that right, Reina?"

A bead of sweat dripped down Mommy's face. We were losing a battle with Iris, and I knew it wouldn't be good if we did.

"I don't know what got into her. She's been a handful lately, my deepest apologies sir," she said.

Felix stayed silent, but his lip was twitching.

"Of course, my dear! I, too, know how stubborn children can be. So now that she's back, we can administer Extium! All will be right and this mess can be forgotten,"

Iris said, as he pulled a small canister of white pills from his lab coat pocket.

I became even more alert at the word Extium—Wren's invention. This would change who I was. I wouldn't know Mommy anymore and I wouldn't be able to remember Daddy's stories. They couldn't give me Extium! For everyone else in the gang, somehow Extium didn't work, but it wasn't guaranteed not to work on me. See, the first time, Mommy just pretended to give it to me. If the Prime Minister made me swallow it, I could be gone. On Distribution Day, Mommy made me run so no one could make me take it. Now, there was nowhere to run.

Prime Minister Iris began to unscrew the bottle and one tiny white capsule appeared in his hand. "Ah, it's beautiful, isn't it?"

"It has changed our society for the better," acknowledged Felix.

Iris then ordered, "Felix, go fetch the little lady a glass of water to get this down."

"Right away, sir," he said as he left.

"Reina," Iris started, "I'm very happy to see you're obliging to the situation. I was worried you wouldn't. This seriously makes some other things I must attend to today, much less complicated."

"The transformation of Laiden is of the utmost importance," Mommy mumbled almost inaudibly.

"Yes, I'm glad we are finally on the same page again. The process finished this morning. The pill has now engrossed the system."

Mommy gave a small smile, but turned it quickly into a frown when Felix reentered the room. I still chose not to say anything. Maybe I'd get lucky. Maybe it wouldn't work. I couldn't risk the others wasting their time trying to save me! I tried to stay brave like Daddy taught me when I took the water from Felix.

"Open wide," Iris instructed tenderly.

I did and just as he placed the capsule on my tongue, Mommy began to shout.

"NO! Byrde, spit it out! Spit it out! No! No!" she screamed wildly, grabbing for me.

I spit the white pill out of my mouth and was quickly swept out of Mommy's reach by Felix who had lifted me off the ground.

The sneer I had been waiting for crossed both Iris's and Felix's faces.

"This is more like it," Iris jeered.

Iris then grabbed a long, pointy needle from the same pocket the pill bottle had come from. He jabbed it into Mommy's arm and she fell to the ground.

I stared wide-eyed, and my mouth hung open for a second. Then I started screaming too.

"Felix, I need you to say here and contain the girl. If Reina stirs, give her another shot from the syringe," Iris said, handing him the needle that was still half full of a golden liquid. "Await further orders. I am going to need you to bring them both down to the chambers after I attend to one last thing…"

"Of course, sir. I will have them under complete control," he said proudly.

He elbowed me and I stopped screaming. I took that moment to look around the lab again. There was just the one entrance that doubled as an exit. And you needed an eye scan to get out. I truly was stuck. At least the chamber would be where the others would meet back up. They could save me. I wished.

"Yes, Byrde, it seems you will see your friends one last time. One last time before you forget they ever existed to begin with." Iris laughed in a way I hadn't heard before.

He scanned his eye and the door slid open and answered, "Thank you for your hard work, Prime Minister. Your valiant efforts to improve Laiden to reach its maximum of perfection are most gratifying."

Fifty-Seven

Masen

"So what do we do now?" I asked Carra and Wren. Even though Carra was an enemy, for some reason she was acting like she was on our side.

"Well, that was the second time we heard of arrivals coming. Is it prudent to assume someone will be bringing along Lennon and Winslett?" Wren inquired.

"Clearly," I said. "But how do we prepare? We have one round of stunning left. Whoever brings in the two of them is sure to be armed more heavily than we are."

Carra, who was still sitting cross-legged at the edge of the cell, piped up, "True. Also, they may not come alone. You are at a clear disadvantage."

"There's no way around it though," Wren said, frustrated.

"You might stand a chance at hand-to-hand combat," she told us.

I tried to wiggle my fingers. This time, I could. It was still immensely painful to try and stand up, but I wasn't a helpless lump anymore. My eyes were fine and only blurred with a sudden head movement. My ears had cleared for the most part besides a slight ringing in the right one. It *seemed* like I was over the fact that Carra tortured me, but I wasn't. The only reason I was acting so cordial toward her was in the case she could be of some use to us.

"Masen is still not in any condition," Wren said in exasperation.

"Masen isn't my concern. Has he ever been taught combat anyway? I'm talking about you and me, Wren. We could take them."

"How can I trust that when an official you're friends with comes in, or Iris himself, that you'd be willing to do that?" Wren rubbed his forehead. It was obvious to me he knew that the options were few.

I craved to input my opinion. Some part of me told me that this was our best bet. I didn't trust her, but I couldn't shake the image of her when she was unconscious. It was easy then to see why Wren was crazy about her. She was very beautiful, and I was a weakling.

"Wren, we've been over this. I was following orders," she said rigidly.

"Exactly, and your job when the guards come will be to help. How can I rely on you then?" Wren asked in a strained voice.

"Wren, I agree with Carra," I stated blandly.

The shock on both their faces was almost laughable.

I continued, "She was only doing her job. I'm not going to get into the ethics behind what this stupid place does. Weren't you just doing your job when you created Extium?" Shame crossed his face, but I didn't let it stop me. "You turned innocent people to slaves. You made loved ones strangers. You were the one who caused the grief for Lennon, Winslett, Byrde, and me. Yet, somehow we decided to come back here and save you and rescue you from almost slipping away into insanity. We came back and decided to return the trust we once gave you. So yeah, maybe I don't know Carra, but you do. You trusted her once and you can trust her again. She's offering to help and I want to take it."

Silence fell over the already too quiet jail. Clearly, my out of character speech had made an impact.

Wren cleared his throat. "I see your point, Masen, but this is a different situation altogether. There is a very real possibility we won't beat them. We could be executed."

I chose to ignore him completely. "Carra, what was your plan?"

She stood up and even though iron bars separated us, she was towering over me.

"Let me out," she said. "Seriously, if I'm in here they'll know something is not right."

"I'm not going back in there," Wren demanded.

Carra rolled her eyes. "I'm not going to lock it, you fool. When they come in, they'll see me holding your stunner and the two of you secured in the cell. They'll believe I accomplished my job like I reported. Only at the perfect moment you'll push open the door and we will attack, the edge of surprise on our hands."

I was stupefied by how much sense this plan made. I couldn't find a flaw as long as Carra kept to her word.

"That's a really solid strategy," I told her.

Wren let his lip curve into a rare, but small smile. "She did quite a few rotations in our strategizing headquarters. She was one of the best they'd ever seen."

"Far from it, Wren," she retorted.

"You're being modest. They recruited her immediately, but she chose the job as an official instead."

"It was where I belonged," she spoke.

"Even though you were one of the only three people to ever make it through a complete round of simulations without losing your head?"

She just shrugged.

"Simulations?" I questioned.

"You clearly don't listen." Wren sighed.

"That's not true, I totally... uh never mind, I don't listen. Explain it again?" I admitted.

"Simulations can invade your mind, throw fears at you, and conjure up scenarios to scare you. It can make you see things, think things, or feel things that aren't true or real at all. Simulations, for most people, besides the three documented, seem like reality," Wren explained in his scientific voice.

"Whom doesn't it work on?" I asked.

"Well, it works on everyone. Some people can work through it better than others."

"Wow," I said.

Carra ended the conversation. "None of it matters. Simulations have nothing to do with our current situation. Are we all on board with the plan?"

Wren and I both nodded.

"Good," she told us. "They could be here in a matter of minutes or in a matter of hours. Unlock me now."

Wren still looked apprehensive. He reached into his pocket very slowly to grab the keys. He took the three steps to the cell, even slower. When the cell finally opened, Carra swiftly exited.

Wren held her gaze for a long time before he turned around to me.

"Remembered me down here, have you now?" I mocked.

Wren walked back over to me and lifted me to my feet. I wrapped my arm around him for support. He did most of the work as I limped into the cell. I barely had any weight on my legs, but it still hurt. I grimaced.

Wren and Carra reached to shut the door at the same time, but Wren backed away. He joined me and sat against the wall.

"Remember, it's not locked, so don't lean on the bars in case it swings open," she reminded us.

I had to trust in the plan. We had given the keys, stunner, and communication device all back to Carra. We were once again in a vulnerable position if she betrayed us.

"It will work," she promised.

Neither Wren nor I responded. All I could think about was the imminent arrival of Lennon and Winslett. They had no idea what had been done to me, the pain I endured. The pain grew as I imagined Winslett with her pretty face potentially mangled from fists, her hair potentially matted with blood. It made me sick.

If this adventure had taught me anything, it taught me how much I would relish the day I came back to the government to tear it down.

Fifty-Eight

Winslett

Water.

I was surrounded by water and enveloped in darkness.

A piercing pressure rang in the back of my head and through my ears. Bubbles escaped from my mouth as I, panic stricken, swiveled my head frantically to find the surface. Defenseless, I closed my eyes and let the remaining bubbles of air leave my lips.

I felt a firm hand entwine into mine and pull me to heaven. I smiled. What a funny way to die, being surrounded by water and all. Never did I think my last dying moments would be spent like this.

The pressure had fully lifted now and my ears stopped ringing. I could tell that I was almost close to heaven now.

Instead, I had been rudely awakened. Rapid waves of salt water crashed around me as I reached the surface.

It took more time for me to see where I was than to react to my surroundings. I gasped as a rush of heavy waves took me under. The salt water stung my eyes. Bobbing up and down, I panicked as the water rushed around me and dunked me once again. The repetitive motion enervated my strength and will to remain alive. I had never been more than a couple feet in water. It was what Laiden had allowed.

"Winslett!" a voice screamed over the crashing waves.

I gasped for oxygen at the sound of Lennon's voice.

"Winslett!" he called again.

"Lennon!" I screamed, but the water had dunked me under and turned my screams into gurgles.

"Winslett, come if you can hear me," Lennon called, before being interrupted by a crash of pounding waves.

I turned my head around rapidly and squinted my eyes to see a small figure making its way toward me.

But I was distracted by something else now. A glint of crystal in a form of a spherical shaped pebble lay on top of a massive rock, piercing through the current. I recognized it immediately as the orb. Waves slapped against the surface of the rock, almost crawling to touch the orb, but sunk back down as if the object had repelled it away.

A surge of adrenaline fueled me now. Lennon's gaze met mine as I excitedly pointed to it.

Lennon stopped me. "Let it go, Winslett! Anyone willing to go near that is insane. It's way too dangerous."

He was right. The rock was jagged and slippery. It would have cut anyone who dared to climb it, but the orb's radiating glow had the powers to mystify me and I persisted on. I couldn't give up on the mission now.

The orb simply stared back at me, regally shining, calling my name.

I was tossed by the water's rapid waves, but I had a reason to stay afloat now. The rock lay only a couple more feet away. I heaved myself toward it with all the strength I could muster. A couple more inches now. The glow was brighter than ever and I could see my reflection in the orb. Leaning one hand against the boulder's jagged surface, I propped my right foot against a sharp crevice. I knew I could reach it if I just…

Ow. My foot had slipped off the rock and I landed back in the water where I had started. Licking my lips, I tasted blood. I rubbed my hand against the side of my cheek and gently felt around the deep wound. Red blots of ink dripped in the water, but that was not my concern.

I propped myself against the rock again and begun to climb. Lifting myself out of the water and onto the rock, I felt a pair of hands pull me down. I landed back in the crashing waves. But this time it hurt. Salt had entered my wound and a searing pain electrified the side of my face.

I glowered at the force that had pulled me away from the orb. I saw Lennon's eyes grow wide, staring at my face. But then as immediately as it had widened, he began to pull me away from the orb and the rock.

"No! Stop, Lennon! We need the orb! This is bigger than all of us right now!" I screamed, raising my voice over the water slapping the shore.

"No. It's not. At least not for me," he answered. "I would rather let the orb go than to see you risk your life for it."

"If I don't get it, we all die!"

Lennon swiftly grabbed my waist and began pulling me away from the main current. We took turns being tousled in the water, gulping more bitter salt water than tolerable.

But finally, I knew that the worst had been behind us. The waves had begun to calm as we pulled ourselves toward the shore.

I sputtered out violent coughs of salt water as I staggered against Lennon's arm for support. We stood in the rippling water in silence.

"Are you okay?" Lennon asked softly, after the hacking had stopped.

I looked at him. He was completely soaked, with hair pressed over his face.

I didn't know what else to do except close my stinging eyes and let tears of salt rush down my face as Lennon opened his arms to cradle me. Death had pardoned me one more time.

Fifty-Nine

Lennon

A hot breeze brushed wisps of Winslett's hair along the side of my face and I felt grounded once again. We were still locked in a tight embrace, her arms were tucked into my chest and her head was buried into the crevice of my shoulder. I took a deep breath and blinked my eyes open.

I blearily looked into the sun, but the light hit me so mercilessly, I had to cover my eyes again. I peaked through my fingers. This time, I was careful to not expose my eyes to too much of the penetrating light, and looked around warily.

Winslett and I stood in a plush green jungle under a bed of a species of trees I didn't recognize.

Rain must have gathered the night before and collected in the bark of the foreign trees, where creatures took the liberty of coming close to Winslett and me to drink the water. Twisted vines wrapped around the base of each tree all the way to the top. The vines connected the roofs of the trees, forming an intricate wreath along the tops of the canopy, hundreds of feet ahead. It served as a valuable method of transportation for those supple, flightless creatures, while exotic birds encircled above us.

However, the peace in the tropics was disturbed by a sound of barking and growling in the distance. The sound grew closer and I darted my eyes across the horizon only to be met with an incredible pack of wild beasts sprinting toward us.

"Winslett, RUN!"

I burst into a sprint, grabbing her hand. She shook my grasp away, clenched her fists, and increased at her own speed. My pace leveled with hers as we barreled our way through the depths of the jungle. The beasts ran closely behind us, and each time I looked back, the space between the beasts and us grew smaller and smaller.

"Lennon, look out!" Winslett called.

She had seen it a fraction of a second before I had, but it had been too late. One, out of the pack of dirty mongrels that had been chasing us, cut me off, screeching Winslett and I to a violent halt. The rest of its pack trapped us in a small circle.

The monstrously tall beasts had dark, mangled hair. Their backs arched like a stray felines', with paws close to the size of my head. I looked at their faces, all pretty similar. Their ears stood pointed, keen to pick up any signs of prey. However, their massive bodies were fairly skinny, obviously not properly fed— bad news for us.

"Lennon," breathed Winslett in disbelief, "the eyes."

I glanced at the growling, wild beasts, and this time looked at the alpha dog's eyes curiously. Its unusual glassy eyes strangely held no hatred. Instead, delicate eyelids glowered around them.

I looked closer and choked.

Instead of its colored iris, a glassy, spherical orb lay in its place. I looked around at the other dogs and saw dozens of the same crystal eyes.

I hurriedly pushed Winslett behind me in a protective sweep.

The pack of animals surrounded us, gleaning and growling. They were ready to pounce at a moments notice. Sweat dripped into my eyes. There was nowhere left to run.

I grabbed Winslett's hand and interlocked her fingers in mine as we braced ourselves for an imminent death.

"Close your eyes," Winslett whispered to me, giving my hand a gentle squeeze. "It's better that way."

Sixty

Lennon

I felt the same jolt of pain and pressure that took over me before, and I knew I was yet in another place. But this was different. I opened my eyes, expecting… well, I didn't know what to expect. I had been terrorized, nearly drowned, and almost eaten. Having experienced a wide range of possible deaths, I was pretty confident I'd survive this one.

Unless I was dead.

Which could be very true.

I looked around to find a familiar room of fluorescent lights. But what prevented me from seeing any farther was a figure that stood directly in front of me. I stared down at the figure's glossy, black leather shoes and slowly looked up to see a well-dressed man with black beady eyes smirking down at me.

I had been wrong about one thing.

I was not prepared for where I was now.

Sixty-One

Lennon

Iris.

I met his smirk with a mixed expression of shock, fear, and anger, probably making my face look pretty deformed.

He chortled haughtily before pulling out an all too familiar glass marble from his right pocket. "Looking for this?"

It surprisingly still glinted in the artificial lighting.

I glared at him this time.

"Were you the one that made us go through all of that?" I exclaimed.

"If by that you mean the stimulations, than yes," Iris ensured. "I am responsible. I set you up from the moment you and your friends entered my government."

I quickly brought myself to my feet and was about to teach him a lesson that would make him feel like he was attacked by a pack of beasts, but immediately sunk back down. I had gotten up too quickly and a heavy pressure made figures in front of me shake.

"Uhhh," I groaned, lying on the cold white tiles.

"Careful now, you don't want to enter in another stimulation," he warned.

"But, how?" I asked weakly.

"Well, just as this isn't my actual office, it wasn't Winslett's bedroom, nor a white water rapid, nor a jungle," Iris pondered. "This is my stimulation room. It has the ability to make you believe you are standing in a new exotic place when, in fact, you never left this room."

"But the wild beasts..." I mulled over. "Weren't they real?"

"No, child, they weren't. They were simply figures of your own imagination. I played into your worst fears, and simply," Iris made a plucking noise, "popped them into the stimulation!"

Regaining some of my strength back, I sat up. "I swear I will..."

Iris tisked.

"Let's not make any rash decisions yet, children," Iris continued. "It wouldn't be worth it."

"Worth what?" I yelled back. "I'd do anything to rip you apart!!"

The room lay silent.

"Anything?" Iris mused, then smiled furtively.

I glowered at him.

"What now?" I barked, fuming.

"No, no, you may continue," Iris stalled, "if you truly agree to do anything to 'rip me apart.' It's just... just... that it would be such a shame to have a row with me, at the cost of the lives of so many others."

"What others?" I asked stupidly.

Iris turned to me in mocked shock. "Why, your friends, of course."

I turned white and heard Winslett gasp behind me for the first time.

"Oh, speaking up for the first time?" Iris sneered. "I'm glad you've decided to wake up."

Changing the subject, he continued to twirl the orb in his fingers.

"A miraculous contraption, is it not?" Iris mused.

He seemed entranced by its reflective beauty.

I was disgusted with the orb by now. It had caused us nothing more than trouble.

"Why don't I strike you a deal, hmm?" Iris inquired.

"We're not crazy enough to make any kind of deal with you!" I shot back.

"Lennon…" Winslett warned behind me.

Irritated, I tried again. "What could you *possibly* want from us?"

Iris smiled. "Information. Nothing that would make you feel uncomfortable, of course."

I stared at him suspiciously, not buying any of it.

"Information about what? We don't know anything you don't know," Winslett piped up from behind me.

"You see, I highly doubt that," Iris murmured, turning his back from us. He began pacing around the room.

I raised an eyebrow.

"Anytime you want to stop stalling and get on with it, would be great," I spat.

Iris sighed, shaking his head. "Now, that tone isn't going to get you anywhere, boy."

He turned back around to face us.

"But, yes, moving forward. I would like to start where this all began." He made an elaborate hand gesture.

"Which is?" Winslett pushed.

Iris grimaced at Winslett. "Why the Cure didn't work."

I pursed my lips.

"Do I have to repeat myself or are your incoherent minds lost in the fact that you think you are so clever."

"No, it's not that," I retorted.

He looked at both Winslett and me. Had I come off across as genuine? But Iris, full of surprises, shocked me once again.

"Oh!" Iris gasped. "Of course, why not see what your friends are up to, hmm?"

Our friends had counted on us for one thing, to retrieve the orb, and Winslett and I had failed to do even that. Now Wren and Masen would feel Iris's full wrath. These would be my last moments.

"Off we go, darlings. Let's take a little trip down memory lane." Iris smirked, his thin lips curling upward and black eyes glinting.

Sixty-Two

Wren

A nervous adrenaline overtook me. It was a feeling I had only experienced once before, and it was too hard to describe. It was the same kind I had on the day I fled. So much waiting and never knowing when or who would be coming. My fate lay in someone else's hands. And out of all hands that it could be laid in, it had to be Carra's.

Seeing her again brought back a pang of guilt. She had once placed her faith in me. We had plans, the two of us. When I ended things with Carra so suddenly, she wouldn't let it go. She had to know why, and eventually she got it out of me. It was the day before I had planned to leave…

I was locking up the lab for the night and all the officials and other scientists in the area had went home, changed shifts, or moved to another part of the never-ending government building.

"Wren, just talk to me!" Carra begged. She had stayed late that night just so she could have me cornered.

"What more do you want me to say?" I snapped.

"You told me you loved me! Tell me how that is true one moment and false the next?" Her walls, when we were alone, always seemed to fall down. She was speaking from her heart of hearts, the one that was only known to me.

"Things change. People change," I said.

"Nothing's changed!"

"I need to focus more on my research here," I said evenly.

"Stop pretending. For the past few months, you've been focusing all your energy on the pill! You've succeeded now. Work is only going to decrease from here on out, so don't lie to me!"

"It's not you, Carra… it's me."

She actually laughed. "Really? You're going to use the most cliché line in the book?"

My face grew cold. "Well, it's true."

For a twenty-year-old girl, Carra had enormous strength. She pressed me against the wall. "You're hiding something. Tell me what it is."

She was strong, but I was stronger. I brushed her hand away.

"You'd tell Iris," I whispered. I hadn't wanted to say it, and I didn't see how she couldn't be mad.

"How could you say that? You know I don't involve work with our relationship," she said as she gestured to the government as a whole.

"You might feel differently if you knew the truth."

"Then tell me, and we'll find out!"

"I'm leaving…" I mumbled dropping her gaze.

"You're quitting your job here?"

"No, I'm leaving Laiden."

She paused for a long moment to let it sink in. "There's nowhere to go, Wren. If there was, maybe I'd have left a long time ago."

"Well, I need to find out if I really believe that this is it."

"It is."

"And if it isn't?" She didn't say anything so I continued. "Carra, I need to do this. I'm going to. I'll live in the depths of the forests until I can figure things out."

For a while, we stood in silence. She bit her lip and then said, "Take me with you."

"What?"

"Let me come with you."

"How can you, Carra?"

"You know how I feel about that. Wren, I've never liked it here. If leaving means being with you, then I don't want to wait another second."

I smiled. "I'd like that."

"Good," she said, returning the smile. "When do we leave for real?"

"I haven't decided that just yet," I mused. "I can't decide what's best, either the day before Distribution Day, or the day after. What do you think?"

"The day after, most definitely," she said with certainty. "Iris won't be suspecting it. You'll have seen if Extium succeeded or failed and then we can bolt out of here together."

"Sounds like a plan. We leave the day after Distribution Day."

I kissed her forehead and we walked out of the building hand in hand.

I had betrayed her though. On the eve of Distribution Day, I couldn't take it. I packed and unpacked, until I just fled, leaving her waiting for me in the dusk. I couldn't pretend it wasn't hard. Did I think I was protecting her? Or did I do it for more selfish reasons? Maybe a bit of both, and I wasn't proud to admit it.

And here we were with another plan, this time hers and not mine. Hence, I was hesitant to trust her. Would she betray us just to spite me? I didn't know.

I heard footsteps and looked at Carra. She put her pointer finger to her lips.

Muffled voices came from behind the door that held a tall staircase heading back into the main floor of the government. It creaked open and I was on the alert. Carra struck a more threatening pose and all of our eyes became trained on the entryway.

Two figures came through. They were silent and didn't run. It was too dark to tell who they were. Closer and closer they came, until it was clear that these people were Lennon and Winslett.

My two friends stopped in front of us. Their eyes and heads were focused downward. From what I could tell they looked a bit ruffled, but there were no visible injuries. A familiar thumping of leather shoes shook my consciousness away from Lennon and Winslett. Prime Minister Iris himself was striding in behind them.

I held my head a little higher and stood up to make sure I was towering at the same level. Iris could not intimidate me.

The five of us stood in silence until he finally broke it. "What a nice little reunion this is." Iris looked around and when he realized none of us were going to respond any time soon he said, "Nice work, Carra. Good to see your silly feelings toward Wren are in the past."

At that, Lennon and Winslett both turned toward the girl that the Prime Minister announced had once loved me. Carra's pale skin turned a fierce red and she looked away.

"It's amusing, Wren, the lengths people will go to be with their loved ones. It is curious how people will continue to risk their lives when there's no doubt all effort and courage put into another's trust, will fail," Iris scorned. No doubt he was still talking about Carra's allegiance.

I looked over at Masen who was trying desperately to catch Winslett's unwavering eyes. Iris seemed to see this too and said, "Go ahead, dear, you may as well talk to him now. There isn't that much time left anyway."

Winslett looked frantically to me and back to Iris, but ultimately decided to come closer to us and whisper to Masen. Lennon followed in a protective sort of way.

"Are you guys alright?" Winslett whispered in pain, because no doubt Iris could hear.

I nodded, and Masen did too.

"Why aren't you standing up?" Winslett then asked with a hint of concern.

"I can't," mumbled Masen.

She fell silent at that remark. I looked toward Masen's closest friend as she knelt down beside him, and took his hand.

"Are we done yet?" Iris asked in a tired voice.

Lennon gave a curt nod.

"Good. I'd like to get things underway."

Lennon, Winslett, and Masen did a three-way look of panic. I even risked a glance at Carra. Her gaze was dogged.

"Carra, I'm going to need the assistance of my daughter," Iris continued. And this is why I was afraid our plan would fall to pieces.

"Yes, of course, father," Carra answered smoothly.

Sixty-Three

Masen

Father? Did I hear that right? When we were talking before, she didn't think it was necessary to be like "oh by the way the Prime Minister of Laiden is my *father*?" My mouth may have actually dropped open. I looked at Wren, but he was rubbing his forehead once again. At least Lennon and Winslett shared the same shocked look as I did.

"*He has a daughter*?" Winslett mouthed to me.

I tried to mouth back, "*How come we never knew*?" But her attention was already elsewhere. Seriously, why hadn't Laiden known? Was he hiding her existence? Probably not… nevertheless, the daughter of Iris would have been treated as royalty!

We were still four against two, but Carra had a stunner. Iris didn't seem to have a weapon, but who knew what was really up his sleeve.

Carra assumed a position adjacent to Iris; they were whispering. I couldn't make out what they were saying, but soon enough, she had swapped communication devices and began walking away.

I couldn't help myself when I frantically asked, "Where's she going?"

"She went on a quick errand for me," Iris replied. "Though that shouldn't concern you at the moment."

"Then what should concern us?" I snapped back. Winslett sent a look to me that screamed, calm-yourself-down-and-shut-up. I shot a nasty look back, but I did stop talking.

"Glad you asked, Masen," Iris said. "You should concern yourself with answering my questions."

Lennon spoke up for the first time. I quickly shut my mouth, not realizing I had opened it to yell another rebuttal. "What makes you think we'll answer anything?"

Iris gave me a coy smile. Sometimes I forgot that he didn't become Prime Minister of Laiden just on his good looks. He was always one step ahead. "I anticipated you all to act like this."

"Did you?" mocked Lennon.

Still, Iris was keeping up a presence of indifference. "Torture just isn't as effective as it used to be. Just ask your friends over there."

I realized he was addressing Wren and me, so I flashed him my pearly whites and said, "Us? We're just dandy!" I even threw in a wink.

The vein in Iris's neck bulged, but his stance remained unbroken. "That's why I've asked Carra to help me out."

Wren looked up for the first time. I knew he still wasn't going to say anything. He was clearly on edge, waiting for Carra to make her final move when she returned.

Iris looked like he was inspecting his hands and said, "You see, I've been mindlessly having Wren tortured for days, but I reaped no results. I could do the same to you three, but my hunches tell me it would be just as fruitless."

"How the hell do you even get away with this?" I cried.

"Masen," hushed Winslett.

"No, no. Let the boy talk," Iris laughed, clearly amused.

"I mean, you call yourself the high and mighty Prime Minister of Laiden. Yet, you go around torturing innocent citizens? There just isn't anything high and mighty in that," I declared.

"Well, like you said, I *am* the Prime Minister which entitles me to do what I deem to be right."

"And you deem torture to be right?" I exclaimed. Lennon, Winslett, and Wren were all watching our show down. Wren didn't look concerned and Lennon had his eyes trained on Winslett, who was still looking fretful.

"When needed, yes," Iris said again.

"The people won't stand for this! They barely put up with the public executions anymore."

He let another chuckle out. "They may not have before, but they will now."

"Well... I..."

No reason could stand up to this. I was defeated by the awful truth. The awful truth was that no one could defy Iris anymore even if they wanted to. The "citizens" had already suffered the worst.

"Has your small human brain finally arrived at the snag in your argument?" Iris jeered. "There isn't a person in Laiden, besides perhaps you four, that would ever dream of defying me! I'm glorified. The people are at my command, to do what I say, when I say. I trust Wren has taught you how Extium works. It invades the mind and wipes it blank. Over time, it ensnares the whole brain rendering it thoughtless. It is ready to be filled with new ideas and morals. I could plant the seed in every newly refurbished mind in Laiden that torture should be looked at as pleasurable! Your argument is silly, my boy."

When Iris looked satisfied by all of our subdued attitudes, he continued where he had originally left off. "So as I was saying, it is clear to me that torturing will get us nowhere. The four of you are as stubborn as ever, so I have an incentive."

Lennon spoke, this time adjusting his body to be slightly in front of Winslett's. "You have nothing we want."

"Don't I, though?" Iris asked with an acidity in his tone. He then took out Carra's communication device from his lab coat pocket. He hit a few buttons and continued talking, only not to us. "We're ready for you."

He shoved the device back into the depths of his pocket. Three seconds passed since he had muttered the four words and I heard a quiet click at the end of the hall. I hoped it was Carra, or maybe I didn't. In spite of my wishes, it soon became apparent that four figures were coming back into view, not just one.

I squinted harder as they came closer. One was a classic male official and one was definitely Carra. Another was a government lab worker with the recognizable white coat, being dragged by the male, half unconscious. The fourth was much smaller in size with unmistakable blonde hair. Byrde hobbled in with her injured knee.

I felt the features of my face sink. Byrde was not a part of our plan. She was supposed to be safe, protected in the dark tunnel. My insides felt cooked alive, and I felt my face grow hot.

Byrde was not smiling either. The only mark on her body came from the injury she already had on her knee. She hobbled to Winslett who gave her a hug. She then hugged Lennon. Her brown eyes looked through the bars at Wren and me.

She mumbled, "I'm sorry, everyone."

"Sorry for what, blondie?" Wren asked, speaking for the first time in a while.

"It's all my fault," she croaked.

"We all got caught, Byrde. Let's just focus now on getting back out again, alright?" Wren winked, instilling a little hope in the small girl's heart.

Byrde slipped underneath Winslett's arm as the other three adults came in.

The man dropped the woman onto the floor and Byrde began whimpering. Something about her face looked familiar, but I couldn't place it.

"Time for a few more introductions, I think," Iris said. He pointed to the man. "This is Felix."

"Pleasure." Felix sneered in a similar fashion to Iris's own signature smirk.

"And this is Reina Faleman. Byrde's mother," Iris added.

So that's why she looked familiar.

Carra moved back to her position in front of the cell. Iris ignored her movements and gestured to Felix to move

Reina's body more central to our view. He rolled her over with his feet.

I didn't know what to say, but then I saw Felix take out a long, sharp bronze knife.

"So my proposition to you all is, you can answer my question like I ask you too or Felix will give Byrde's mommy a nice, slow death." Iris dragged out the word "slow."

Just to give us a taste of how serious the matter was, Felix gently pressed the knife into Reina's leg.

Sixty-Four

Winslett

I was about to yell, "Stop!" but anything I could've said would've been drowned out by Byrde's horrified screams.

"Hush, Byrde, it's alright. It's all going to be alright," I said gently to the little girl beside me as we both watched blood spill onto the floor from the body of her mother. It would most certainly not be all right, not after seeing this.

"Enough," bellowed Wren in a powerful voice. The old Wren always emitted a feeling of power, but his voice was never raised. This projection was so intimidating that I stopped talking. Byrde silenced her tears. Felix lifted up the knife. It was eerily quiet, however, Felix's sick look of thrill did not leave his face.

Iris cleared his throat. "Very well. Felix, stop that for now."

I grabbed Byrde's hand and stroked her hair. Tears began to roll down her face again. She reminded me so much of Evelyn. How could I fail to protect her in this time of need?

Iris continued, interrupting my thoughts. "I take it you'll answer the questions now?"

I didn't want to be the one who had to answer this. I didn't want to say yes and betray my friends, yet I couldn't say no and watch Byrde's mother suffer. Little girls need their moms. I could vouch for that better than anyone. So I looked to Wren whose face had hardened. Masen was only looking at me, telling me I could make the call. Why didn't he see I didn't want to?

I finally looked to Lennon. He knew. He grazed his hand on my shoulder and took a few steps forward. I couldn't see his face anymore.

"We'll answer," Lennon responded shakily, "if Felix puts away the knife."

Iris's lip curled. "Very well. Felix?"

Felix shoved the knife into its holder tied to his black belt.

Iris's bemused expression darkened. "I want to know why Extium didn't work on you. Wren, obviously, seeing as he was the creator, did not take it. Byrde, because of Reina, dodged having to take it herself. You three though… you three swallowed the pill."

"We'd like to know that ourselves actually," Masen said.

"Tell me, did Wren have a hand in this? Did he know it might not work on some?"

Lennon put his hand up to us all. He was going to answer the question. "To tell the truth, we've discussed this with Wren. He was just as confused that it hadn't worked on us. None of us have any idea how it happened, but thankfully it did."

Iris's jaw clenched. "You won't be thankful for long. Now answer me this, what drew you to this orb?" He brought it back out of his pocket. He seemed to keep taunting Lennon and me with it. However, I got to see the small smiles threatening on the lips of Byrde, Masen, and Wren. See, we hadn't totally failed!

One thing was odd to me though, Carra looked intrigued as well. She was waiting for the answer just as much as Iris was.

However, Lennon was at a loss. This wasn't a question that could go answered since it would ruin our whole plan. Iris would never let us go if we told him we were planning on bringing down the barrier. He wanted control, not chaos.

"Well, um," he stuttered.

"Felix," Iris sneered.

Felix withdrew his knife again and this time made a slash across Reina's jaw. This brought her to consciousness, and to pain. I could tell Reina didn't want to show the pain in front of her daughter, but it must have been too much. She screamed, and her shrieks intertwined with Byrde's.

"Iris, enough! The boy is about to answer you!" Wren said through gritted teeth.

Iris looked toward Lennon. "When you please," he gestured, clearly content with himself.

I kneeled down to be on level with Byrde, and tried to get her attention away from her mother. The tears in her eyes brought tears to my own. Byrde's small fingers brushed them away. I kissed her cheek and we were both quiet for a while.

"We were just interested in seeing the hologram file, that's all," Lennon lied.

"That's the best you can come up with?" Iris asked.

"It's the truth," he mustered.

"You're going to have to do better than that if you want to stop Felix."

"Just finish asking your questions so we can leave!"

"Oh, you won't be leaving, Lennon."

At this remark, I found the courage to speak. "You said if we answered your questions you'd let us go!"

"*Let you go?* I promised nothing of the sort. I said I wouldn't torture you. I said nothing about killing," Iris proclaimed.

"Killing?" stumbled Lennon. "You're going to kill us?" He retreated back to take my hand that wasn't holding Byrde's.

"That's not fair!" I squeaked wildly.

Iris sighed. "I've been nothing but fair."

"But, but… but I thought…" I stammered.

"You thought I'd let you go, scamper back into the forest unharmed? For a girl so smart, you are so naïve."

Wren spoke again. "Then what's the point of all this, if you tell us that we are as good as dead? They aren't going to help you now!"

"Clearly. Don't mistake me for a fool, Wren," Iris told him.

"Then why?" Masen said bewildered.

"Because I can. You still don't understand. I can manipulate you even without Extium. Look at how you bend to my will when someone is in harm. You all care too much. That's your weakness," Iris said as his eye gave a manic twitch. He had cracked. The older man had finally fallen off his rocker.

I saw his daughter reach for the stunner and I went on defense. Did Iris have a plan established with her? Was she going to stun us so they could drag us away and kill us without a struggle? What were we going to do? I could only dodge for so long…

"NOW!" Carra shrieked.

Wren was moving within seconds. He grabbed Masen and shoved me forward. Lennon didn't miss a beat and dragged Byrde along.

"Come on, Winslett!" Wren shouted behind my shoulder. He had already gone a distance ahead of me. Where was he running?

Wren shoved me forward again. "Keep moving, head up to where you had come from."

"The weapons room?" I asked breathlessly.

He gave a curt nod, readjusting a limp Masen hanging over his shoulder.

"Mommy!" cried Byrde as she struggled against me. It took everything I had to ignore her and keep pushing her forward.

Iris was quite agile for a middle-aged man. I looked back again and saw he had lunged for Felix's knife. Reina was moaning, but was more alert than she was earlier. In his mad fall for the only other weapon in the room, Iris's orb had dropped to the ground and began rolling toward us. I gaped at the glowing sphere with the same awe I had in the simulations, in the water, and in the jungle. It was real this time.

"Get out of here!" I heard Reina yell. The blood was flowing too rapidly. I wanted to go back for her, but the sad truth was that Byrde's mom wasn't going to make it anyway.

"What are you waiting for?" Lennon screamed to me, pulling my arm.

"The orb, Lennon, it fell! I can get it!"

"No, forget about it, Winslett. We'll find another way."

"There is no other way!" I yelled, breaking from his grip and running for the orb.

I was too close to Iris for comfort and he was swinging the bloody knife around like a madman. I grabbed the orb, not realizing he was getting closer with his arm thrusts. My face felt wet above the wound on my cheek that had already started to dry. Had Reina's blood splattered on me? No. I brought a shaking hand up to meet my face once again. It burned. Iris lifted the knife back up ready for another swing. But instead of swinging forward once more, it was he who suddenly fell back. Carra had sent a kick to her father's chest. At that moment, my hands clenched the orb and I shot back up, not knowing whether or not he had regained his breath.

I dashed back to the group as fast as I could run. I caught back up with them and firmly seized Byrde's hand so she wouldn't go back like I had.

We were almost back to the door we had come from originally, the one that led to the arsenal.

As we started to turn a corner, Iris bellowed, "Stop!"

He was kneeling over Reina's chest, gripping the knife far above his head. Fresh blood was smeared across his right cheekbone and dotted against his crisp, white shirt.

The knife was still dripping red, and without looking down, he plunged the blade deep into Reina Faleman's heart.

Her screams barely escaped her lips, but they overlapped once again with her daughter's. I had failed to think about her. I didn't even cover her eyes. Byrde didn't deserve to see her mother die like that, not like how my parents died. I cringed at the flashbacks.

The girl, Carra, grabbed Byrde before she could utter another scream.

Wren yelled, "We have to keep moving!"

I caught his words and ran with the other five around me. No one talked anymore; we were all silenced by Byrde's continued screams of horror. We turned the corner and were faced with the ladder leading back to the arsenal.

Carra addressed Byrde for the first time as she put her down. "Can you climb?"

Byrde didn't respond, but her small hands gripped the bars and she led us up. Carra followed her, then Lennon, then me. Masen was leaning his full body weight on Wren and they seemed perplexed on how to get him up.

"Don't worry, Wren. My arm strength is strong enough to get me there, if you go before me and pull me up when you reach the top," Masen said.

It was clear that Iris hadn't followed us, and neither had Felix. But if Iris changed his mind, he could reach us in a matter of seconds.

Wren nodded and walked him to the bars where he firmly placed his hands. I turned away and continued to climb. Wren was quickly at my heels. We all reached the top, but Masen grunted from below. I knew Masen was strong, but it really took all his strength to propel himself upward. When he made it to the last rung, he was breathless. Wren heaved him up and he once again collapsed his weight into Wren.

I wanted to help Masen too. I wanted to help everyone lately, but I was powerless. We all resumed our quick pace even with Wren and Masen lagging a bit behind.

Byrde's voice was getting hoarse, so she switched over to sobs. They were only a little bit quieter. Hopefully this all would end. Hopefully she'd cry herself dry. I knew it sounded insensitive, I just didn't know what to do. I was petrified myself, but it must have been ten times worse for Byrde.

I was lost in my own world and had to be shaken back by Lennon who was shoving a new stunner in my face.

"Everybody take one," he commanded as he dispensed the weapons. He even gave one to Byrde and Carra. Carra... what was she doing? Was she a traitor? Was she a double agent?

"Lennon, stop!" I shouted.

"What, Winslett? We have to take the weapons and get out of here!" he responded.

"That's Iris's daughter you just gave the stunner too!" I cried.

Carra rolled her eyes and it was Masen who answered me, "She's on our side, Wins. Trust me. It was an act. She's coming with us."

Carra still had hold of Byrde and we kept running, finally making it back into the dark tunnels.

"Hang on, everyone," Carra insisted, stopping us in our tracks. "Where does this tunnel lead?"

“It’s a hidden shaft that leads near Hero’s Point,” Masen answered her.

“You’re going to have to fill me in on Hero’s Point, but from what I know, these tunnels have been closed off for a long time.”

“Yeah, we know,” interrupted Lennon. “We took a shuttle to get here.”

“But you still had to walk from the platform to the shuttle,” Carra shot back. “It takes forever to get anywhere through them. And from the state we’re in…” She paused to glance at Masen and readjust Byrde on her back. “The Prime Minister will be sending people after us in no time.”

“So what are you suggesting?” Wren yelled. “Come on, Carra, we’re losing time!”

“I’m suggesting we take a hovercraft.”

Wren pondered the thought, but quickly agreed. “Okay, the garage isn’t too far from here. I know a back entrance.”

He fled in a direction opposite of the tunnels and through a set of doors leading to a clear, winding staircase, all while supporting Masen who was clinging onto his shoulder. We ran after him, through the staircases and through multiple sets of swinging doors. I panted alongside Lennon, who stopped to hold the door for Carra and Byrde.

“How much farther?” groaned Masen.

“Not much, just one more...” Wren replied, pushing yet another door forcefully open.

Slipping past the door, I ran into a huge open space, with the rest of my companions closely behind. I could only guess what lay before me was the government building’s garage. Dozens of hovercrafts had been lined meticulously in number order, all in their impressive black coating.

"Wren?" asked a voice behind Hovercraft 2.

"Jarem, we need to fly out of the headquarters immediately," barked Carra.

"I'm afraid I can't do that," answered the man meekly. He shrunk lower behind the hovercraft.

"Jarem!" yelled Wren.

The man had pulled a communication gadget from his back pocket. "I'm sorry, but you can't leave this time." His voice trembled.

"Don't!" screamed Masen, as Wren shrugged himself loose from Masen's grip and leapt toward Jarem.

I caught Masen from the crook of his elbow before he could roughly collide with the ground.

Wren fumbled with the gadget, trying to swipe it from Jarem's hands. The older man clutched onto the gadget until Wren gave him a hard shove. Jarem smacked onto the ground, wheezing and holding his chest. He looked nastily up toward Wren, but Wren had run for the communication gadget that slid from Jarem's hands and across the garage.

"Lennon, get everyone aboard a hovercraft!" Wren ordered. "Carra, grab the tablet from Jarem's back pocket and get the silver disk from the ring around his belt." He stomped on the communication gadget with a hard crunch as a touch of finality.

Lennon took Masen's weight from under my forearms just as Carra gently handed a whimpering Byrde off to me and onto my back. Carra rushed to push Jarem to the ground again and fish through his pockets. Whipping out the tablet, she handled the device expertly.

Lennon led the three of us from behind into Hovercraft 1.

"Hey!" Carra shouted.

We turned to look as she tossed a silver disk with an engraved “one” on its surface toward our direction. Snatching it from of the air, I nodded once. Lennon put Masen down briefly and pulled the door of the hovercraft open with a loud groan.

“Here, Byrde,” I said, placing her on a seat and buckling her in. She kept her eyes squeezed shut. Stepping in behind her, I held out my arms to grab Masen. Lennon handed him over and I slid him onto a chair next to Byrde.

“Come on.” I gestured to Lennon.

He looked over to Wren, who had grabbed Carra’s hand and was sprinting back to us. Lennon leapt in the hovercraft and held the door open for them both.

“Let’s go!” he shouted, grabbing the silver disk from my outstretched hand.

“Is everyone buckled in?” asked Carra. “I’m driving!”

Wren tossed her the key, and she revved the engine, pounding on the lit buttons.

“Wren, we forgot to retract the roof!” she screamed over the whining motor.

Wren groaned out of frustration, but quickly rose from the passenger seat.

“Over there!” a hoarse voice screamed from a distance.

I whipped my head around and looked out the windows of the hovercraft, searching for the voice.

It was Jarem. He had crawled his way over to his office in the corner of the garage, looking over to a dozen or so officials on top of a set of stairs, pointing their weapons toward us in Hovercraft 1. Iris stood beside them.

“Release fire on my count.”

Sixty-Five

Lennon

Byrde screamed the minute a bullet shot the window of the hovercraft. It had only made an indent, but the scream was still appropriate.

Winslett shut her eyes and slammed her palms against her ears, trembling against the back of her chair. I saw Wren and Carra exchange a worried glance.

"Don't," commanded Wren.

"Don't tell me what to do," Carra snapped back.

Another bullet struck the side of the hovercraft with a great bang, and Byrde cowered lower into her seat. This time, Masen grabbed her little hand and held it to his chest.

Carra forcefully kicked the driver's seat door open, walking out of the vehicle with her hands above her head. Iris immediately commanded the open fire to stop.

"Father, don't do this," she begged.

"How dare you try to command me, Carra." Like father like daughter.

"I'm apologizing. Please stop shooting, and I'll come back to you."

I swallowed a hard lump in my throat as I watched her carefully. A tap on my shoulder shook my attention away from the family drama.

"I'll be right back," Wren whispered to me.

I nodded once and watched him creep behind the row of hovercrafts, toward a red lever not too far from us.

Turning my attention back to Carra and Iris, she continued. "You knew I was in love with Wren, father. I thought that if I could leave with him, I'd have a chance of being with him again."

"You thought wrong," Iris snarled.

"I know. I was foolish. You were right from the beginning. I cannot have both love and power."

Iris seemed to settle down a small fraction. He let out a sigh and released minimal tension in his shoulders.

"What are you proposing I do with the traitors then?"

I snuck a look at Wren, who had made it to the end of the line of hovercrafts. Reaching toward the red lever with an outstretched hand, beads of sweat ran down his face and mine.

"Let them go. They are harmless."

"They plan to use those orbs against me!" His pointer finger grazed over us, twitching slightly.

"You are too powerful for them, father."

"Carra, my sweet child, you must take me as a fool." He turned toward his officials. "Open fire!"

"I do not! Please stop!" Carra screamed, dodging behind the door, escaping the flood of bullets pounding against the vehicle's metal. Before swinging her legs over the seat, she glanced up at the retracting roof.

My heartbeat quickened as I looked back to Wren, releasing the red lever and sprinting back to our direction behind the row of hovercrafts.

"Down there!" Jarem shrieked.

Iris narrowed his eyes to the moving target, growling when he caught sight of Wren. "Get him!"

The fire of bullets quickly switched direction, as Iris commanded his officials to close in on Hovercraft 1. They jogged down the stairs as a unit and sauntered to us, firing at will.

"Wren! Watch out!" Carra screamed.

"Hurry up and circle in around them!" I heard Iris bark, kicking one of the officials roughly in the back.

I looked back to Wren. He was so close now, but Iris was getting closer.

"Go!" Wren yelled as loud as his voice could carry. He was panting madly, and I could see his legs begin to start to buckle beneath him. The exhaustion was killing him.

"What are you saying?" Carra yelled back. "Don't stop!"

Wren shook his head, and motioned for Carra to ride the hovercraft up into the sky.

I crawled to the front of the vehicle and held the door open for him. "You're almost there!" I encouraged.

Wren hit the floor and grasped his upper arm in response.

"He's been hit!" Carra gasped next to me and leapt out after him.

Struggling to stand, he only collapsed again, but this time into Carra's arms. She dragged him toward Hovercraft 1, and I ran out to help her.

"Shoot away!" Iris laughed madly.

I grabbed for Wren's good arm, and hoisted it over my shoulder. Carra strode behind, shielding us from the oncoming officials who had broken into a run.

"We're here," I breathed.

Winslett came to the door of the hovercraft and helped lift the rest of Wren inside and onto the floor of the vehicle. Carra slammed the door behind her as she rushed to position herself in the driver's seat. Yanking a stick shift backward, we ascended into the sky. I looked down through the window of the hovercraft to see Iris and his officials shooting their guns directly below us.

Sixty-Six

Byrde

Masen was holding me like a baby. Only I'm not a baby, I'm an orphan. My face was dry because tears wouldn't fall anymore. I guess I was all out. The Prime Minister of our society had just killed Mommy. Mommy was dead. Mommy was dead… I couldn't stop saying it to myself.

And now Wren was hurt. Masen cradled me and told me to close my eyes, but I couldn't look away. Wren was in so much pain, and I could see it all over his face. He was holding his bloody arm tightly to his chest.

Lennon had ripped off a piece of cloth from the arm of his shirt, and tightly wrapped it around Wren's wound. Wren had told him the bullet had only nicked his arm, but I didn't know what that meant.

I looked at Winslett, who was helping Carra find our way to Hero's Point, but I really didn't want to go anywhere. I wanted a place to cry alone, but there were too many people around, so much dying.

"Incoming!" Carra screamed, her voice shaking.

We looked to the back window of the hovercraft, and I saw more hovercrafts rising into the sky and coming after us. One was flying closely to our right, and another flying closely to our left. We sped over the tops of the forest, over our campgrounds, and over the edge of Laiden.

"Don't worry. We're almost there," Winslett comforted.

I turned back to Wren and picked up his hand.

"I'm sorry, Wren. I'm sorry I let you be caught by the bad men, and I'm sorry you got hurt. I'm sorry I didn't tell you everything," I told him, tears falling quickly from my face. "Please don't die."

He began to laugh, but quickly stopped to wince. "It's only my arm. I'll be okay, blondie. You don't need to apologize for anything."

I squeezed his hand, and leaned into kiss Wren's cheek, just like Daddy used to kiss mine. He smiled at that, and the pain left his face for a moment, almost making me believe I was forgiven.

Sixty-Seven

Winslett

"Guys, stop fussing over him so much. He said he wanted some breathing room," Masen told Lennon and me.

I took a hesitant step from Wren as Lennon helped him to his feet and moved him to the passenger seat next to Carra in the front of the hovercraft.

Wren grunted a thank you, as Carra gave him repeated worried glances.

He caught her long stares. "Eyes on the sky."

Had Carra mentioned something to Iris about being in love with Wren? I eyed them curiously. She chuckled humorlessly and changed the subject. "How are we looking back there?"

"The other hovercrafts don't seem to be advancing on us too much, but they're still coming," Lennon warned.

"It'd be better to land soon, Carra," Wren started. "The last thing we want is to run into the barrier in this huge machine and repel backward a hundred yards."

She nodded and began to descend the vehicle, frequently pressing buttons and turning on lights. "Are we within walking distance?"

Wren nodded. "Yes, but it doesn't hurt to hurry. We need to get beyond the barrier as fast as we can."

I walked over to Masen and rested my hand on his shoulder. "Do you think you'll be okay to stand?"

Byrde removed her buried forehead from the crevice of his shoulder and awaited a response too.

Shifting in his seat uncomfortably, he replied, "I think I'll be fine, not for too long though."

Carra yanked the stick shift of the hovercraft forward, and the vehicle stopped its surge, resuming into a comfortable glide. The whine of the motor began to slow into a groan, as its feet itched to touch the ground.

I looked out the window and saw the grass below, waving furiously against the wind. The hovercraft landed gently, and Carra ran to open the door for Wren. I took hold of Byrde from Masen's grasp, and Lennon took Masen's arm and lifted it over his shoulder. Masen leaned nearly half of his weight against him.

No guards came, but three hovercrafts flew overhead. This was not good.

The six of us did not go undetected. Sirens wailed and Lennon lost hold of Masen, who fell to his knees. Embarrassed, he took hold of Lennon's forearm and Lennon lifted him back to a standing position.

"Back to Hero's Point!" Wren ordered.

Sixty-Eight

Wren

What a disaster. My rag tag group of misfits was falling apart. I had my wounded arm clutched to my chest, and Lennon forcefully dragged Masen along. Masen was in way more pain than I was. Part of me was ashamed that I was annoyed at him for moving the group so slowly. I knew Masen didn't want us to lag behind and he was doing everything in his capability to act like it wasn't so bad. I appreciated his strength, like always.

We had just broken through the trees. For the most part they kept us covered, but from time to time, the undergrowth became sparser, leaving us vulnerable to the hovercrafts that could appear.

I wondered why no one was following us. I was sure the others were too, yet no one was talking. The only noise was our heavy breathing. We were tired, hungry, and scared. But we were alive—that was what I kept telling myself. We also had the two orbs, meaning we could open the barrier if, and when, we reached it. The sound of the hovercrafts grew louder. My hope dwindled. It couldn't be long before they came, and we were too visible. The sun shone down too bright.

Carra caught my sleeve. "Don't worry, Wren, it is going to rain. It'll help conceal our tracks better."

I was about to respond that that was a ludicrous wish. There wasn't a rain cloud in the sky, but then I felt a drop of wetness hit my nose. More rain immediately followed the drop and soon it was a torrential shower. Maybe fate wasn't trying to dupe us. Maybe fate was actually on our side. Nevertheless, though the rain now provided the ultimate coverage from the hovercrafts, it was harder to see where we were going, and it was harder to run in fear of slipping as the hard ground turned to mud.

I heard Carra fiddling around for something. I also heard some mumbling, muted out by the storm. Suddenly there was a small stream of light, her flashlight.

"Carra!" I tried yelling over the rain. "You can't turn that on!"

"They aren't going to see it. The sky is dark, and a little light won't make a difference now," she replied. She was probably right, and we did need it.

I wiped the rain from my eyes.

I couldn't hear the hovercrafts anymore, but I doubted they were gone. This rain had come on too fast to last a long while. Surely the officials were waiting for their opportunity. Extium would have no survivors.

Sixty-Nine

Masen

It was going too fast and too slow all at the same time, and I was still trying to figure out how. My leg was numb in parts and excruciatingly painful in others. I wasn't helping Wren at all, and I knew we wouldn't make it much further especially with this rain. The rain was turning the ground to mud and I couldn't keep pace.

I pushed through the pain though, not wanting to fall behind the others. But then it happened. The ground was muddy and unlevel to begin with, and I fell down hard, taking Lennon with me.

The others had to halt their run as we scrambled to get up. I held back a cry. My wound now stung and Carra shone the light quickly upon it. I wished she hadn't. Winslett covered her mouth in shock and even Lennon winced. I didn't blame them.

Wren gritted his teeth. "We have to keep on going, and fast." He looked to the sky where the hovercrafts were surely hidden behind the haze. I could read his mind. I could read all of their minds. I was a burden.

"Thanks," I muttered to Lennon.

Winslett ran up with Wren, and the sprint continued.

I was surprised that no one complained to take a rest. I knew we couldn't afford one, but I sure needed it. I was honestly afraid I would collapse.

The rain was still heavy, but the sky was a light shade of gray where a sliver of daylight shone. It was in that spot of the sky that I saw a beam shine through. It was a clear beam from a hovercraft. Byrde started crying again and I heard Winslett soothe her as she continuously glanced down, trying not to trip, while carrying Byrde.

I heard a rustling of footsteps behind me as the wind sped up. I looked back, but there was no one in sight.

I summoned my strength and yelled over the raging storm. "I think someone is coming!"

Wren heard me. He stopped and turned around, his eyes wide in a craze.

Winslett kept running, but halted when she finally noticed Wren was no longer beside her.

"No one was following us on foot!" I heard her yell back, but her voice wavered.

Now was not the time to fight, though. We had already spent precious time pausing to assess the situation. This time, I was not the only one who heard the rustling.

"He's right," Carra said. "They've gotten closer."

She bolted with Byrde, knowing we would all take the clue to follow, but I couldn't get my feet moving. Lennon, in a moment of panic, forgot about my leg and pulled me along too fast.

Once again, I fell to the ground. My face was immersed in the mud and I couldn't find the surface. When my lungs finally found air, it was my eyes' turn to fail me. I couldn't see anyone. Had they abandoned me in the attempt to save themselves?

I tried to get up, but this time, I couldn't. It was like my body was in a horizontal state, and didn't want to try anymore. Part of me whispered to myself to stay lying there, that it was an okay time to go. The world didn't need me here and the others could make it without me. Now that I was crippled, I wasn't really aiding anyone. I could lie in the sodden ground until the end came. Then I heard her voice.

"Masen." The call of my name was barely audible.

A pair of rough hands hoisted me up. A wet sleeve then scraped against my eyes, returning my sight. I looked upon Winslett. Her hair was caked in blood and mud. Her face was dirty and cut. I felt hazy still and wobbled once more. But Lennon's hands, the ones who had returned my sense, pulled me back into a sprint. The six of us began running again. Too much time had been lost, and this time, when I looked behind me, I saw an outline of two dark figures.

We weren't even slow, and running faster, if even humanly possible would not help us now. An odd mixture of salt and dirt rested on my tongue. Oh dear god, I was crying. Man, I was turning into a wimp. But all I could think about was Winslett. If she could get away, I would sacrifice us all. Instinct. Sometimes you had to put someone you cared about before you. For me, that someone was Winslett, and I'd put her before anyone.

Crunch.

Branches were breaking all around Lennon and me. I looked back for the third time and I could see some subtle features of the two officials' faces now. They raised a shadow of a gun, from what I could make out. There was too much rain to see the details of the two men's mouths, but I imagined them laughing hysterically.

Lennon hissed, "Keep going!"

"Don't you see that behind us?"

He turned to glance. "All I see is rain."

"No! That's not true!" I protested. Had I been hallucinating? Were the officials only a figure of my imagination?

We had already run a far distance. It had been so long that whatever sun the morning had shown us, wasn't just behind the clouds, was gone altogether.

Winslett ran back to us as Wren, Carra, and Byrde continued at a pace I no longer thought possible.

"You guys okay?" she urged meaningfully to both of us. Lennon reached out and stroked her face.

"I'm sorry you got hurt," he said, never taking his eyes off of her.

"We all got hurt," she replied.

"It was my fault though," he responded, and I could hear the pain rise in his voice.

"Lennon, I'm fine. There was nothing you could've done. It could have been much worse."

"You almost lost your sight."

A chill went up my spine.

"But I didn't," she said curtly.

He nodded his head and she squeezed his hand. She gave me one last look, and it was one of pity. I did not like that look at all.

"Wins," I cried before she ran back to Wren.

"Save your energy," she admonished between ragged breaths.

I beamed, though I knew my own breaths were just as staggered. "What are you talking about? I've got loads of energy!"

Lennon cut me off. "Guys!" he screamed. "There's the shaft door we took to the shuttle. We should be nearing Hero's Point soon!"

I took a mental note of the familiar, vine-covered door I had cut my forearm against.

"I recognize it too!" Winslett yelled across the rain, a shrill in her voice.

"I have no idea where I'm going," Carra panted. "Winslett, you lead us."

"It should be close," Winslett said. "The orbs should glow when we are there."

Just as she said it, a blue glow emitted from the figures of Byrde and Winslett. The orbs.

It seemed that we had reached the barrier with the keys at long last, and even the rain was beginning to quickly let up.

And you know what? For once I had a little faith in something.

Seventy

Lennon

Winslett held her hand out for us all to see that the orb had glowed increasingly brighter.

"Ouch!" Winslett and Byrde exclaimed in unison.

Winslett dropped the orb to the ground, leaving a scorched mark in her skin. We all watched her as she shook her hand violently.

I quickly untied the orb from Byrde's neck and handed her the string.

"Guys, look." Carra had interrupted my train of thought.

The orbs were glowing brighter and brighter until the whole place held a tinge of blue.

"What's going on? This is because of the orbs, isn't it?" Carra pointed out.

"Way to state the obvious," Masen mumbled and Carra shot him a glare.

Byrde whispered, "Three will free. Two will open. One will point you in the right direction."

"Two orbs will bring down the barrier. But, probably only temporarily," Wren warned.

The glow was soft, and nothing happened. The barrier was still there. It was unnerving.

The whole gang looked to Wren, but he had his eyes trained upward.

I squeezed Byrde's shoulder reassuringly. And for the first time I stopped to really look at her. This kid had been through a hell of a lot. Those brown eyes were no longer the scared, innocent doe eyes I had first met. They had witnessed death and experienced the fears and the tortures of being a fugitive. The scars on her face were there to prove it. I opened my arms to give her a hug and she fell into them. I smoothed her dirty, mangled blonde hair. I squeezed my arms around her fit but skinny body gently, and pulled her into a closer embrace.

I glanced up to look at the sky, like Wren. I knew I was only several feet away from the invisible barrier that would free us from Laiden's looming government and keep us safe from the intense watch of Iris. This was it. The Outlanders were behind this wall.

Wren and I both had our eyes fixed upon a quivering blur. Was the barrier slowly unraveling? We kept waiting for more to happen, each with our own set of expectations. To be honest, I was looking forward to a brilliant flash of light or a startling eruption, but none came.

A bead of sweat dripped down my face and my hands moistened. I had to readjust Masen several times. I didn't want any hovercrafts reaching us before we could cross the barrier.

Just like that, an intense ripple of color swallowed the barrier, making it visible. It was as if someone had poured a vat of oil all over Laiden's walls, creating a surreal rainbow-ish tint that slowly melted the barrier away, blurring the projection of trees and wildlife. It was an almost beautiful sight. A slow shiver rose up my spine and I braced myself for the other side.

Byrde backed away and stood with Wren and Carra, as the barrier melted away to meet the earth. The blue glow dissipated.

My heart pounded as the blur of the fake landscape began to clear. I heard a gasp escape from Carra's lips and froze. My journey since the arrival of Extium and apart from Laiden had officially come around a full circle. Just as I had met Wren in the woods, I was welcomed with a deadly greeting of ten massive men and their guns.

PART 4: The Resistance

Seventy-One

Wren

I swept my hand down to pick up the two fallen orbs and swiftly placed them in my pocket before throwing my hands up in the air in surrender.

With a quick glance around, I saw Carra, Lennon, Masen, Winslett, and Byrde following suit and staying silent.

I took a step forward. "I am Wren Casterra. My friends and I mean no harm in coming here."

No one responded, but I remained in a confident stance. A gruff man with a thick brown mustache grunted and nodded to another shorter plump man with a rather thick gray beard.

The men ranged in age from twenty-five to the oldest being somewhere in his sixties. They were all very muscular, surely more built than Masen, Lennon, or I. These had to be the Outlanders… and maybe, the Resistance.

The man with the beard grunted and said, "Well I can't say I thought this would happen in my time. Now that it has, I don't suppose we can do nothing but take you fellows in."

"Follow us, Wren Casterra, and friends," said another man from the crowd, nodding toward Byrde, whose arms were still tightly wrapped around Carra's cat-like uniform, her head buried into Carra's long braid. I then looked at Masen, whose arm was soon swept over the sturdy shoulders of the man with the brown facial hair. Masen leaned against him willingly, too exhausted to argue, as the man supported his weight easily. I felt gratitude toward him. Clearly they weren't intending to hurt us, rather they were merely sizing up who we were and why we had come.

Lennon looked relieved and sauntered over to me. Winslett stayed by Masen's side while we all walked, now surrounded by the small army of men. Somehow, I felt oddly at peace, whether it was because we had reached our intended destination over these several weeks or that I was simply relieved to leave my rotting state in the government cell, I wasn't sure.

"So, after all this time, the Outlanders were right here," Lennon stated, interrupting my thoughts.

"I guess so," I mustered.

"And they could see us?"

"I guess so."

"So they saw us before, when we were at Hero's Point?"

"Maybe."

"You okay, Wren?" Lennon asked me.

"Sorry, Lennon, you know just as well as me what a long day it has been. For once, I am not in the mood to find out answers. I just want to let things happen."

"So you don't think we should be worried then?" Lennon chuckled. "Sorry. Right, no more questions."

"It's okay. I'm sure more will come soon enough."

Lennon smirked. "Okay, well just answer me one." I rolled my eyes purposefully, but knew I'd be answering the kid's question. "What do you think they know about us?"

"More than we think."

He nodded solemnly and walked back to Winslett, eyeing the guns suspiciously and taking up a protective guard.

Carra, who began talking in a rapid whisper because of Byrde, quickly replaced Lennon's spot next to me.

"Wren," she said in an accusing tone, "what are you doing trusting them so easily? There were ten large men pointing guns at us and you think it's a good idea to not even ask why and willingly follow them?"

"Carra," I started, "we crossed the barrier and this is what we found. This is what we wanted to find. If they meant us harm they could've hurt us twenty times over by now."

She glowered, but I knew she felt I was right. "I just hope we get wherever they want us to go, soon."

"Me too," I assured her.

We walked in silence. Clearly we were all lost in individual thoughts and working out individual worries. The last few hours were a daze that made little sense, but I was beyond questioning it. I selfishly wished I could just sit down.

The man carrying Masen grunted again and said, "Almost there."

"Almost where, exactly?" I questioned in the manner my old self would have. I realized that perhaps I couldn't lead my friends into the unknown so blindly.

He looked smug, but not in the same conniving manner that the government officials did. "I think you know, Mr. Casterra."

It was Winslett's turn to delve into the strange scenario we had landed ourselves in. "Are you the Resistance?"

"Not here girl, not here," the man said in a rushed mutter.

Lennon dared to speak again, but the man had already continued. "I can promise we will get everything sorted out once we reach the village. I fear the worst is about to begin."

Masen then came out of his groggy daze. I hadn't thought he had processed much of anything. "Then why aren't we running?" he asked.

The man gave a hearty laugh. "They are going to come, and whether or not we arrive a few minutes early won't matter, my boy."

"Fair enough," Masen said as he grimaced with what was probably an attempt at a smile. "You're not worried though?"

"Worried?" the kindly man retorted. "We've been waiting."

"You knew we were coming, didn't you?" Lennon asked dryly.

The man looked at him rather quizzically and shook his head without a response.

I held Carra's all-knowing gaze once more. I was beginning to doubt my first instinct of blind trust, yet the options were few. We escaped death of the free-willed mind and we escaped death at the hands of Iris. If death were to find us here, far from the place we once called home, then I welcomed the chance to escape it once again. I would see my mission out to the end.

The ten burly men gracefully stepped over all the undergrowth like seasoned journeyers. The rest of us stumbled embarrassingly through all the twists and turns of the thickening forest.

We turned a sharp bend and I saw some of the men's arms slacken.

"Welcome," I heard one say.

Seventy-Two

Masen

The camp of the Outlanders wasn't what I expected, not that there was something I was expecting. It was an extremely small-scaled society. I had to keep blinking my eyes open to see, not wanting to faint just yet from the pain. I was tired of feeling this inferior, but the robust man who helped me support my own weight was friendly enough. He had told me Brock was his name and reassured me that they were the Resistance. We had made it after all this time.

There were about sixteen cabin-like homes forming a semicircle in front of us. A large bonfire glowed brightly in the middle. Women and children alike ran around playing and chatting. They ate things I had never seen before. They wore outfits different from the plain drab one's Laiden provided for us, and I could see the many different styles as they were hung out to dry on various strings. Life seemed different here. It seemed good.

A woman of about forty sauntered out of the first cabin and over to Brock, kissing him on the cheek. My thoughts immediately drifted to Winslett and me. I wondered if we could ever make a life here, together.

Brock smiled, looked to her, and said, "Honey, look what we've found."

Her face darkened in concern, but then brightened just as instantly. Her smile gave me such a warm feeling of security that I had to return it.

"This is Masen," Brock introduced. "And Masen, this is my wife, Eden." She had faded blonde hair and rosy cheeks to match Brock's. They had to have been married at least twenty years, and still looked in love.

"What happened to you, Masen?" she asked politely.

"Ack- I- don't," I mumbled, finally fading somewhat.

"I don't know either, hun, but it looks bad," Brock said in my stead.

"Bring him to our cabin, dear, and I can get Doc to help me fix him up," she ensured.

Brock nodded and good-heartedly signaled to the other man with the thick gray beard and wrinkled eyes. The man with the beard stood quickly from his seat, and sauntered over to me. Although he looked decades older than Brock, he seemed just as mobile.

He held out a wrinkled, calloused hand for me to shake. "Hendrick is the name," he introduced, grinning boyishly.

Wren looked over and stopped us, as I figured he would. "Hey, where are you taking him?"

Brock politely responded, "He is in a grave condition as I'm sure you've realized. We are having a doctor look at him."

Wren eyed me and I think I tried to nod. Whatever happened, he let me go.

Hendrick winked. "Now ain't you be worrying, Masen. I'll take a right good care of your friends here."

I heard Wren begin to talk, but what he said I would never know…

I awoke to an indescribably pleasant, but unfamiliar smell. Blinking my eyes open, I looked around a cozy, clean room. A small fire pit was built in the corner, and the walls and floors had been made with wood. I lay in a comfortable bed with a quilted blanket covering bundles of hay that acted similarly to a mattress. My leg had been elevated and wrapped in white gauze I had only seen in government-issued health buildings in the Square. Wow, I had been gone a long time. My hair was damp with sweat, but I felt immensely better and the pain had diminished almost completely.

Eden walked in with a smoking mug of the pleasant smelling stuff.

"This is coffee, with some milk," she explained. "It should warm you up, give you a speck of energy, and it tastes good too." Her smile was warm and motherly. It had been a long time since someone had acted this way toward me.

"Thank you," I said with a twinge of awkwardness because I was being coddled so much.

"Are you feeling better?" she asked as I took a sip of the dark liquid. It tasted creamy and sweet with just a touch of bitterness. It wasn't something you could drink in gulps, but every sip left me wanting more. It was wonderful and warmed me down to my bones.

"Much, I can barely feel any pain."

"That'll be the pain meds kicking in."

I hastily tried to get up.

Eden rushed to gently push me back down. "Where do you think you're going?"

"My friends… my friends…" I muttered.

"Your friends are all fine and are speaking to Brock, Hendrick, and a few other villagers. It doesn't concern you now. You need your strength back."

"But…"

"But nothing, Masen. The pain will flare back up in an hour or so and you'll need more medication. Just take a moment and relax." She took my mug and told me she would fetch some more coffee.

I gazed out the window in Eden and Brock's cabin. I could make out Winslett's wispy red hair and Carra's long braid. I wondered how much they were telling these people. Part of me wished they would tell them everything. We could not take down Iris by ourselves. This was the Resistance and they would help... right?

I just wanted to be with them. Had they so swiftly moved on to configure a game plan? Or did they even know that these people were truly the Resistance?

Eden returned with the coffee and another treat. She called it a chocolate chip cookie. I tucked half of it away to share later with Winslett, if I could.

"Get some more rest," Eden ordered me, and I heeded her words, quickly falling back into the calmest sleep I'd had in months.

Seventy-Three

Byrde

A few of the bigger men moved us closer to the glowing flames. Wren introduced our family, but I got a feeling that when he said my name, the others already knew who I was.

We waited calmly, waiting for them to speak first, and they did.

"We are the Resistance. I'm Hendrick," a fat old man said. "The man who just left is Brock. The two of us run things 'round here."

He eyed up Wren, like he already knew his strong personality might mean trouble.

A few of the other men stayed around Hendrick, probably curious about us too.

"We want to hear your story of course, but a lot we have already guessed. We want you to feel at ease here. You're one of us now," Hendrick told us, with a smile that didn't leave his eyes. "The Resistance has been alive for as long as Iris came into power, and since then, both our concern for Laiden and our fear toward its monarchy have grown stronger. Not only have I been a leader of the Resistance for many decades, but I was also the brother to an original starter of our group, Zakarias. Zak is Byrde's grandfather."

I rubbed my tired eyes at the sound of his words. Had I heard them right? Hendrick picked me up and sat me on his knee. He was Daddy's Daddy's brother. He was my real family.

I wrapped my arms around him in a hug. He felt warm.

"It's nice to finally meet you, Byrde."

"You too," I whispered. The others were watching us. Winslett looked happy for me.

Hendrick started to talk to the others again. "My family, Byrde's family, has always been involved in the Resistance." He smiled down at me again. "Her grandfather, Zakarias, was one of the three original starters of the Resistance, a constructor of the orbs."

"Three orbs, three men…" Winslett whispered aloud.

"Yes, Winslett," Uncle Hendrick said. "One orb, you have told me Byrde possessed, helped you find the secret entrance to the government. That was Zak's idea. Two orbs together temporarily unlock the barrier. That's how ya'll got here."

Wren had guessed this.

Uncle Hendrick continued, "It takes three orbs to break it."

"Three will free. Two will open. One will point you in the right direction," Wren recited.

Hendrick nodded. "Steffan's song."

I smiled at the sound of Daddy's name.

"So where is the third?" Lennon mused.

Uncle Hendrick readjusted me, and out from his shirt pocket he pulled a sparkly blue orb that matched the one dangling around my neck. I smiled as he did, and I heard Winslett and Carra gasp behind me.

"Now that you have come with the other two orbs, the Resistance has in its possession all three orbs. We can now, thanks to you, break the barrier."

Lennon opened his mouth again. "You just said the Resistance had all three, but we still have two."

Uncle Hendrick good-heartedly chortled. "My boy, do you not think yourself to be a part of the Resistance?"

I smiled and so did Lennon. Daddy would be proud of me, and Grandpa Zakarias. Just like them, I was now a part of the Resistance.

"I guess so," Lennon said.

Winslett chimed in, "Mr. Hendrick, I'm still confused though. How is it that the orbs were made? And that Zakarias ended up here while Byrde's father was inside Laiden with Reina?"

I scrunched my eyebrows together. I never thought about how Daddy and Grandfather were separated, and now I was curious.

"You can just call me Hendrick, Winslett. But, it is a right fair question. And I'm sure Byrde is just as curious." He paused for a brief moment. "Long before the barrier was constructed, Zak was in cahoots with the Resistance, the original anti-government coup."

"I'm sorry Hendrick, but how was the Resistance discovered? I thought the entire group was kept a secret," Wren interrupted.

Hendrick nodded. "Our original members continued to explore unregistered Laiden territory, and Iris decided that enough was enough." He cleared his throat. "When word was let out about the possible construction of a barrier, the Resistance started work on the orbs. The first orb Zak gave to your father, Byrde, and so it was left inside Laiden. The second fell into the hands of a member of the Resistance who turned his back to us and gave into the power of the government, which is, as you now suspect, how it came to be with Iris. The last orb we had here, waiting for the day all three were returned." Uncle Hendrick breathed and we waited for him to finish. I loved listening to him talk. Having him here made me feel like I was with Daddy, or maybe even Mommy.

"The barrier sprang up suddenly and it happened the day Zak and I were deep into the undiscovered territory. He was going home back to his wife and son, but, of course, the barrier would not let him. Later on, his wife realized what must have happened and she joined a force of people who were a secret, inside-the-barrier type of resistance." He then looked at me. "Your father and mother were a part of that. Your grandfather left many notes and letters inside his house for Steffan, explaining everything in case he was ever killed or separated somehow. That is how your father came to know all he did, and helped tell you what he could."

It kind of made sense to me, what Uncle Hendrick said, and I was proud of my Daddy that he knew who the bad men were.

Everyone was nodding at Uncle Hendrick and I think they were proud of Daddy too.

"Speaking of things that had been written, I have one more thing for you, Byrde." Uncle Hendrick reached in his pocket once again. He pulled out a folded, yellowed envelope stained brown in some places. He held it out to me.

From the envelope was another folded sheet of paper dyed the same kind of yellow. It was not crisp, but soft when I touched it. It was a letter from Grandpa to Daddy. I read it and it felt like I heard his voice in his last couple words.

Connect the dots, child. When the time is right, your destiny will be certain. The dreams the Resistance had, can still come true. Wish on the stars, my son—they will always guide you. There is no doubt in my mind that you will make me proud.

Always,
Your father

I would have cried if I had had any tears left. I touched my sockets and they were dry.

I passed it around for the others to read and perhaps things made sense to them now too. Daddy had taught me all about the stars and Perseus for the reason we had thought. He was the reason we found the orbs and made it across to the rest of our family. Daddy truly was the best.

Wren was the last to read it. He folded it, and handed it back to me. I held the letter to my heart and looked to the sky. I was hoping Daddy and Grandpa Zak could see me.

"So now what, if we have all the three orbs?" Wren asked.

"We break the barrier of course," Uncle Hendrick said, poking my stomach, sending me into a fit of giggles. I think I liked it here.

Seventy-Four

Lennon

Hendrick had stayed silent as he listened intently to Wren, who gave him a full rundown of the past month.

"And her?" Hendrick asked Wren, after he had finished, gesturing toward Carra.

"You didn't explain how you had met up with her," Hendrick pointed out.

Wren hesitated, pulling at his shirt and fumbling with his words. I looked at Winslett who was fiddling with her nails and Byrde who stayed silent. I turned to Carra, who looked annoyed and rolled her eyes.

"Why don't I just introduce myself?" She frowned at us.

She looked up at Hendrick and began, "I met Wren while working in the government building. After Wren and I had planned to leave Laiden, we were separated for a brief time until I found him being kept in one of the government cells. I helped him escape with the rest of them."

"Anything else you're not telling me, by the looks of everyone's faces?" Hendrick questioned, looking at all of us.

I swallowed the lump forming in the middle of my throat.

"Oh yeah, Prime Minister Iris is my father," Carra answered casually, looking at her nails.

I looked up at Hendrick, along with Wren, to see his expression. He seemed irritated, but calmer than I would have expected.

I decided to help her case. "Before you say anything, we all thought through the same things, and we've all had the same suspicions. But we can trust Carra. She is nothing like Iris and wants to help Laiden and us, not hurt it."

Wren nodded in approval and squeezed Carra's hand.

Hendrick's face seemed to simmer down a bit, but still looked at Carra disapprovingly.

Winslett changed the subject. "But, Hendrick, it still doesn't make sense how Extium didn't work on us. How was it possible?"

Hendrick cleared his throat and answered, "Well, years later after the barrier had been built and the whole fixation with the Resistance took place, Iris had been getting finicky. There were rumors within the government of him wanting to create some sort of memory wiping, brainwashing device. Of course, the whole idea seemed preposterous, even though nobody said anything."

Hendrick paused to collect his thoughts. "However, Byrde's father, Steffan, was wary of these rumors and the brilliant scientist he was, created a sort of hope… an insurance, more like, in case something were to ever happen… in which it did." He glanced at Wren.

Wren had turned red and suddenly found the grass beneath his feet much more interesting.

"What did he do?" Carra urged on, intrigued.

Hendrick nodded. "There happened to be complications from several mothers who were not able to give a natural birth. Steffan, having the knowledge about the Resistance from his mother, used these similar aged surrogates from these mothers to alter their genetic material, the components needed to create such a pill wouldn't be able to affect their babies, which you can probably guess by now are Lennon, Winslett, and Masen, since Extium obviously didn't worked on them." Hendrick gestured toward us and I gulped, containing my shock to listen to the rest of his story.

Hendrick looked around at all of us as we watched him with intent curiosity and continued, "Having a drug that may not work with a patient's genotype is known as 'pharmacogenomics.' It took years of research from a team of doctors and scientists, led by Steffan. In most cases, when a drug does not match up with a patient's genes, it is a mistake and needs to be altered. But in this case, Steffen wanted to ensure it. Of course, he never knew if this could possibly work from the genetic makeup he had created. He never found out in his lifetime."

"So what, we were an experiment?" asked Winslett harshly.

"I understand that you may be upset. And you have a right to be. Again, Steffan understood the possibility that Iris could create such a mind molder. These children would not be affected by it, but instead, they could eventually find us, the Resistance, and help save Laiden," Hendrick explained. "So, as a matter of fact, we've been waiting for ya'll."

"Surely he must've known the danger he put these kids in? It's pretty unethical," Wren stated.

"And I would agree with you. It would automatically have put a target on these youngster's backs. But, you see, this was a far, far reach. So much so that Steffan even doubted it would work. It is a miracle that it did, and if you look at the outcome now, I'm sure you're glad it happened. Laiden actually has a future now because of you kids." Hendrick replied.

He acknowledged Brock, who had just walked into the room and added, "You should also know that there were four mothers that were unable to give birth, but the fourth child Steffen altered died during childbirth, along with its mother."

I sat dazed as questions ran through my head. There could have been another one of us? It was known I would find the Resistance? My future had been mapped out before I had been born?

Hendrick read my mind. "I wish to give you all more time to think about this now, but we need to focus on the present. This place will never be the same."

Seventy-Five

Winslett

"Winslett?" Lennon asked from behind me.

I turned and smiled into his encapsulating stare. The golden flakes were as prominent as ever.

He took my hand. "I wanted to ask if you were okay, you know, with the whole surrogate mother thing?"

I grimaced uneasily. "I'm not sure yet. I know Steffan was only trying to help, but the entire idea of being an experiment is still unsettling. Wren was right. Our lives had been put in danger before we could even begin them."

"That's true, but you know, if our genes hadn't been the ones chosen to be altered, this would've never happened," Lennon said, motioning around the Outlander's territory. He drew closer, wrapping his arms around me, and I could feel his cool sweet breath on my neck. "And I wouldn't have been able to meet this incredible girl. You know, the one with fiery, red hair and beautiful gray eyes. You wouldn't happen to know her, would you?" He tickled the sides of my waist, and I squirmed out of his hold to return a smile.

Wren walked over from behind us, doing a poor job of trying to hide the smirk that ran across his face. "So this happened while I was gone?"

Lennon reddened slightly. "We were doing some discussing of our own."

"About Extium?" Wren asked.

Lennon's jaw tightened a bit. "No, but speaking of... do you know if you'll be able to reverse it?"

Wren cleared his throat. "I can't be sure. When I was working back in the lab, Iris had never requested me to create a way to possibly reverse Extium's power. I never gave it any thought. I can try to make a legitimate substance the citizens could take to remove Extium's effects immediately, but it seems pretty unlikely. Our best bet is to make some sort of medication that will alter their DNA to repel the mind molder."

"I need to write this down," he mumbled. "I'll see you guys later. I need talk to Hendrick." He shuffled quickly from us, Carra following closely behind.

I turned my face back to Lennon and sighed. "I need to go check on Masen."

His face fell and I knew he was disappointed.

"I'm sorry."

"Don't be sorry," he said, but his golden eyes were sad. "He's your best friend. You should see how he is doing."

I nodded and called to Carra, "I'm going to go check on Masen, okay?"

It was Brock who answered me though, with his big rosy-cheeked smile. “That’s a good idea.” He pointed to a cabin to the far right. “He is in that one with my wife.”

It was so nice here in the Outlanders mini society. It was different than Laiden had ever been. I got warm smiles from everyone. I tossed a young boy his ball back as it rolled down to my feet.

I hesitantly knocked on the door of the cabin and it opened slowly by whom I could only guess to be Brock’s wife. Such an odd thing it was to do. In Laiden, it would’ve been considered impolite to knock on the door of someone’s house you didn’t know.

“Hello, you must be Winslett,” she said.

“Yes, that’s me.”

“Masen spoke so fondly of you. He’s sleeping, but feel free to wait next to him.”

I stepped inside her cozy home and spotted Masen sleeping peacefully on a bed. He always looked happier in sleep. It brought a smile to my face.

“Thank you,” I told the lady. I sat down at the foot of the couch near Masen’s head and placed my hand on top of his, waiting for him to wake up.

Seventy-Six

Masen

I was having the best dream. Winslett's stormy gray eyes were alight with sparkles and they were staring straight at me.

"How do you feel?" she cooed.

"Better, now," I told her.

"You've been asleep a while," she told me, and I realized I was no longer dreaming. She was actually here.

"Wins, I have something for you!" I exclaimed.

She laughed, not expecting the sudden burst of enthusiasm.

I pulled out half of the cookie I had saved for her.

"It's called a chocolate chip cookie."

Eyes wide with wonder, she split it in another two and gave me back half. We both ate it. "Mmmm," she told me.

I noticed Eden in the corner of the room smiling at us. We both turned around and I didn't hesitate in asking for what I wanted. I got the feeling she liked this role of caretaker.

"Eden?" I asked.

"I'll be right back with two cups of coffee and a plate of cookies," she said and disappeared. It was unreal she knew exactly what I needed. I pictured this was what it was like to have a parent who loved you.

"Coffee?" Winslett asked. "Is that something you eat too?"

"No, but trust me, you'll like it."

Eden came back quickly and Winslett actually did not like the coffee. Eden shrugged and said, "Don't worry, it isn't a taste for everyone."

She left us alone after that, and Winslett and I enjoyed a good six cookies each.

"You don't realize how much Laiden didn't have until you come to a place like this," I told her.

"Evelyn would love this," she mused. She didn't say this with regret, but in an uplifting way, in a way that was optimistic that one day Evelyn would be here too.

"Thanks for coming to keep me company, Winslett," I told her.

"I couldn't let you have all the fun!"

"Fun!" I scoffed.

We smiled at each other, just staring into the other's eyes and it felt right. I dared to say what I was feeling. "You know I love you, right?"

"I know," she replied after a minute or so, in a tone that was different from what I knew. It seemed genuinely torn.

"You're going to have to choose eventually," I persisted sadly.

"Not today. Let's just focus on now."

I didn't want to push her, or make her aggravated at me for doing so. I really was happy she came here and I was happy to just have time away from Lennon and be with her.

Her cool lips met my forehead and I sighed. I felt part of her knew this was how it was supposed to be.

I changed the subject. "So tell me what you all have been up to? What's happening out there?"

Winslett quickly fell back into a regular conversation and began filling me in on what the Resistance was and what we were all about to do. Yet, as she was speaking I couldn't look away from her soft pink lips forming word after word, and I couldn't stop imagining how they would feel moving against mine.

Seventy-Seven

Wren

"So you really think it can be done?" Carra asked Brock.

"We have all three orbs and from what you have told us, Laiden has grown worse than we feared. We must proceed with a plan to reverse Extium, or as Wren discussed with Hendrick earlier, alter the citizens' genotypes to repel Extium's effects. Either way, we do not have the resources available beyond the border for such advanced technology. Wren said himself that he needs his tools and research from the research lab in the government building. Therefore, our mission must be a team effort. While Wren and some of our best healers make their way back to the government building, our strongest men and women will be put on guard to defend Wren and his research process from any interruptions," Brock said assertively.

"Like government officials and the Prime Minister Iris!" Byrde piped up.

Brock nodded and continued, “Hendrick and some of the older Resistance members have agreed to break the barrier with the orbs and guide some of Laiden’s citizens into our territory, just as a safer refuge away from Iris. The preparations are still in the process of completion.”

“Do we really have the manpower here?” I questioned.

Brock answered, “From what you’ve told us all, the only real people that pose a threat to us are the most high of government officials.”

“Yes, but the Prime Minister, because of Extium, has the power to make the citizens into an army at a moment’s notice if he so desired,” Carra spoke my thoughts, but it was odd to hear her speak of her father in such a detached way.

I wanted to talk to her more than anything, to hold her, to brush her hair behind her ear like I used to. It had to have been hard to see her father act the way he did.

“True,” Lennon began to respond to Carra’s statement, “but I don’t think he would. I think no matter what Prime Minister Iris will always underestimate the Resistance. He thinks too much of himself.”

Brock nodded in assent. “I believe the boy.”

“I’m feeling more optimistic than usual, that is for sure. The Resistance knows a lot, a lot more than I thought they ever would,” Carra amended.

“Yes, we have been planning this siege for years now. We also had the hopes of seeing Steffan’s pre-altered genotype children burst through the barrier, guided by our clues,” Brock continued.

I looked around my rag-tag group of delinquents and chuckled.

"We'll be needing Hendrick back," Brock laughed along. He got up and approached the old man. Little Byrde was still giggling.

"I'm happy she can be happy for just even a moment," Carra told me.

"I know. She seems to have been dealt all the wrong cards." I shook my head.

"But now she has Hendrick, and all of us. We won't be going anywhere once the barrier is broken forever you know." I smiled at her and she continued. "I'm not going anywhere, Wren."

Lennon awkwardly moved away to join Brock, Byrde, and Hendrick. They were trying to get Byrde to cooperate in taking a nap, and she jokingly ran around, dodging their clumsy grasps.

I moved closer to Carra and grazed her face. Her eyes were unwavering. It had been a long time since I was this close to her and once again I could see the soft sprinkling of freckles across her cheeks that reminded me that she was in fact human and that this was not, in fact, a dream.

"Never again," I whispered as I twirled her tangled hair through my fingers.

She placed her palm on my chest and I ran my fingers down her smooth cheek. We enjoyed the moment and then I closed my eyes and went the last step. Our lips melded against each other and it felt natural, like it had those many weeks ago. She tasted sweet and fresh and I didn't want to break away from her, but as her hand fell from my chest I knew we had to.

We broke apart and a small smile graced her face.

"You two about ready to go then?" Hendrick asked innocently.

I cleared my throat, highly embarrassed that he had witnessed our private moment. "Sounds good to us."

The four others walked in front of us as we headed to Brock's cabin where Masen and Winslett waited.

I knew no one could see us, but I wasn't sure that it mattered even if they could. I linked Carra's hand through mine as we neared the threshold.

Only Brock entered though, and I heard some muffled talking from within.

"I like this," Carra said letting her guard down a little.

I smiled. "I think I'm just starting to realize how different it will all be, once Iris goes down."

"It won't be Laiden anymore."

"I don't want Laiden."

"What do you want, Wren?"

"I want you and me, and I want it forever, Carra." I drew her close for another kiss. The feel of her lips lingered as she pulled away.

"In that case," she said with smoldering eyes, "we better get preparing."

At that moment, Brock exited the cabin with his wife and Winslett, who held onto Masen's arm as he mostly propped himself up on what looked like a wooden staff.

He was smiling. No, he was grinning his wolfish grin ear to ear.

"Masen!" exclaimed Byrde, giving him a hug.

"Hey, blondie," he said, ruffling her hair.

"Have you met my uncle?" she squealed, running back to hug Hendrick.

"Nice to meet you, officially that is, sir," Masen said with a kind of respect he would never muster toward me.

"You as well." He took Byrde's little hand and started walking away.

"Where are they off to?" inquired Carra.

Brock answered, "Oh just to the bonfire. I have called a meeting for the entire Outlander population."

We followed them and watched as fifty or more people came out of the cabins and the nearest forests to gather around as a unit.

It was eerily like the town meeting Iris used to hold, except I could tell people were genuinely happy to gather. There was an ease that was not felt in Laiden. There was freeness. It was a place where not only could you speak your mind, but what you said actually mattered.

Lennon joined Winslett and Masen. He leaned to whisper something in her ear, but I couldn't hear what. Carra and I went to join the three, and we all strayed toward the front of the crowd. A sea of friendly faces swarmed us.

Brock and Hendrick stood on a small platform next to the raging fire. Byrde was at Hendrick's side. I waved and her little hand answered me.

"Hello, everyone!" Brock addressed the crowd rather informally, but for some reason, that was what I liked best about it here.

Murmurs of hello chorused around me.

"I'm sure you've all noticed the few new faces around." He smiled down at us and we sheepishly nodded or waved.

A woman next to us gently patted Carra's shoulder.

"And no doubt, rumors have already circled as to why they are here," he continued. "To dispel anything that may be negative or wrong, I am telling you that they have temporarily unlocked the barrier, bringing with them two orbs. As you know we have had the third in our possession for quite some time. We now have the power to take down the barrier for good, enter into Laiden, and save those who have been cursed by the pill and Iris for far too long."

A light applause erupted, but at Hendrick's gesture of "down" with his hands, it quickly simmered away.

Hendrick began to speak. "While this is good news, it also is serious news. The pill that we once feared has taken over Laiden. The citizens are slowly losing their memories due to Extium. It won't be long before they forget humanity completely."

I was entranced by the reactions of the audience. They seemed genuinely concerned for their neighbors across the border, people they had never known.

"The time is now to take down the Prime Minister and to teach Laiden the rich life that we have found here. A community as you all know is about love, trust, and sharing," Hendrick stated surely. "The Resistance also has hopes to reverse the effects of those afflicted by the curse, Extium."

The crowd nodded enthusiastically, especially Winslett. I stared at the ground in shame.

Brock took over from Hendrick. "We must make a motion to start preparation to temporarily leave our territory and overthrow Laiden's government, a task that our Resistance ancestors left for us to complete. We do not have long to turn it to a public vote or discuss this in great depths. We leave now, or I fear we will have lost our greatest opportunity to right a small part of our world. I urge you all to think about this. Your opinions are the only ones that matter after all."

He paused to let it sink in.

A woman clad in navy pants and a loose blouse shirt piped up, "What about the children?"

Hendrick smiled as always. "The children and the very elderly will stay behind, with perhaps a few mothers who do not feel capable of fighting. Any able men or women wanting to fight are advised to take up arms."

She nodded, as did several others.

"We have waited for this for too long," a fit man of maybe thirty said. "And I'm ready to save our kin."

"Laiden would be our home if we weren't lucky enough to end up in a place like this," a middle aged woman spoke. "I am ready to show them what life can be like."

"It's not fair to leave those from Laiden in that state," another cried.

The crowd then erupted in a lively chat, but one would be a fool to call it a debate, for everyone seemed to share the same opinion. I, too, was inspired by the will of the crowd, to take Laiden by storm and not only restore the people, but give them something better.

Brock gathered the attention back in an instance. "All who object to the final siege speak up now please." No one did.

"Then," Hendrick roared, "it is time to get ready."

The Outlanders quickly segregated themselves. The scarce elders chatted idly, probably envying the youth preparing to fight. The older mothers gathered all of the youngest children who couldn't fight. The younger women went to join every male, with equal fierceness. It seemed

Carra, Lennon, Winslett, Masen, and I were the only ones left dazed and confused.

Hendrick took Byrde to the other children; finally she would be categorized into her age group, not left on the battlefield to see things not meant for her eyes.

Brock approached us. "Amazing, isn't it?"

"That you can all agree so readily?" asked Winslett. "Sure is."

"We aren't just the Outlanders. Primarily, we are the Resistance. Our purpose has always been, when we finally became able, to take down Laiden's government. Our people are simply answering the call."

"We are grateful, Brock. We really are," Lennon said seriously.

"How long until we leave?" I asked.

"Three days time seems apt," Brock answered.

"So soon," Masen said. "Will my leg be healed?"

"So quick to fight, eh? Time will tell," Brock replied.

Masen nodded his head gravely. He would make sure his leg was fine; he wasn't going to be left out of a battle.

"What can we do now?" Carra questioned further.

"Wren, I'd suggest you meet out healers in Cabin 6." He held my gaze and I knew that he judged me slightly for the parts I had played in all this, but now was my time to fix my mistakes and redeem myself.

"Carra," Brock continued, "go find my wife, Eden. I think you could be of use to distributing the weapons we have in stock."

She nodded and squeezed my hand.

"Lennon, rally with the men. Not all have heard your incredible story. Give them a rundown on what it is like inside the government building."

"Winslett, go with the children." Her face was surprised, with a hint of bitterness nobody missed. Brock quickly put her at ease. "Just for today, dear. I'm going to need Hendrick back in a jiff, and I want Byrde to still feel comforted." She smiled, clearly happy that she wasn't going to be left out of the impending fight.

Masen was the only one who had not been assigned a duty. "Masen, I don't know what's going to happen. For now, go with the elders. They like to feel included even though they won't be involved directly. Tell them what's going on. Be their friend."

"Okay," Masen said, clearly crestfallen and frustrated at his leg, and probably Carra. But I had no doubt he would be ready when the time came.

Brock was not done speaking. "This next part goes for all of you. Hendrick and I will reassess things within the next two days before we start for Laiden. Until then, remember, you are the Resistance."

Brock disbanded us at that moment. Clearly, he was a man of many responsibilities who had to attend to the rest of the Resistance and the Outlanders, not just us new kids.

It was the five of us. Byrde was elsewhere, but it didn't make this moment any less emotional. There was a sad finality that we knew our group that had started in the woods would never be completely the same again. Then, quite suddenly and in sync, we turned our backs on one another and walked away. Walked away knowing that when we met again, it would be time for everything we were ever familiar with to end and for something new to begin.

Seventy-Eight

Iris

I watched them closely from a distance away. The Resistance. Images from the Outlanders' territory glowed upon a screen before me.

The scene flashed to men preparing cargo and ammunition. Then to women securing their children behind closed doors. Then to others cowering over a skew of papers, deep into their work.

Lastly, the screen flashed to a man I had once known in another life. Three orbs glowed from within the clutches of his aged palms. He had one purpose only—to break the barrier that encapsulated my Laiden.

I owed my sight to Carra, and the tiny camera I had embedded into her uniform. Refocusing the lens, I scoffed at them all.

Their efforts would be futile.

If a war was what they wanted, then I could promise a war would come.

ACKNOWLEDGMENTS:

Editor Chuck Sambucchino, for his guidance and advice.

Myongson Rha and Debbie Gewirtz, our mothers, for their unwavering faith.

Rachel Rha, Chris Rha, and Terry Johnston Jr. for being our first readers.

Jonathan Gewirtz and Michael Rha, our fathers, for their encouragement.

Arden Gewirtz and Mark Levine, for their counsel.

Mrs. Manos, for her enthusiasm and support.

The I.W.W.G., for welcoming us into their community with open arms and ears, literally.

ABOUT THE AUTHORS

High school seniors Katie Rha and Emery Gewirtz discovered their shared passion for writing at an early age.

Both members of the International Women's Writing Guild, they recently published their first joint young adult novel, *Extium.*

Rha and Gewirtz currently reside in New Jersey and are heading off to college in the fall of 2014.